Home to Texas

Home to Texas

Thom Nicholson

FIVE STAR
A part of Gale, Cengage Learning

GALE
CENGAGE Learning

Farmington Hills, Mich • San Francisco • New York • Waterville, Maine
Meriden, Conn • Mason, Ohio • Chicago

GALE
CENGAGE Learning

Five Star™ Publishing, a part of Cengage Learning, Inc.

LIBRARY OF CONGRESS CATALOGING-IN-PUBLICATION DATA

Names: Nicholson, Thom, author.
Title: Home to Texas / by Thom Nicholson.
Description: First edition. | Waterville, Maine : Five Star, Cengage Learning, Inc. [2016]
Identifiers: LCCN 2016007142 (print) | LCCN 2016012453 (ebook) | ISBN 9781432832902 (hardcover) | ISBN 1432832905 (hardcover) | ISBN 9781432832858 (ebook) | ISBN 1432832859 (ebook) | ISBN 9781432833381 (ebook) | ISBN 1432833383 (ebook)
Subjects: LCSH: Ranchers—Texas—Fiction. | GSAFD: Western stories.
Classification: LCC PS3614.I3535 H66 2016 (print) | LCC PS3614.I3535 (ebook) | DDC 813/.6—dc23
LC record available at http://lccn.loc.gov/2016007142

First Edition. First Printing: October 2016
Find us on Facebook– https://www.facebook.com/FiveStarCengage
Visit our website– http://www.gale.cengage.com/fivestar/
Contact Five Star™ Publishing at FiveStar@cengage.com

Printed in the United States of America
1 2 3 4 5 6 7 20 19 18 17 16

Home to Texas

CHAPTER 1

Captain Travis Glenn Sasser, the chief battle surgeon of General John Bell Hood's Texas Volunteers, wearily shook his head, hoping he could clear away the fog of fatigue from his brain. He stepped closer to the wooden table in the small kitchen of the old farmhouse, pressed into service as a temporary field hospital. This bloody fight, already being called the Battle of Chickamauga Creek, was two days along and he had yet to sleep.

Upon arrival at the dilapidated farm home, he had immediately set up his hospital and then spent the next thirty-six hours frantically sawing ruined arms and legs from screaming, blood-soaked, young soldiers. On the tabletop smeared with blood lay another man, semiconscious, waiting his turn under the knife. His agonized groan cut through the chorus of sounds made by the hundreds of wounded men scattered around the house, like discarded cordwood. Travis forced himself to concentrate. The shredded bone and flesh that once was a human leg demanded his attention.

A sharp scalpel was placed in his hand by his medical orderly, Homer Waites. Travis could smell the raw odor of the alcohol that Homer had washed the knife in only seconds earlier. The wounded limb of the unfortunate soldier lying helpless before him quivered and oozed fresh red blood. A white stump of shinbone, shattered by the deadly minié ball fired from a Yankee rifle, had pushed its way through the skin. A shadow briefly fell against the leg and passed on, another wounded man arriving. The flickering candlelight softened as Travis placed his whole concentration into his first cut. Without looking up, he ordered, "Homer, keep that tourniquet tight. This damned leg's bleeding like a stuck hog."

With skill honed by far too many previous young men under his surgeon's knife, Travis slashed the white skin, cutting deep into the red muscle underneath. His fingers moved with practiced speed. He had amputated limbs so often, he could do it in his sleep. He tied off the numerous bleeders with the fine silk thread he'd been fortunate enough to find last week at the medical storehouse back in Richmond. As he finished, he held out his hand for the bone saw that Homer had waiting for him.

Poor Homer, Travis thought to himself. Dirty, blood-spattered, with beads of sweat standing out above his upper lip, the bespectacled young orderly nodded and twisted the tourniquet a little tighter with one hand as he passed the saw with the other. Dried blood from some soldier's spurting artery remained on the lens of his thick glasses. The slight, young assistant was subdued and wan as he struggled with the terrible job of providing aid to the suffering men who surrounded him. At the beginning of the war, the Confederate army had rejected Homer as unfit to serve. Travis shook his head in amazement at the absurdity of the notion.

Instead of carrying a rifle, his faithful assistant fought to save injured comrades, not to kill the enemy. Homer had more than once risked his own life to rescue a wounded man exposed to enemy fire. He'd worked hours without rest, cleaning and caring for suffering wounded, both blue and gray. He had gallantly served Travis as medical orderly for over a year without complaint, never asking for more than the opportunity to provide care for the wounded men of Hood's division.

The stifling interior of the house reeked of the dirt, sweat, and blood from the many men who packed its interior. Travis hadn't seen so many wounded men at once since Gettysburg, during the terrible battle fought last July with General Lee's Army of Northern Virginia.

Now, here he was, two months later, between the Georgia and Tennessee border near Chattanooga, at the bloody fight near Chickamauga Creek. Someone mentioned to him that the Indian word "Chickamauga" meant "River of Death." It was an appropriate name if ever there was one, he thought. The first two days' fighting had produced over ten thousand casualties from the opposing armies and nothing had yet been decided. The mighty armies would clash again in the morning and fill the dusty clay soil of northwest Georgia with more blood.

As his practiced hands continued to save a man's life by maiming his body forever, Travis thought of the restful days spent in Richmond after the mind-numbing agony of the long retreat from Gettysburg in July. It had been a wonderfully peaceful respite, for a moment shutting out the bloody specter of war that was scouring the country.

Travis had slowly recovered from the days and nights of never-ending work trying to save the uncounted wounded from the savage fighting near the small crossroads town in Pennsylvania. The fierce battle at the Devil's Den, near Little Round Top Mountain, the afternoon of the second day, had filled his operating room with injured men from his division. The long retreat south to the home soil of the Confederacy was written by the dying youths he had lost en route, their graves serving as morbid milestones to the victorious Yankees chasing the once proud Army of Northern Virginia back to its home soil.

Travis had spent several hours late that second day at Gettysburg working to save the left arm of his friend, General John Bell Hood. A small cannonball had torn away most of the muscle above the elbow. Before Travis put him to sleep with some of the precious ether he still had available, Hood had begged Travis to save his arm, and perhaps he had, yet Travis knew the dashing bachelor general would never again hold a comely Southern maiden in his arms while twirling her around the dance floor. The arm would forevermore be nothing more than a floppy appendage hanging from the shoulder of General Hood.

Travis had to employ all the skills he had learned from two years of surgery on wounded men just to save the life of his friend and commander. After one last, careful inspection of his work, he was satisfied he had done all he possibly could for the badly injured general. About midnight, he placed the unconscious Hood in an ambulance with three other wounded men. Instructing the driver to deliver the general to the hospital at Culpepper Court House, across the Potomac River in Virginia, he stepped back onto the porch of the residence near the Seminary College at Gettysburg.

Morosely watching the wagon pull away holding the man who had recruited him two years before from his brand-new practice back in Nacogdoches, Texas. Travis didn't envy the injured general's next few days. The long trip in the hot ambulance jostling along rutted, country roads would be a constant and painful reminder of the wound that nearly cost the fiery soldier his left arm.

The next morning, the third of July, Travis walked out of the Lutheran Seminary classroom that was being used by the Confederate army as a field hospital to get a breath of fresh air. It was shortly after midday when roaring cannons shattered the morning quiet. Startled, he turned toward the sound of death and destruction. Watching the gun smoke of the largest and most vicious cannon engagement of the war drift above the tree line, he was momentarily awestruck at the ferociousness of the fire. More than two hundred cannons were hurling shot and shell at each other across the mile-wide field that lay between the ridge named after the Seminary College and a local cemetery on a smaller hill just outside the town of Gettysburg.

He had watched the cannonade for a few minutes with some friends, while the cannons' roar increased in ferocity, if that was possible. Travis remembered the despair he felt. He knew that his skills would be in great demand again before the day was over. Then he walked back inside the makeshift hospital to attend the many patients he had received since Hood's soldiers failed in their attempt to gain control of the enemy's left flank, a hellhole called Little Round Top, the previous afternoon.

Travis shook the memories from his mind and returned to the present, here in north Georgia. He finished sewing the flap of skin and muscle over the stump and dropped the amputated limb into the tub at the foot of the kitchen table. It landed with a sickening splat on the twelve other legs and seven arms he had removed from pitiful young boys whose luck at the gaming tables of war had gone sour.

"Easy, Homer. Release the tourniquet and let's see if there are any leaking blood vessels." Travis studied the stump for a moment and nodded. "Looks good, so far. Wash the stump and wrap it lightly." Pushing his back straight, he concluded, "I'm going to get a breath of fresh air and then sleep a bit. Call me in three hours if you don't need me earlier."

"Yes, sir, Doctor Sasser. Good night." Homer watched as Travis slowly walked out of the room. He knew how tired Travis was and nodded in admiration.

Standing on the porch, Travis stared up at the starry sky. It must be well after midnight, he thought, as he stretched the kinks out of his back. He shuffled across the yard to the tent Homer had erected for him behind the cabin. He recalled again that fateful day in July, two months earlier. Doctor Hillman, who at the time was the chief surgeon of General Lee's Army of

Northern Virginia, had stopped him as he entered the recovery ward at the seminary. The aging doctor from Alexandria was killed several days later during an artillery barrage at Falling Waters, Maryland. It was to be the last time they would ever see one another.

Doctor Hillman remarked as he pointed toward the cannons' roar. "We'll be busy tonight, Doctor Sasser. Longstreet's corps is going to attack the Yankee center in a few minutes. Fifteen thousand of our boys will be breaking through the Union line over at Cemetery Hill, yonder. You'll be able to see it from the balcony if you care to join me. I'll supply the brandy."

Travis was about to decline, when he reconsidered. This would perhaps be the final big battle of this accursed war and he owed it to those who were about to make the ultimate sacrifice for the South to watch their heroic effort.

"I'll be honored to join you, sir. Just give me a few moments to check my patients. From the sound of those guns, the main assault will be a while in coming."

For the next hour he checked the many wounded Texas men from his division. There wasn't enough opium to reduce their pain and several moaned as they tried to rest. Those awake looked at him with the same unasked question he saw on nearly every face in a wound ward. *"Am I going to live, Doctor?"*

Smiling in his most reassuring manner, he moved from man to man, talking and checking their dressings, feeling their pulses and brows. They never asked, and he never said otherwise. He knew from bitter experience that half of those he looked at today would be dead in a few days or weeks.

As mid-afternoon approached, he had returned to the balcony and joined Doctor Hillman and several other medical staff officers. The roar of the cannons had not abated a decibel from the unholy roar of the first minute. Travis knew that thousands of shells must have been fired, and if only one in ten caused injury, there would be an abundance of carnage to deal with that night. He wondered if the Yankee doctors on the other side were dreading the coming rush of casualties as he was at this moment.

"Looks as if the Yankee guns are slacking off, Doctor Sasser. You got here just in time." Doctor Hillman passed him a small glass of peach brandy. The burning sensation from the alcohol sliding down his throat brought fresh vigor to his tired body.

Almost as suddenly as it started, the firing stopped. An eerie silence rode the billowing gray-white clouds of windblown gun smoke across the gently waving field of grain to his front. The slight breeze was blowing directly toward the balcony where he stood, so he could both smell and taste the pungent odor of black powder in the air. As the smoke dissipated, the far hill and cemetery became visible to the silent men on the crowded balcony. Travis could see activity, and putting his binoculars to his eyes watched as streams of blue-coated men rushed to the barricades along the crest of the hilltop. Travis felt an uneasy stirring in the pit of his stomach.

Before he could say a word, however, the battlefield melody of hundreds of bugles and the rattling of as many drums sounded. The call to advance swept down the row upon row of kneeling men patiently awaiting the order. Out of the white smoke marched the twelve thousand brave soldiers of Pickett's First Virginia Division on their doomed assault to everlasting glory.

The heart-stopping sight of the battle flags billowing at the vanguard of the many regiments, and the soldiers' parade field precision as they marched into death would stay with the young Texan until the day he died. The gray-clad men marched with pride and determination across the field toward the grove of trees that marked the center of the Yankee lines. For several minutes, not a sound was heard, save the drums and the marching feet of the doomed legion.

Abruptly, the Yankee guns started their roar of destruction, and Doctor Travis Sasser knew this was not the last day of this war, only the next. With a heavy heart, he left the stunned company of spectators and returned to his ward to prepare for the stream of broken bodies, which would soon flood the hospital.

The retreat back into Virginia for Travis and his wounded patients was, thankfully, a misty memory dulled by weariness and unending work, as the beaten Army of Northern Virginia slogged through incessant rains to the safety of the South. Fatigue was his ever-constant companion during the endless struggle to save those men he could.

He called on the last of his reserve energy as he sought to apply his medical skill to the unfortunate wounded men in his care. The muddy roads at least made the jarring ambulances a little less agonizing for the wounded. After an exhausting six days, they reached Richmond, where he turned over his charges to the hospital and slept and slept, slowly recovering his strength, as had the exhausted and tattered Texan soldiers who had survived the hell of that awful summer of 1863.

Here he was just two months later, all the way over in Tennessee, thanks to a hurried train ride, again trying to save a man another man had just tried to kill. While in Richmond, he had replenished his medical wagon, written several letters home to Ma and Clarissa back in Nacogdoches, and purchased a new saddle for Duke, his trusty horse. Mostly though, he had slept and eaten anything he could get his hands on.

Last week, President Davis had reassigned General Lee's most able commander, James Longstreet and his corps of tested veterans, including Hood's Texas Division, which included Travis Sasser, Chief Surgeon. Their new job was to help Braxton Bragg's Army of Tennessee stop the Army of the Cumberland under the command of General Rosecrans from driving into

Georgia and if possible, push the bluecoats back to the Ohio River. Crippled and weak as he still was, General Hood had insisted on accompanying his men.

Travis had tried to convince the wounded Hood to stay in the hospital at Richmond, but the sad-eyed Texan, with his gray-fringed beard and dashing heart filled with the love of battle, would not listen. "I appreciate your concern, Doctor Sasser, but I must be with my men and you must keep me well and fit enough to lead them. Besides, we're gonna whip 'em once and fer all. I don't wanta miss that."

The general's left arm was strapped to his side and riding was painful, but he was where he loved to be, at the head of his fighting Texas Volunteers. The men deserved no less, for they had fought the Yankees to a bloody standstill every time they had met. Their commander had been with them from the start. They deserved no less now.

Travis smiled as he remembered that summer day in 1861 when Hood had ridden into Nacogdoches with his battle flags waving and bands playing. Nearly every young man in town had joined up on the spot, himself included. Hood had shaken his hand and promised him very little work, except on Yankee prisoners. "Believe me, Travis, my boy," he had confidently remarked, "we'll be done with this war by Christmas, and home before spring planting, or you can call me a horse's rump."

Travis still called him General Rump when they were relaxing together, much to Hood's delight and his staff's dismay. The tall, dark-haired Texas general was a fire-breathing, battle-loving maverick. His soldiers loved the fighting general and seemed willing to follow him anywhere. Travis hoped it wouldn't be straight into Hell.

He listened to the sounds of the night before stepping into his tent. The dark Georgia air was filled with the continuous roar of rifle shots and cannon fire as the two huge armies probed and maneuvered in the early morning hours of the twentieth of September 1863. The dawn would bring more combat as the two rival commanders attempted to take the key terrain overlooking the river town of Chattanooga. The doorway into Georgia was straight through this spot, where Travis lay down fully clothed, too exhausted to undress, on his field cot.

As he drifted off into fitful slumber, he wondered if he would get any letters soon from his ma and Clarissa. To his distress, he had only received one from his new girlfriend whom he had met during his leave last December. The mails were terrible, especially since the Yanks gained control of the Mississippi River, but he'd heard from his mother three times since he had last heard from Clarissa.

Travis recalled the dance held where they first met. She had just moved to town with her father, who bought the Emporium Dry Goods Store. He had worn his finest dress uniform, with the blood-red sash of the Confederate Medical Department around his waist. "Who is that beautiful girl by the punch bowl?" he'd asked his sister Molly.

"That's the new Emporium owner's daughter, Clarissa Watkins. They're just up from San Antonio. Pretty thing, isn't she? That is, if you like sassy blondes." His older sister had smiled mischievously at him.

John grinned and begged Molly to introduce him. Accepting his incessant pleas, Molly gave in to her handsome brother and led him over to the pretty young woman, standing with a short dour-faced man, who turned out to be her father. "Clair, this good-looking rake, whom you'll run off with a buggy whip if you're smart, is my little brother, Travis. He's home on leave from General Hood's Texas Brigade. Would you do me a favor and dance with him once, so I can get some punch and dance with my husband? Mr. Watkins, may I introduce my brother, Captain Travis Sasser."

John flashed his most gallant grin. "I'm happy to meet such a beautiful addition to our town." Quickly he shook hands with her father. "My pleasure, sir." The old man grumped his reply, and shifted his gaze between Travis and his daughter with frosty eyes. Travis was too smitten by the blonde-haired loveliness of his daughter to notice.

"My goodness, Captain," she had airily replied, "you soldiers do think of the sweetest things to say to a girl."

They had danced every dance and spent as much time as they could together in the next three weeks. He hadn't told his ma or pa whom he was seeing, but it was obvious they knew the love bug had bitten him hard. He'd planned to take her out the next Sunday to meet his family and see the ranch his father had carved out of the wild country next to the Sabine River. The unexpected orders to return to Richmond had spoiled his plans.

Their last afternoon together, they had ridden out to the special place they had discovered in the willow grove next to Parson's Creek. They sat on the grassy bank and pledged their eternal love and devotion to each other.

"Clair," he had whispered in her ear, "when I come back from this cursed war, I'll be asking you to make an important decision. Will you wait for me?"

"Oh, Travis, how can I let you go? I'll be so lost and alone without you." Crying as she held him tightly, Clair had begged him, "Stay well and take care of yourself, my darling. Try and get another leave as soon as you can. You must hurry back to me. I'll be so lonely. I just don't know how I'll be able to wait for you."

Travis had a very good reason for living. "I promise Clarissa, my dearest, I'll return as soon as I possibly can."

Their passions and the moment took command, and soon they were kissing with an intensity and urgency fueled by his impending departure. Travis quickly unbuttoned Clair's bodice and placed his sun-browned hands on the white, silky softness of her breasts. She moaned softly in his ear, enjoying the gentleness of his touch. Her whisper recalled him to his senses and he realized what he was doing. "My, God, forgive me, Clair. I didn't realize. I must have lost my head. Please forgive me." He jerked the offending hands away from her.

Blushing, Clair buttoned her clothing. "Hush, darling. I understand. It's all right. I love you, I always will. You can do anything you want, it's all right."

To Travis, that had sealed their promise to marry, and he fell into a deep sleep thinking of his love for his darling Clarissa. He longed for another letter from her, and soon, just to affirm the life awaiting him at the end of this death and suffering. The noise of the coming battle didn't prevent him from falling into a deep, exhausted sleep.

Morning came far too quickly for the tired doctor, and he groggily arose to Homer's persistent shaking. "Wake up, Doctor, the sun's a'risin'. Here's some acorn coffee and hardtack for breakfast."

The day started slowly, and it was nearly noon before the sounds of battle peaked toward the front. During the early morning calm, Travis rode to the headquarters of Hood and General Law, who were sharing a small house captured by the Texas troops the day before. Waiting until the tall figure of the general climbed on his horse and secured his useless arm in its sling, Travis rode over and delivered his report.

"One hundred seventy-three treated yesterday, General, and nine more this morning so far. Only fourteen died during the night."

"Morning, Doctor," the busy general responded. "Not too bad, so far, I reckon. I'm going to inspect the lines one more time before we attack the Yanks. Ride with me a bit if you have a moment."

Travis and Hood, followed by several young aides, rode through the trees toward the steady sounds of rifle fire. The general acted as if they were on a Sunday ride to church, oblivious to the wizz of minié balls cutting through the leaves of the forest.

At the edge of the woods, they came upon the main defensive line. A long row of fallen trees faced a similar row of fallen trees across a grassy field. Behind the two barricades, the opposing soldiers fired at one another as fast as they could reload their weapons. Turning to his left, General Hood slowly rode behind his men, grimly surveying the enemy breastworks he would assault within the hour.

Turning to one of his aides, he shouted, "Tell Perry to bring his batteries to this spot immediately. He's to suppress the enemy fire as the attack starts. Hurry, I'll be down at Wilmont's brigade when you return."

As the general turned to ride on his way, a cannonball exploded at his horse's feet. The unfortunate horse was killed instantly and Hood was thrown off its back to land in the brush by the trail. Travis and the others leaped from their horses and ran to their downed commander's side. The general was barely conscious and murmured to an aide, "Tell General Shannon to take command and press the attack. Longstreet is counting on us."

Gathering the bloody Hood in his arms, Travis ran behind a tangle of fallen trees, and ripped the pants leg away from Hood's right thigh. "Easy, General, I'll take care of this and have you back in the saddle shortly," he reassured his wounded commander.

It was a fearsome wound, high up the thigh, nearly shearing the leg away from the body. Travis would have to demonstrate all the skill he possessed to save his commander. Quickly tying a belt around the bleeding leg, he sent one of the aides for a stretcher. As soon as the unconscious general was picked up and put into the horse-drawn ambulance, Travis galloped ahead to prepare for the operation to follow. *"Damn those Yankee gunners,"* he thought savagely, *"why couldn't they have been less proficient in their work?"*

As General Hood was placed on the operating table, several additional wounded men arrived from the raging battle on Snodgrass Hill, near where he was riding with the general. Travis put on his dark operating smock, still stained with yesterday's blood. "Well, Homer," he remarked to his assistant, his voice grim and worried. "We'll have a bitch of a time with this leg, I'm afraid. See how high the wound is? I doubt General Hood will ever again ride in front of his troops as they attack the enemy."

Dipping his hands in the corn liquor kept just for that purpose, sighing in frustration at the immense burden he faced, he started cutting on the bloody leg. Homer placed a wooden tub at the foot of the table, where Travis could drop the severed limb.

By the end of the day, Doctor Travis Sasser was a spent man. He'd beaten yesterday's record of bloody amputations hands down and still had more to go. General Hood was still alive when Travis had him placed in the field ambulance. Once again the general would have to endure the agony of a rough wagon trip. This time it was to Ringgold, Georgia, where a train to the hospital in Atlanta awaited him. What would happen there was debatable because Hood was so desperately wounded, but Travis knew his friend had a fierce will to live, so there was hope.

For Travis, the next few days passed as they had at Gettysburg, with Travis laboring without sleep or respite to save as many young men in butternut and gray as possible, and even a few blue bellies as well. The wounded men could not be distinguished when he worked on their naked and torn bodies.

On his operating table he could not tell Yank from Rebel. He was so tired of this damned war. Would it never end?

Chapter 2

Following the route of the Yankee forces by the determined soldiers of the South, the Yankees retreated into Chattanooga, but to the bitter disappointment of the Confederate soldiers, General Bragg contented himself with building defensive positions, which Bragg anchored around the massive and forbidding sheer-sided rock called Lookout Mountain. The Confederate lines were impregnable, it was claimed, yet Travis had seen just what determined men could do if they were willing to die in the process. If the Yankees made an assault on the Confederate lines, many would suffer. That didn't seem to be a consideration in the minds of the generals in charge.

The president of the Confederacy, Jefferson Davis, had arrived from Richmond to visit the army. Rumors were rampant that the other generals insisted that Braxton Bragg be replaced as Army of Tennessee commander, but nothing had happened. Since Davis and Bragg were the very best of friends, it was no surprise to Travis.

After the fateful meeting with the Southern generals, where President Davis firmly insisted that Bragg was his commander of choice, the Confederate president had toured the rear area. Homer had scrubbed the little cabin spotless when the great leader arrived. President Davis quickly glanced around and stepped out into the sunlit front yard. He pointedly ignored the clusters of wounded men lying before him everywhere and merely hemmed and hawed a bit, and then turned away from the maimed, human remnants of the battle. As it ended, Davis shook Travis's hand and remarked, "Very nice field hospital, Doctor Sasser. Have you received enough supplies to properly treat the wounded? The South needs every man you can return to the field."

Travis looked directly into the eyes of the lanky, aloof chief executive. "Sir, we never have enough, yet somehow we make do. Thanks to people like my assistants, Doctor Reynolds and Corporal Waites, the men are receiving the best care possible. If you can improve the flow of medical supplies to us, even more of them could be saved."

The president of the Confederacy said nothing, merely nodded his head and then smiled wanly at Travis. "Doctor Sasser, General Hood asked that I pin the rank of major, Medical Corps, on you myself. It is my pleasure." With that, he made the promotion advancing Travis to his new rank and immediately thereafter indicated to his aide to bring up his horse. His visit complete, the president and his party mounted and rode on their way. "Doggone, Doctor Sasser," Homer exclaimed, "I seen the president of the Confederacy hisself. Just wait till Ma reads about this in my next letter home. Who'd a'thought it? To think he pinned your promotion on, personal."

Travis watched the president's party ride off, wondering if he had made the man understand how desperate was his need for more medical supplies. Shaking his head, he jotted a quick note to General Hood, who clung to life in the hospital at Atlanta, telling him how much he appreciated the promotion. Travis was sure that Hood's latest wound would force the general into military retirement, if he survived at all. The Texicans missed their fiery commander, but had settled in under the new man, General Shannon, the former commander of artillery for the Texas Division.

The last of September was as beautiful as any in Travis's

memory. The broadleaf trees were ablaze in gold and red, a brilliant contrast to the numerous evergreens, which covered the hills around Chattanooga. The days were relatively quiet, with an occasional skirmish and intelligence raid to break the monotony of the stalemate. Even so, Travis and Homer stayed busy treating wounded survivors of the skirmishes.

They also took advantage of the lull to replenish what they could of their stock of medicine and supplies for the battles sure to come. He wrote several letters home to his mother and Clair, describing the lovely region of Georgia and Tennessee where he was living. Unfortunately, no mail came to anyone from across the Mississippi. Every week he prayed the next would be the one when mail from home arrived. Eventually, some mail was certain to cross the river, Yankee gunboats or not. He reminded himself that he had to be patient.

The last day of September was warm and pleasant, as had been its predecessors. The bad news that morning was from the Seventeenth Arkansas Volunteers, which was located to the left of Hood's Texas Division. Their doctor requested that Travis ride over and inspect some of the sick in their field hospital. The message said numerous men were too sick to soldier. The old doctor feared it might be smallpox. The dread disease had killed too many soldiers for anyone to take the information lightly.

Travis called for his orderly. "Homer, have the fellows hitch up an ambulance. We'll ride over and take a look at those sick soldiers. If it is smallpox, we'll have to move the sick men away from the others. There's a small hospital at Crawfish Springs where we can take them and set that up as a quarantine area."

The two men drove a small ambulance over to the Arkansas unit's location in a somber mood. Smallpox was a feared scourge for men packed in close quarters as the Rebel army was presently. The deadly illness killed nearly every man who contracted it.

Travis and the Arkansas doctor examined the five suspects. Both were in sad agreement; it was almost certainly the dreaded pox. The sick men were in a separate tent from the rest of the wounded in the little clearing the Arkansas unit used as a hospital. Travis and Homer put the sick soldiers into the cramped interior of the ambulance and started down the wooded trail toward Crawfish Springs.

It was a warm afternoon, so Travis soon shed his woolen gray coat with its shiny new major's star sewn on the collar. He was more comfortable in his old denim shirt and gray cavalry pants with his New Orleans boots. He carried the .36-caliber Colt revolver his father, Big Tom Sasser, had given him as a farewell gift two years earlier. The trail was devoid of any other traffic, and the singing birds serenaded the passing horseman and swaying wagon.

The ominous silence slowly worked its way into the young doctor's consciousness. The birds had quit singing, how long ago? Turning to look back at Homer on the wagon, Travis started to give warning when the brush to the side of the road erupted in rifle fire. A bullet tore off his hat and another fanned his cheek so close he felt the heat of its passing. Drawing his pistol, he fired into the dense darkness of the bushy hillside.

"Whip 'em, Homer," he shouted to the startled Homer. "Yank ambush."

Homer snapped the reins while Travis emptied his gun into the brush. The concealed Yank soldiers' next volley dropped the lead animal of the ambulance and its fall tangled the second animal until it was immobilized. The wagon skewed to a sudden halt. Homer was jerked out of the wagon seat and fell heavily at the side of the trail, not moving. Without any hesitation, Travis leaped off the seat and gathered the stunned Homer in his arms. Holding up his pistol, he shouted, "Ambulance and wounded, don't shoot. We surrender. Be careful, there are sick men aboard."

Out of the brush stepped six bearded men dressed in the hated blue of the enemy. Motioning for Travis to keep his hands up, the sergeant in charge took the pistol from him. Stuffing it in his pants belt, the captor motioned with his head. "What's in the wagin, Reb?"

Travis stepped to the canvas side and raised it until the interior was visible to the men who stood along the road with their rifles ready for action. "Sick men that I'm taking to the hospital in Crawfish Springs. I ask that you allow us to proceed without interruption. You know your people and mine have been exchanging sick and wounded, anyway. There's a possibility these men have the pox."

The old sergeant hissed in surprise and stepped back. He peered at the silent men lying on their stretchers in the dim interior. Looking over at Travis, he asked, "You a sawbones? Air you a officer in the Reb army?"

Nodding vigorously and pointing at his jacket tied to the seat of the ambulance, he answered, "Yes, Sergeant, I'm a medical major with Hood's Texas Volunteers." Pointing to Homer he continued, "That is Corporal Waites, my medical orderly. Won't you please allow us to transport these men to the hospital? They are very sick and possibly contagious."

The Yankee NCO shook his head, and motioned with his rifle, "Nope, I'm suppose to brang a Reb prisoner back to the colonel, and I'm a'taking you folks, so jus come along and do like yer told and nobody gits hurt. If they got the pox, our sawbones can take care a 'em."

Hurrying, the ambushers cut the downed horse free and pulled the ambulance around its body. Travis checked Homer's head, but there was no visible injury. He'd just been knocked senseless by the fall. Motioning his men toward the gap at

Frick's crossing, the Yankee sergeant led his party with their prisoners over the hill toward the river crossing at Bridgeport, northwest of Chattanooga. Travis tried to reason with the stubborn Yankee sergeant, but it became obvious that he would have to speak with the raiders' commander before they would be freed and allowed to finish their delivery of the sick men in the ambulance.

Their arrival at the Yankee headquarters at Bridgeport was uneventful, although everyone was tired from the quick trip away from the Confederate lines back to the safety across the river in Tennessee. As soon as they arrived, Travis requested he be allowed to speak to the commander. The young officer who had come out to take the information from the returning raiders shrugged his shoulders and replied, "Yes sir, Major, I'll be happy to speak with him as soon as he finishes the staff meeting he's having with General Rosecrans. You can wait here until then."

He opened the door to the room next to the main parlor of the home where the headquarters was located. The young captain concluded, "I'll put your men in the holding pen by the stables until the colonel decides if he's gonna pardon you back to the other side of the river or not."

Travis stepped into the small room being used as an extra office. Sitting down on a hard wooden chair, he gave in to his weariness and leaned against the wall. He realized he could plainly hear the discussion going on in the adjoining room. It must have been General Rosecrans speaking. Travis listened, his eyes closed as if asleep.

"Colonel Wells, you will take your entire command across the river on Friday and sweep the enemy rear as far as Dalton if you can without becoming decisively engaged. Destroy all stores and obtain as much information as possible. Return only when you must to avoid engagement with superior forces."

Travis realized he had heard some valuable information to pass to Bragg's headquarters when he was paroled back to his army. He smiled and pushed his ear close to the wall to hear more. He didn't hear the outside door opening.

"What's this? What are you doing there?" A bewhiskered Yankee colonel rushed into the room and looked suspiciously at the startled Travis.

"Nothing, sir. I was only resting my eyes for a moment," Travis quickly replied. It was too late. The door into the room where the conversation was taking place opened and the general and colonel stepped through.

"Colonel Sullivan, what's going on here? Who is this Rebel officer?" General Rosecrans was in no mood for problems at this time. His stature with Washington was on shaky grounds as it was, since the disaster at Chickamauga Creek.

The staff officer replied, "Sir, I caught this Reb listening to you and Colonel Wells discussing your plans."

They all turned and glared at Travis. He lamely sputtered, "Sir, I'm a surgeon with General Hood's division, and I assure you that I heard nothing of importance while I awaited an audience with Colonel Wells."

Turning to Travis's accuser, the general motioned, "Get this officer out of here until I decide what to do with him. Don't be the least bit careless and allow him to escape or your next assignment will be counting procuring horses in northern Minnesota." The general whirled and walked back into the parlor.

As the colonel followed his general into the main office, Travis was led out of the house under guard to the pen where Homer and the sick men were being held.

The slight orderly moved close to Travis. "Doctor, are they returning us soon? We'll not make Crawfish Springs before late tonight if they don't release us soon."

"Damned if I know, Homer, but listen to what I just heard."

Travis spoke in a soft whisper. "If you get back to our lines before I do, pass it on to General Bragg's staff." He outlined the plan he had overheard in the house. Homer repeated the information and committed it to his memory.

Meanwhile, the Union general was trying to decide what to do with the Rebel officer who likely overheard him planning the sweep around the Confederate's rear. "Colonel Wells, send that Reb officer and his men back as prisoners under heavy guard. I'll write instructions that they are to be kept incommunicado until I personally rescind the order. That should keep word of our plans quiet." The necessary orders were issued.

Protesting vigorously, Travis, Homer, and the sick men were put on the prisoner train for Memphis, the written instructions put in the hands of the captain in charge. To Travis's dismay, the Yankee doctor disputed the sick men had the pox. "Just chicken fever." He airily dismissed the distraught young physician.

Under the instructions that sealed from the rest of the world information that they were now captives of the Union army, Travis and his unfortunate comrades began their way into the prisoner-of-war custody of their enemy. General Rosecrans was relieved the next week, and Colonel Wells fell in battle the day after that. The very man who issued it forgot the damning letter of instructions, and neither Travis nor those with him were aware of it and the bitter consequences it would bring to their lives in the next few months.

The tired and sick men arrived in Memphis the next evening and were placed in a large lot that once was the holding pen for the local slaughterhouse. There were no cots or blankets for the prisoners, leaving every man to sleep in the filth and mud of the pen. As the number of captured Rebel soldiers grew, Travis grew more fearful that a full-scale epidemic of smallpox would break out. He bribed a guard with a Union ten-dollar greenback to bring the local doctor to the holding pen.

The Yankee doctor recognized the threat and returned with what medicine he could, but the men in Travis's care steadily grew sicker and weaker. The five original soldiers had all died by the end of the second week. Regrettably, other prisoners were now infected in turn, as the three hundred or so men in the POW holding pen were loaded on to a grimy side-wheeler for the trip upriver.

"Where we goin'?" Homer asked a friendly guard.

"To the new prison camp just constructed at Rock Island, Illinois. You Rebs'll never git outta thar till Abe Lincoln lets ya go."

"You've got to let me separate the sick men from the rest of the prisoners," Travis insisted to the harried Union officer checking the prisoners as they loaded the boat. "We may be able to stop the spread if we act now."

"Sorry, Major, I can't help you. The orders are that you all go upriver to the stockade at Rock Island, Illinois. You'll have to wait till you get there to do your segregatin'."

"Damn it, you fool," Travis grabbed the arm of the Union officer. "Can't you see what a mistake you're making?"

A nearby guard swiftly smashed the butt of his rifle into Travis's head, dropping him in the mud like a shot turkey. "Damn Reb. I'll larn ya to grab a Union officer like that."

The Yankee major looked at his unconscious Rebel counterpart. The Reb doctor sure seemed intent on getting his head busted. Well, he'd done all he could. There were Union boys to take care of. He spoke to Homer, who was on his knees cradling Travis's head in his lap. "He'll be all right. Maybe it'll teach him some manners. Have him checked by the doctor at Rock Island." He walked out of the holding pen, other matters on his mind.

Travis drifted in and out of consciousness the four days of

the journey to the federal prison. Homer worked an unending schedule trying to provide relief to both his friend and the latest sick soldiers. The guards were coarse men with little concern for the sick and wounded Rebel soldiers. There was no doctor on board and very little medicine. The small amount that Travis had received from the doctor in Memphis was about gone.

Travis came to a groggy awakening just before they arrived at the island prison. "Ooh, my aching head. How long have I been out?"

"Better 'n four days," his exhausted assistant replied. "I was afraid you were hurt real bad. A guard smacked you upside the head with his rifle butt, back at Memphis." He helped the dazed doctor to the railing of the old steamer.

Travis leaned against the railing, watching the lights on the bank from farmhouses as the dilapidated steamer chugged past. He berated himself for not convincing the stubborn Yankee doctor about the existence of smallpox in his patients. Homer stayed with him for a few minutes of fresh air before they returned to the stench and misery of the ship's hold, where the prisoners were crowded together like cattle on the way to the slaughterhouse.

"I'll bet a fellow could float a mighty long way down this river toward home if he was of a mind, don't you, Homer? What say, shall we go over the side right now?"

The faithful little orderly giggled. "Major Sasser, you know we'd make better time riding the stage after we get our parole as medical personnel. I sure don't relish the idea of gittin' cold in my bones from that black water. I'll wait, if you don't mind."

Travis laughed, "All right for you, Homer, but you could use the washing a swim would give you. So could I, for that matter."

Before dawn the next morning, the steamer pulled up to the dock at their destination. The island, called Rock Island by the local folks, was smack in the middle of the Mississippi River, near a destroyed bridge to the Iowa side. Apparently, all needed supplies were barged out to the prison from the towns on either side of the river, Quincy, Illinois, and Davenport, Iowa.

The prison was midway down the mile-long island, surrounded by ten-foot-high logs. The enclosed space was immense. Travis later measured it as nine hundred feet by eleven hundred feet. The construction of the logged walls had almost denuded the island of trees. There was a small grove down on the far end, and a large number of brush piles from the discarded limbs. Inside the compound were row after row of two-story buildings. The green wood, which had been used in their construction, was warped and split. The huts would be as cold in winter as the freezing temperatures outside.

There wasn't a spot of paint or any other thing resembling color throughout the compound, save the brown mud and raw wood.

"Damn, Homer," Travis proclaimed. "What a dismal spot to end up in." He pointed at the huge piles of brush. "At least, we should have enough wood to stay warm this winter, if we can get close enough to the stove," Travis remarked to Homer.

"Don't you fret, Doctor Sasser. We'll be back in Texas long before the snows come, mark my words," the loyal orderly replied.

The Union army had shipped sixteen thousand captured soldiers to the newly constructed prison within the last month. The three hundred most recent arrivals were marched off the steamer, many helping to carry the sick and wounded. Glumly, they shuffled into their first day behind the log walls that would comprise their world until the war ended, they were paroled, managed to escape, or died.

Chapter 3

After the next morning's roll call, a daily burden that every prisoner had to endure for the first two hours of his morning, Travis went to the front gate of the prison compound with Homer. He waited patiently until a guard walked by and inquired, "What'd you want, Reb?" The young, pimply-faced Union soldier peered suspiciously at Travis, as if daring the captured Texan to try anything.

"Private, I am Major Travis Sasser, chief surgeon of Hood's Texas Division. Would you please tell the commandant I request a meeting with him. Please tell him it's very urgent."

"All right, Reb, jus step back from the gate and wait over by that rock. I'll tell Major Fitz what you asked and then he'll decide iffen he has the time."

The guard ambled toward a bare, wooden structure, which was apparently the headquarters building for the prison commander on the island. Travis and Homer waited at the huge boulder pointed out by the guard. It was nearly four feet high and twice that in diameter. By standing on it, a person could barely see over the ten-foot-high logs that formed the walls of the prison. Climbing up to the top, Travis took his first look around the outside of his wooden cage.

The high ground of the island was filled with wooden barracks and storage buildings for the large detachment of guards assigned to the prison. The massive log barricade that comprised the prison itself was constructed along the north side of the island, just a few feet above the edge of the muddy water flowing slowly on its way to the Gulf of Mexico.

The east side of the island was covered by the last stand of trees left after the walls were constructed. He couldn't see past the crown of the island to the south. There were too many of the bare, wooden buildings housing the Yankee guards in the way.

To the west, the denuded land dropped off to the surrounding water, with the piers from a long-gone bridge across to Iowa the only man-made object in sight. The place seemed to be a foreboding and desolate place to wait out the rest of the war. Travis was grateful that he and Homer would shortly be paroled, as was the custom for medical personnel. Meanwhile, he'd tell the commandant about the smallpox presence among the prisoners and pray there wouldn't be a full-scale epidemic.

The guard returned and motioned Travis to come to the main gate. Pointing him out to the bored sentry standing in the guard tower above the massive main gate, he spoke importantly, "The major wants me to escort this Reb officer to his office. He'll be in my custody until he returns."

The armed sentry nodded. "Okay, Dan. He's your problem." He watched impassively as Travis stepped through the iron-barred door into the comparative freedom outside the walls.

With the escort at his heels, he walked swiftly over to the headquarters building and entered the door. The front room was filled with busy clerks and a cluster of varnished wood storage files. Near the back wall, a burly senior sergeant major sat behind a bare, wooden desk guarding the office of the camp commander, a Major Samuel FitzPatrick, according to the sign on the closed door.

Without waiting for his self-important escort to speak, Travis walked up to the sergeant and announced, "Major Sasser to speak with Major FitzPatrick on urgent medical business."

The senior sergeant looked up with a raised eyebrow at this uppity Rebel officer and slowly nodded his head. "Stand over there with yer toes on the red line and I'll announce you to the commandant."

Sighing at the little game he was being forced to play, Travis moved to the red line painted on the floor in front of the commandant's door. After a moment, just to show him who was boss, the sergeant moved to the door, knocked, and entered, shutting the door behind him.

He emerged in a few minutes and nodded at the young doctor. "The commandant will give you two minutes, Major. Stop at the red line in front of the desk. Wait until you are spoken to before you start talking. Unnerstand?"

Swallowing his resentment at the brusque treatment, Travis nodded grimly and stepped into the commandant's office. Sitting behind the desk was an immense, red-haired man wearing the gold oak leaves of a major. The huge shaggy red beard wavered as the camp commander looked up at the prisoner standing with his toes touching the painted line and spoke. "Well?"

Travis assumed the question was his permission to speak. "Sir, I am Doctor Travis Sasser, Hood's Texas Volunteers. I was captured outside of Chattanooga a week ago with five very sick men. I believe they were infected with smallpox. While they have all died of fever since, chances are they have passed it on to some of the prisoners that shared the holding pen with them."

"So what are you telling me, Major Sasser?" the commandant asked.

"Sir, you must have better than ten thousand men behind the walls out there, all jammed in tight as fleas on a dog's back." Travis waved his hand in the general direction of the barracks. "You also must have several hundred of your men close by, serving as guards. I implore you to inform your doctor and instruct him set up in an isolated area where he can quarantine the sick from the rest of the prisoners and your people."

Travis waited for the commandant to decide. The burly, red-bearded major started at Travis for a moment, then rose to his feet and walked over to the door. Sticking his head out, he ordered his adjutant to send for the post doctor. Then he called the sergeant major to come in the room.

"Have a seat, Major Sasser, while we wait for Doctor Gutnick to arrive. Sergeant Bossemy, would you pour the major and me a small helping of whiskey, please? You will have a touch of the spirit with me won't you, Reb?"

Nodding his head, Travis sat and accepted the small silver cup of dark fluid. It made a delicious burn down to his stomach. "Thank you, sir. That's the first taste of Scotch whiskey for me in several years. It was excellent."

Major FitzPatrick glanced down at his desk, where the order signed by General Rosecrans lay beside other papers he was reviewing. He wondered if this Rebel officer knew what the order said about his custody, and what had been the reason for such a drastic decision. FitzPatrick leaned back in his chair, carefully scrutinizing his newest prisoner.

"Major Sasser, my orders are to maintain a secure prison at this place for soldiers in rebellion against the government of the United States. I was formerly the assistant warden of the federal prison at Fort Leavenworth and I know my business. I hope you aren't contemplating some foolish plan to escape or other such mischief."

"Major FitzPatrick, I assure you I am only doing my duty as a doctor. I fully expect to be paroled in a few days, so why would I try anything so foolish. Believe me, sir, if a full-scale epidemic of smallpox breaks out in this camp, as poor a physical shape as most of the Southern men are in, you could lose thousands. Your superiors in Washington would take a dim view

of that, I hope."

They were interrupted by the arrival of the camp doctor, an elderly contract physician who was introduced as Doctor Gutnick. The commandant passed along Travis's warning of smallpox among the new arrivals.

"Oh, dear," the old doctor lamented. "We'll need to set up a quarantine barracks immediately. Major FitzPatrick, can you reassign the men in the most remote building somewhere else? We'll need an isolation hospital, and I'll need to order fever suppressant from Saint Louis. We will have to burn all the clothing and linen of those who become sick. You must also inform the assigning provost marshal at Memphis that the camp is restricted for new prisoners until the epidemic has run its course." Looking at Travis and then at the major, he concluded, "I can use this doctor as my assistant, if you don't object."

"Go ahead, Doctor Gutnick, I'm sure Major Sasser is anxious to save all the Rebs that he possibly can. Right, Doctor?" The commandant smiled at Travis as he escorted them to the door. "Tell Sergeant Bossemy which barracks you want for your hospital. He'll make the necessary arrangements."

Following the fussing Doctor Gutnick out of the building, Travis sighed in defeat. He'd just have to help all he could until his parole came through. He had a feeling he and Homer were in for some long days and nights. In addition to the extra work, they would have to take care not to come down with the disease themselves.

Major FitzPatrick reread the order signed by the new commander of the Missouri Region. He guessed this General Roscrans knew what he was doing, but it would be hard on the two prisoners. He would have to stop all mail to or from them and they would not be paroled or even certified as being in custody until the recession order came from the same man who had sentenced them to the extraordinary confinement.

Travis and Homer went to work for the old doctor and, as Travis had feared, spent three months vainly fighting a full-blown smallpox epidemic. The death rate was horrendous and until the sickness abated, one thousand four hundred sixty-one men died and were buried in the muddy cemetery across the little island from the compound. The days and nights merged into an endless blur of activity as the overwhelmed medical staff of the prison, plus Travis and the four men he recruited as orderlies, worked to save those they could and comfort those who were dying of the dread disease.

When he found the time, he wrote to his folks and Clarissa and sent a formal request up to the Yankee headquarters at Saint Louis, asking for immediate parole. The rest of his waking hours he labored at the barracks that had been converted into a hospital. When it became apparent the worst was over, the provost marshal at Memphis started sending new captives to replace those lost to sickness.

Doctor Gutnick and Travis convinced Major FitzPatrick to build a small hospital outside the walls of the main prison. The men arriving from the battlefields into captivity were undernourished and easily stricken with illness. Fortunately, because the Union army had food and medicine, the loss of life to disease dropped to a much lower level than if the soldiers were in a Southern army camp.

Major FitzPatrick received favorable mention from his superiors on the quality of care given the prisoners during the epidemic, so he was amenable to requests from his medical officers, as long as they didn't try to ask for the moon. He placed the letters from Travis and Homer to their families in a folder marked "Hold Until Further Notice" and kept them in a locked file cabinet. He said nothing about the unusual orders denying them mail access, but he wondered what they had done to deserve such a restriction.

Travis and Homer convinced Doctor Gutnick that they should sleep at the little hospital and take their meals with the patients. He and the Union doctor became close, both as doctors and as friends. He had worked hard and impressed the old doctor with his skill as a physician during the epidemic. In return, Doctor Gutnick tried to help Travis in every way he could to make imprisonment as tolerable as possible.

Travis recruited an ex-miner's cook from the prison population and had a small kitchen built next to the hospital. He was able to live in relative comfort and relieved Doctor Gutnick of much of the day-to-day responsibility of administering to the sick and wounded prisoners. This suited the old doctor, as it gave him more time to sit in his rocker and sample the brandy he cherished.

Travis and Homer waited eagerly for their first letters from home, but without any satisfaction as the days and weeks slowly passed. Their disappointment was tempered only by the daily demands on their skill at administering to the health needs of the ten thousand soldiers penned inside the huge stockade.

On the last day of March 1864, the steam packet from Memphis arrived with a newly captured batch of Rebel soldiers. Travis and Doctor Gutnick examined each man before he went into the log enclosure. Separating those who needed medical attention from those more healthy, the two captive medical men worked through the entire group. The last man Travis checked was a wounded sergeant, his left leg wrapped in bloody bandages and tied to a fence rail.

Travis gently unwrapped the bloody rags. "Homer, please wash the wound area with the carbolic acid." As he bent over the leg, he asked the weathered sergeant, "What's this grass doing stuffed into the bullet hole?" With his forceps, he pulled a bloody mass of green stuff from the wound.

"Moss, Doc. It's a old Injun trick I larned when I was trapping up on the Sawtooth Range in forty-six. It keeps the septus from getting in a arrow hole fur them, so I suspect it'll work fur me." The old mountain man shifted his weight gingerly. "Doc, my leg's broke bad, I know, but I ain't gonna let you cut her off. Save my leg or let me die with it still attached."

Travis was going to give the man his standard answer, when the old man grabbed his arm in a vice-like grip. "I mean it, Doc. Iffen you cain't save my leg, leave me alone to die a whole man. You take my leg, and I'll have to carve your heart out and feed it to the buzzards."

"Let me take a look Sergeant . . . ?"

"Jacob Wheeler, Doc. Call me Jake iffen you like. I'm part mountain man, grizzly bar, trapper, Injun fighter, and lately first sergeant, A Troop, Sixth Arkansas Cavalry, Nathan Bedford Forrest's division." He hissed in pain as Travis gently probed the wound in his leg.

The feisty sergeant was right, Travis thought. There was no sign of infection in the wound, even though it was obviously several days old. His leg was severely broken and by all general procedures should be amputated immediately. Turning the leg gently, he saw the bullet had not exited the leg. He'd have to cut into the leg and remove the lead slug before he set the bone and put the splint in place.

"All right, Sergeant Wheeler, I'll try and save your leg for you. Lord knows, I've cut enough off to last my lifetime, anyway. I'll have to go in and take a look at the damage to the bone and extract the bullet. If I don't think I can fix you up, I'll wait until you wake up from the operation and give you the news. You can then decide what you want to do. Live or die, you can decide."

"Fair enough, Doc, 'cept I don't plan to be asleep when you cut on me. I'll take a drop or two of firewater and then you can go to cuttin'." The old man glared fiercely at his tormentor.

Travis smiled at the bold statement. He'd seen the effect of intense pain on brave soldiers before. Most either fainted or screamed their lungs out when he went to work on their wounded limb. Fortunately for the determined Jake, he had an ample supply of opiate syrup. He would give the wounded man a shot glass full of that to drink. Even with the opium, it would take a tough man to stand the coming operation.

Travis looked around the hospital room. Doctor Gutnick was working on a young man's shoulder and the other orderlies were bandaging some minor injuries on a couple of ragged and tired boys from a Mississippi volunteer brigade. "Homer, give me a hand with Sergeant Wheeler. We'll see if we can save his leg for him, and save my heart from the skunks as well."

Together, they washed the injured leg and prepared the operating table while waiting on the laudanum that Jake drank to take effect. He soon was mumbling in a semiconscious doze. Quickly, they placed him on the table and Travis and Homer rinsed their hands in the grain alcohol that Major FitzPatrick swore they were wasting by not drinking. He never quite believed that it was as poisonous as Travis insisted.

Fortunately, Doctor Gutnick backed Travis up in its use, even though he never used it himself. The old doctor did not believe the stories about little critters living in dirt and filth. He listened politely as Travis told of the success he had achieved reducing infection by cleaning his hands and equipment between operations, but the old doctor refused to change his habits of thirty years. "An old dog doesn't change its spots," he grumped.

The alcohol certainly did a better job of cleaning hands than the home brew they used back when they were with Hood's army, Homer proclaimed the first time they had used it. "It's just too bad it doesn't drink as easily as it washes."

Travis tied a tourniquet above the oozing wound and strapped Jake's arms and other leg to the table. He didn't want any sudden moves while he was cutting inside the leg. Taking the shiny scalpel, he dipped it in the tray of alcohol and positioned it precisely at the spot on Jake's leg where he would start the operation. The sharp, tangy smell of alcohol tickled his nose. With practiced skill he cut through the skin and muscle of the thigh. Working fast, he tied off the many small bleeders and touched them with the tip of the hot knife that Homer then replaced in the glowing-red coals of the stove.

He inspected the sciatic nerve and femoral artery. They both seemed undamaged. The femur, or thighbone, was broken and the distorted lead minié ball that inflicted the damage was still against the broken bone. Sergeant Wheeler had been lucky. The shot that hit his leg had been fired from some distance away. The bullet had slowed enough that by the time it hit his leg, it didn't have enough velocity to shatter the bone and penetrate out the back of the leg, carrying away bone and tissue which couldn't be replaced.

Travis cleaned all the bits of clothing and loose tissue from the bullet hole. He wiped the shiny white bone with a swab soaked in alcohol and grabbed the foot of the broken leg. Pulling with all his might, he pulled the broken bone into position. He heard the hiss of agony from his patient. "Hang on, Sergeant, I'm almost done with the hard stuff," he told the old mountain man. He checked the position of the bone and then started to sew his way out of the leg. Soon, he was stitching the skin together and then wrapped the leg in long rolls of bandages, supported by a wooden slate for a brace. Carefully, he and Homer moved the man to his bed and laid the broken leg on the board tied to the end of the bedstead. Tying a weight to the foot, they stepped back to view their handiwork. The leg was immobile and in traction; now only time would tell if they had succeeded.

Wiping the sweating forehead of their patient, Travis smiled down at him. "Try and sleep now, Sergeant. Rest and time are the next steps in your recovery."

"Am I gonna keep my leg, Doc?" the dazed man slurred.

"Sergeant Wheeler, you old grizzly bear, I'd bet my best horse on it," the satisfied young doctor replied. "That is, if I had a horse."

"Thanks, Doc. I'm not gonna forget this. You have a favor coming and Jake Wheeler pays in full, count on it." The wounded man fell into an exhausted sleep.

Doctor Travis Sasser smiled down at his sleeping patient and wiped his hands on the alcohol-soaked rag handed to him by Homer. "One never knows, does he, old fellow? One never knows."

Chapter 4

The days slowly grew into weeks. Spring turned to summer and then almost before it seemed possible, a year had passed since Travis and Homer had been captured. Travis sat at his little desk in the prisoners' hospital, a frown on his face, and spoke to Homer busily folding freshly washed bandages.

"Homer, it's been a year since we arrived and still neither of us has received any mail. The Yanks have control of the whole state of Texas now, I reckon. You'd think something would be getting through."

Homer looked up as Jake stepped around his workbench. The grizzled mountain man was starting to show improvement after a long six months on his back, while his leg healed. Homer smiled shyly at the grizzled old mountain man and then answered Travis. "Yessir, Doctor Sasser. I sure hope everything's all right with my mom. She's all alone, down in Austin. I write her every two weeks, as faithful as the sunrise, but I don't even know if she knows I'm here."

"Shucks," Jake chimed in. "I ain't had a letter from nobody since I jined up. Sides"—he scratched at the scar on his skinny leg—"I couldn't read it nohow. Would it help iffen I wrote a love letter to the both of you homely-looking scarecrows? That is, iffen I could write." Jake glanced around, a sly look of conspiracy on his weather-beaten face. "I'll pass the word among the other boys. See if anyone from yur part of the state is gettin' mail. Someone'll have an ideer what's up. You two have done enough fer them, these last twelve months, I reckon."

"We only do what we're trained to do," Travis modestly replied. "But if you can find out somethin', I'd be mighty grateful. I haven't heard from Clarissa in better 'n eighteen months, now."

"What's she see in you anyway, Doc?" Jake teasingly queried. "You're as skinny as a rail, brown as a Injun, dressed like a dirt farmer's scarecrow, and smelly as a hog in a waller hole."

Travis laughed. "Hell, Jake, if you think we're shabby now, you should have seen us when we arrived. Right, Homer? At least, we've got decent food to eat and a warm bed to sleep in. I don't know about you Arkansas boys, but us Texicans did without most everything civilized when we were in the field with General Hood."

Jake always responded when his beloved Arkansas soldiers were put down. "Well, we was famous in the whole Confederacy as how we did more'n with less'n than anybody in the whole danged army. Sides," he concluded smugly, "I know fer certain that you Texas boys asked us to show you how to get by on nothin' since we was the best at it, so there."

Homer, smiling, pointed Jake back toward his bed. "Time to take a breather, Jake," he remarked. "The doctor and I have to get over to the guards' dispensary and hold sick call for Doc Gutnick. He's feeling a bit under the weather. It's this cold rain. No wonder he's got the miseries."

"All right," Jake grumbled, "I'll lay down fur a spell while you all tend the good Yankee doctor, but I'm a gettin' up shortly. If you two had laid on yer backsides as long as I have, you'd appreciate just how dad-burned hard these here beds git after a while."

Jake limped off to his bed, good-naturedly complaining the whole way, making sure every man in the small infirmary had a smile on his face. Travis and Homer gathered their meager supply of medical implements and stepped out into the cool drizzle.

Waving at the guard looking down upon them from the corner blockhouse, Travis and Homer walked swiftly toward the guards' compound, built apart from the forbidding log enclosure that was the prison. Travis looked through the misty rain at the mighty river that acted as the barrier to most escapes. The sluggish brown water had an oily sheen as the raindrops sprinkled their design on its surface. "Look at that water, Homer." He sighed, "It's heading right down the Mississip past the Louisiana turnoff to Texas and home. In the meantime, here we sit, not hearing from my folks and no idea how everything is with them or Clair or your ma."

"I understand, Doc, but what can we do?" the slight orderly replied. "The war seems to be going on forever, and ain't no one being paroled no more, unless a person's so sick that even the South don't want him back." Homer shifted his torn slicker, trying to cover the annoying drip of cold water down his back. "I don't see why we can't get some mail, though. Even the Alabama boys are hearin' from their families. And the Yanks don't control half of it, yet."

"I know, damn it. Maybe I shoulda insisted that we get our chance at escape the last time I talked to Colonel R." Travis flicked his cape, reflecting the anger and frustration he was feeling.

The last time Travis mentioned escape to Colonel Richardson, the Confederate senior prisoner and head of the camp escape committee, the old colonel had set him down and forcefully informed him that his duty was to stay in prison and take care of the many sick and wounded soldiers coming in from the battles around Atlanta. Travis didn't like it, but because he was a good soldier, he quit asking.

The Yankee army, under its new general, the dreaded Sherman, who had obtained great success since replacing

Rosecrans, had busted through the Confederate lines at Lookout Mountain. Soon they were certain to capture Atlanta, the South's second-largest city.

Travis believed the war was close to being over and the South was going to lose, badly. He worried what would happen to the defeated South. The newspapers carried stories with frightfully vengeful threats associated with what was being called "Reconstruction." The South was in for some hard times after the war ended, as if it hadn't suffered enough already. He hoped that General McClellan would win the coming election in the North, as he was talking in the newspapers about a negotiated settlement to the fighting. If Lincoln won, the war would go on until the bloody end, and Travis wondered if the South could stand that. Already, there wasn't a family in the South that had not suffered the grief of the loss or maiming of a loved one.

Jumping across the mud puddles in front of Doctor Gutnick's small quarters, which were built behind the guards' infirmary, Travis and Homer entered the cluttered living room. The old doctor was sitting in his favorite rocker, with a woolen shawl over his shoulders. The ruddy-faced man with huge, mutton-chop whiskers wheezed and coughed as he motioned the two prisoners inside. "There ya are, Doctor Sasser. I was about to hold sick call myself."

Giving the doctor a quick but careful examination, Travis stepped back and sat on the corner of the table where Doctor Gutnick had been writing. "Doctor, you need to get a few days' rest, and you'll be just fine. You've just plum wore yourself out trying to keep up with the job on this here island." Travis glanced at the cheery fire, which the locked-up Confederate prisoners would have traded their last possession for, and continued. "The wet weather has inflamed your bronchial passage. You need to find a dryer place to stay for a while."

"That's exactly what I'm gonna do, sir. I've got a three-week furlough coming, and I'm going to my daughter's place in Cincinnati. I've spoken to Major FitzPatrick, and he's agreed that you can hold sick call for the guards while I'm gone."

Travis nodded. It would be a lot of extra work, but he'd be able to trade with the Yankee troops for some of the luxuries they always had in such numbers. A day or two of bed rest or a prescription for sick leave was worth a lot to the bored guards. Coffee, sweets, liquor, and decent food from their kitchen were always a possibility. "I'll take care of things, Doctor. You just take it easy and get to feelin' better. If you can, bring back some Eastern newspapers, so Homer and I can find out what's going on with the rest of the world."

Gutnick nodded and laid his head back on the pillow. He had worked hard to provide the best care he was capable of to the men on this island, both blue and gray, and Travis respected him for it. He was soon sound asleep, snoring softly. After pouring some of the old doctor's ample stock of brandy into a little bottle marked "Laxative," Travis and Homer left his room and returned to the prisoners' small hospital. The sick Southern soldiers would appreciate a sip of good drinking whiskey before lights out.

They had a seriously sick soldier to worry about. The young private from a Louisiana regiment had come down with a bad infection in his lungs. He'd been close to death when he arrived at the hospital, but Travis and Homer had just about got him through the worst, and he seemed on the way to recovering. After a short stay in the cold, drafty barracks where the prisoners lived, he had fallen ill again, even more so. Doc Gutnick had signed a certificate that he was unfit to ever serve as a soldier again and recommended he be paroled.

The patient, Robert Amos, was grinning from ear to ear when they walked in, his palid face beaming with suppressed news. "Doc, I'm going home. Can you believe it? I've been paroled as unfit for duty. Great day in the morning, I'm going home." He suffered through a long coughing spell, spit a pink froth into a nearby rag and then continued. "You'll sign my travel papers, won't you?"

"Wonderful, Robert. Both Homer and I are as pleased as you are by the good news. Of course I'll sign your papers. When do you leave?"

"I'm going on the next steamer to New Orleans, probably 'bout Friday, if you say I can."

"Be happy to oblige," the young doctor replied. "I'll get you well enough to travel if I have to work around the clock." As he examined the young soldier, he had an idea. "Robert, you could do Homer and me a big favor, if you would. You live in Shreveport, right? If we give you the addresses, would you sneak out a letter for us and mail it in Shreveport to our folks over in Texas? Neither of us has gotten a letter yet, so nobody at home must have any idea that we're here."

"Sure, Doc, be glad to, seeing how you two saved my life fur me. Something else, Doc." He glanced around to insure nobody was eavesdropping on the conversation. "I was saving this in case I ever tried to bust out." He coughed again, and then went on. "There's a rowboat sunk up at the little cove at the south end of the island. You know where I mean, don't you? I found it one foggy morning while on wood detail. It was floating down the river, as slick as you please. I swum out and got it back to shore afore the guards saw it, and sunk it in about three feet of water, six feet out from shore. There's a rope from the boat tied to a root down near the water's edge. All you'd have to do is pull it up, dump the water, and row away. I'll not have any use for it now, so take it if you want. Iffen you don't want it, pass it on to someone else."

"Thanks, Robert, that's handy information to have. I'll make sure someone gets to use it, if not me," Travis replied.

The following Friday, they watched young Robert and one other lucky soldier who was going home on parole being carried aboard the paddle wheeler for New Orleans. Those who watched fought back envy and resentment towards the happy ones leaving, even though most of those watching knew the two men were so sick that they'd probably not live to see the New Year.

Travis hoped the letters mailed by the paroled Robert after he reached Louisiana would finally reach his family and Clarissa. He was desperate for some word from his loved ones and could not understand why he had not heard from home like the other Texas boys, even though their mail delivery was sporadic at best. Every month, he had turned in his two allotted letters, one to Ma and one to Clair. None had ever gotten through, he supposed.

Travis and Homer doubled their workload the next three weeks. Keeping up with both the guard and prisoner sick calls forced them to miss sleep and most of their leisure time off. It was with relief that they greeted Doc Gutnick upon his return. The old man had relaxed and seemed much improved in health. He returned with several copies of the New York and Washington papers. Sherman had taken Atlanta, and Grant was besieging Richmond. The war was surely drawing to a devastating finish.

Jake was up and walking with hardly any noticeable limp. He managed to stay on as the hospital gofer and handyman. The old mountain man thought a great deal of Travis and Homer. He knew that most doctors would have sawed off his leg and not bothered trying to save it. His gratitude was boundless, and he worked to make himself useful. Travis and Homer enjoyed Jake's company, and never worried again about food, clothing, or the small luxuries available around a military encampment. Jake was a natural born dog-robber, the army term for scrounger, and kept the storeroom of the dispensary filled with items he "found" or traded for. The three friends settled into the routine of prison life and the daily effort of providing health care to their fellow captives.

As January 1865 arrived on the cold and clammy island, a letter arrived for Doctor Travis Sasser, from Nacogdoches, Texas. Another was for Corporal Homer Waites, from Austin. Major FitzPatrick looked at the envelopes pensively. The two Rebels had been captives for well over a year. It didn't seem possible that they should have been held so long as nonpersons. The two had worked hard to maintain camp health and deserved a break. Taking the initiative, the ex-warden wrote a message up through channels requesting clarification as to their current status.

His message was passed through channels to the commander, Department of Missouri, the very same General Rosecrans who signed the original order that put the two men in the nonperson status. After a few minutes' thought, he remembered the incident. The need for secrecy was long past. He had simply forgotten about his original order, in the stress of running the battles around Chattanooga. Without explanation, the general signed a countermand order and just as rapidly forgot about it.

The order releasing Travis and Homer from their "non-status" meandered back down the system until it finally reached Rock Island Prison. The last day of January, Travis reported to the prison commander as ordered. "Major Sasser, I have a letter for you from Texas and one for Corporal Waites. Will you see that he gets it, please? I will accept your letter in return even though it is not the end of the month. You've probably been waiting a long time for this."

Travis flashed the commandant a broad grin as he carefully placed the letter in a shirt pocket for later reading. "Yes, sir, I have. Thank you for your consideration," Travis politely replied. After a few minutes listening to the commandant talk about health problems in the camp, Travis was released and hurried back to his office. He called for Homer and delivered to him his letter. "Homer, at last, mail from home."

Homer frowned as he looked at his envelope. "It's from Mrs. Foster. That's Ma's best friend. Why would she write me?"

Travis delayed opening his envelope as Homer quickly tore open his letter and scanned its contents. His face blanched and tears glistened in his eyes. "Oh, God, my ma's died. She died last July, and I didn't even know it. Damn it all, why didn't I get home to her first?" The slight man allowed bitter tears to course down his bespectacled face.

Travis and Jake moved to their friend's side and did their best to console him. Wiping his tears away, he dried his face and excused himself. "I'd like to go over and talk with Reverend Chardon for a while. I'll be back in a bit if that's all right, Doctor Sasser."

"Sure, Homer, you go right ahead. Take your time. We'll be here when you get back. If you need anything, let me know." Travis sadly shook his head. Pray nothing like that awaited him in his letter, he thought. Excusing himself, he sat down at his little desk and opened his mail somewhat hesitantly. The letter was from his family, and Travis forced himself to crush the little pang of regret that it wasn't from Clarissa. He hoped she had sought out his folks and introduced herself to them. If so, maybe they had some news of her.

Scanning the written lines in his mother's familiar hen scratching, as she liked to say, he sighed in relief. No deaths to report. They had received word over a year ago from Captain Reynolds back in Georgia that Travis was missing and presumed dead. "Son, you don't know just how hard I've been praying that you were still among the living," she wrote. "I hope that this isn't some vile Yankee trick and this letter will reach you soon. Pa is fine and working hard to keep the ranch going. Vernon has come home, discharged from the service for wounds.

He lost his arm at Vicksburg back in the Spring of '63. I wasn't certain if you got my letter about his injury or not."

Travis was surprised; the last he'd heard about his older brother, he'd been a cotton broker in New Orleans. Molly and June, his two married sisters, were fine. They had new young ones to show him as soon as he returned. Both of their husbands had been captured in the fall of Vicksburg, and paroled two months ago from the Yankee prison in Chicago. Both were run down and weak, but getting better every day. His ma had closed, begging him to write as soon as possible.

"Good news, I hope, Doc?" Jake remarked when Travis walked back into the ward. "The news Homer was hit with, a body can do without. At least until he gits outta this here hog pen."

"Yep, my friend," Travis replied, "everything's all right with my family, thank goodness. In fact, they're all home but me. I guess I'm stuck here on this dreary island until the war is over. At least, this year will be a little brighter knowing my family is alive and well." He frowned, and again wished he would hear from Clarissa. If she only knew what a letter from her would mean to him.

"Well, Doc," the old scout cheerfully replied, "tell me all about what's happening with yer folks." He patted the side of his bed, and scooted over to the side until there was room for Travis to sit next to him.

By the time Travis had brought the inquisitive Jake up to date on the news from home, it was supper time for the bedridden inhabitants of the hospital. Since Homer was still with the camp chaplain, Jake and Travis performed the necessary duty of delivering the meals. Then Travis wrote a long letter home telling of his capture and time as a Yankee prisoner. He hoped this letter would get back to his folks through the regular channels, just like Major FitzPatrick promised.

Homer came in late that evening, sneaking past the evening guard, since it was well past curfew. "Are you all right, Homer?" Travis asked. The grim news from home must have been too painful to imagine. He hurt for his slight friend and assistant. He was determined to console Homer to the best of his ability. The loyal medical orderly deserved no less.

"Yes, sir, I'm going to make it. The chaplain and me have talked it out. It was God's will, and nothing can be done about it now, so I'm not gonna moan and wail about what's right and what's not. The only thing is," he sighed, "I don't have anyone to go home to."

"Homer, you're the best medical assistant and friend I ever had. There's always a place for you with me. You and I will return to the ranch together. We'll work something out after that about what we'll do. That is, if it is all right with you?"

"Yes, sir, and thanks. I'm gonna try and sleep if I can. I need to pray for my ma, that she's happy up there. Night, sir." Homer headed for his cot, at the far end of the ward.

"Good night, Homer. I'll say a prayer for your ma, too." Travis did just that, right then, and wished he could do more.

The days seemed to pass easier now that Travis had heard from his family. He eagerly looked forward to the next mail delivery, as the days slowly passed. He surmised 1865 would be the last year of the war, if the papers he got to read were accurate. Grant was closing in on Richmond, and Sherman was tearing up the South from Atlanta to the coast. Travis sighed. At least he could get back to his home and his beloved Clarissa, once he got out of this dank prison.

As the cold month of February finally concluded, another letter from his mother shattered the daily routine. Travis was reading the latest news from his mother when he suddenly sat upright in his chair and half shouted. "Damn it, Jake, I've got to get outta here and quick."

"What's the matter, Doc?" the old scout asked worriedly, absentmindedly rubbing his healing leg. The old man was walking without a limp, now, and seemed none the worst for his wound.

Travis looked up at his friend, the letter crumpled in his hand. "The Yankees have put an outragous tax on the ranch. If it's not paid soon, the folks will lose it at a tax auction. Ma says that Pa got so mad he had a stroke and can't do anything. Nobody has any money in Texas these days, so they don't know what to do." He glanced around angrily. "The folks built their ranch out of nothing, and now the damned carpetbaggers are gonna get it if I don't stop them. I have to get home right now and come up with some money."

The old mountain man scratched his fuzzy chin. "The war is bound to be over soon, iffen you want to wait fer that, I reckon. Or would you just as soon bust out of here right away?"

Travis answered promptly, "Now, Jake, because I've got to come up with the tax money before the first of July." Travis frowned at the immensity of his problem. "I might be able to borrow some from some medical friends of mine. If they don't have any, I don't have any idea as to what I'll do." He paused, thinking. "Maybe I can sell some of our cattle."

Jake glanced around the room and softly spoke. "Doc, I think I know where some Yankee greenbacks is. In fact, there's a whole lot of money, if we're lucky. I'll help you git it and save your folks' place iffen you'll let me."

"What are you talking about Jake? Where would you get your hands on Yankee money? And even if you could, why would you?"

"Well, it's like this," the old scout replied. "Yer my friend, and I owe ya fer savin' my leg, so jus' hush up about why." He carefully looked around and lowered his voice. "When me and General Forrest made the raid up to Paducah, where I was wounded, we busted open the local bank. It was full of payroll money for the Yankee soldiers in the district. We filled eight saddlebags with Yankee dollars. All brand-new greenbacks. Must have been thousands. General Forrest had me put the bags on a ledge in the cave where we had our headquarters. I stood up in my saddle and pushed the bags into an animal hole. You couldn't even see 'em from the floor."

Jake glanced around the room again and continued. "When we was a'leaving, things were in a tizzy, and I told the adjutant to grab the bags. Then I took off to check on the troops. Later, I asked him did he git the saddlebags. He said, 'Yep, all six of them.' I knowed there was eight of them rascals, 'cause I put 'em in the hole. I'm almost sure two bags full of Yankee money is still in that cave. I was gonna tell the general when I catched up with him. But later that same morning, I was hit by the Yankee sniper and left behind. I'd say if the money's still thar, it belongs to anyone who gits to it first, don't you?"

Travis shook his head. "I don't know, Jake." He looked out the small window by his desk. "We can't just ride over to Paducah and help ourselves to the bags. We need a plan. And we've got to break outta here without being shot."

"Well, then," Jake replied, "we'll just have to figger out a way to git in there and out without causing no suspicion. First thing is, we gotta git away from this damn island."

Travis remembered the sunken boat. Quickly, he told Jake about it. "Jake, you find out from the escape committee just who we'd need to find between here and Paducah. I understand there are some secessionist farmers in this part of the country who have been helping escapees get back to the South. We'll take it a step at a time. Let's think about what we must do and talk again tomorrow. Keep it quiet; you know I'm not supposed to even think about escaping." Smiling wide, Travis concluded,

"But by God, that's just what I'm gonna do." He grinned at Jake. "And, so are you, I guess."

Chapter 5

Travis looked up from his medical logbook as Jake entered the dispensary office, stomping mud off of his tattered boots. “Morning, Jake. How are you feeling this cold dreary day?”

“Fine, Doc, and I have some good news, for a change,” he replied as he scratched his shaggy chin whiskers. The old scout’s face reflected his excitement.

Travis looked at him expectantly. “You found out the name of a contact we can use to help us in our escape to the South?”

Jake smacked his lips. “Yep, I was talking with Sergeant Major Greer of the Fourteenth Arkansas and mentioned that I was in need of any names he was familiar with ’cause I was thinkin’ of bustin’ out shortly. He said there’s a farmer down by Saint Louis name of James Tosh who’d helped some boys from his unit get back after they slipped out of Camp Douglas prison up to Chicago. Course, he didn’t know iffen this Tosh fellow was still in business, since Greer was captured over three months ago.”

“Wonderful, Jake,” Travis replied. “Did he tell you how to find this farmer?”

“No problem to it, Doc,” Jake airily responded. “We look fur a big rock next to the river, what’s got a Yankee flag painted on it. That marks the corner of the Jim Tosh farm. It’s north of Saint Louie, right outside a town called Belle Fontaine. Sergeant Major Greer said this Belle Fontaine place has a big sign you can read right from the river, so’s you can’t miss it. Then we go to the farmhouse and knock like we was traveling through on business. We ask if he knows a family name of Wright in the area. He'll answer that they're good folks, and he'll ask us in while he gets 'em. Then we're in his care until he can move us on to the next stop on the trip home."

Travis clapped his friend on the back. "Great news, Jake. Now we best gather some supplies. Can you rustle up some civilian pants and shirts for us? Also, jackets or capes to keep warm. That river is going to be colder than a Yankee grave digger's butt this time of year."

Looking through the door into the ward, Travis called, "Homer, will you please come in here a minute?"

As soon as the three were in the room alone, Travis outlined his plan to escape with Jake. "Homer, you don't have to come. It'll likely be a rough trip and the war will be over soon. I'll leave it up to you."

Thrilled at the prospect of freedom, Homer answered immediately, "I'm with you, sir. I already told you that."

"All right, we'll go as soon as the weather clears, and we have gathered enough supplies to reach Saint Louis. Homer, you start collecting food that we can carry and not have to cook. Jake is getting clothes and warm jackets. I'll see what I can lift from Doc Gutnick's closet when I'm over there."

"Speaking of Doc Gutnick, here he comes," Jake remarked, from his position by the window.

Motioning the two others to return to the front ward, Travis picked up his pen and started making entries in his medical log as the old doctor entered the room. "Good morning, Doctor Gutnick," he greeted the visitor. "What brings you over to this side of the island on such a cold day? Are you feeling all right?"

"Yes, yes, I'm fine," the older man replied, blowing on his hands to warm them. "We're having important visitors next Friday and I wanted to tell you so your people have plenty of time to scrub this place good and clean."

"Oh, and who would be interested in inspecting this pitiful excuse for a dispensary?" Travis inquired.

"The regional supervisor of the US Sanitary Commission and some of her staff of doctors and do-gooders will be looking the prison over for a report that goes directly to the president's attention, that's who." Doctor Gutnick was clearly agitated by the impending visit of such high-powered big shots into his domain.

Travis spoke confidently, "That's all right, Doctor Gutnick. We'll have this place in first-class shape for them, don't you fret."

"They'll also want to see our records, Doctor Sasser, so please bring your medical log over to my room as soon as you can. I'll want to incorporate your log with mine." Fussing and mumbling the old physician hurried from the room.

Travis sighed; the preparation for the visit would interfere with his plans to escape, but the gathering of goods might be enhanced by the confusion. Calling Homer and Jake in again, he explained the reason for Doctor Gutnick's visit.

"Don't fret, Doc," Jake reminded him. "Them Yankee doctors will be carrying their travel orders with them. If I can get ahold of one, maybe we can use it to make ourselves copies. They might come in mighty handy."

"Good idea, Jake. We'll all have to keep our eyes open for any chance to grab their papers."

For the next few days, Travis spent more time with a mop and broom than he did dispensing medicine. All of his little staff worked to scrub the rough wooden hut from top to bottom. Doctor Gutnick worked himself up into a nervous frenzy. His nerves were close to the breaking point and Travis was hard-pressed to keep the old doctor from snapping. At last all was ready, just before the inspection committee arrived early

Friday by ferryboat from Quincy.

The head inspector was none other than Mrs. Mary Marie Livermore, one of the founders of the commission. Another woman named Mrs. Sheldon, two doctors from the Army Medical Department, and three other escort officers completed the party. The party swept through the prison and its little hospital like a blue-coated whirlwind.

Lieutenant Colonel Chase, the chief military doctor, was cold and aloof toward both Travis and Doctor Gutnick. It was obvious he didn't have much enthusiasm for the visit, but was simply fulfilling an unpleasant assignment. However, under the energetic supervision of Mrs. Livermore, the inspectors looked into every nook and corner. Travis and his orderlies had done their job well and the prison hospital was cleaner than it had been since it was first built.

Travis accompanied the party while they inspected both dispensaries and reviewed the medical logbooks, freshly updated by both Doctor Gutnick and himself. They inspected the kitchens and sleeping arrangements in the prisoner barracks. Travis invited them to eat with the prisoners to sample a typical meal, an offer that Mrs. Livermore promptly accepted, much to the disdain of the arrogant Doctor Chase and his assistants.

"Jake, please take the coats of our guests while they have dinner with us," Travis instructed. Jake and Homer were quick to help the grumbling Doctor Chase and the other reluctant officers with their overcoats. During the simple fare of cornbread and beans, with a hint of salted pork, he saw Jake smile happily at him. He had an idea the stuffy Chase was short one very important wallet of papers. The odds were that the pompous doctor would claim he had left his wallet anywhere except where prisoners might get their hands on it.

Travis politely conversed with the two females of the commission and received a condensed history on its background and purpose. The dedicated women truly wanted to improve the well-being of the soldiers, both Yankee and Confederate. They worked to ensure that all camps and prisons were as healthy as possible under the circumstances. Travis was impressed by their fervor and gained useful information to use in his escape plans.

The inspection committee left on the steamer for Saint Louis late in the afternoon. The prison staff breathed a sigh of relief and dispersed to their everyday duties. Travis motioned for Jake and Homer to join him in his little office. "Quick, Jake," Travis whispered, "what did you find in the 'Stuffed Shirt's' coat?"

Grinning like a cat that had swallowed a canary, Jake showed his treasure. The colonel's fat leather wallet had his pay book and travel orders as well as thirty dollars in greenback and a twenty-dollar gold piece. "This is all we'll need to go where we want, Doc. And look, the orders say he is to be given every courtesy by all Union camp commanders. These Sanitary Commission fellows must have some clout back in Washington."

"Marvelous, Jake! However, it also means we'd have to travel in Yankee uniforms. If we are caught, it could go badly for us."

"Don't you fret, Doc," the feisty old scout replied. "We're not gonna get caught. Don't forget, these are Yankees we'll be dealing with."

"Yeah," Homer replied sarcastically, "the same ones who caught us and penned us up here, or have you forgotten? Not that I'd be surprised if you had, being's you're an Arkansas man."

Sputtering and arguing, the two unlikely friends left to serve the evening meal to their patients. Travis smiled; it might work out to their advantage. At least they would have some money to use while working their way south. He'd decide whether or not to use the military papers when the time came, and hold onto them until then.

Travis traded his gray overcoat for a heavy wool navy pea jacket from a Confederate sailor he was treating for camp fever. The dark coat looked more civilian than military and the worn trousers he "borrowed" from Doc Gutnick would do for his escape clothes. Jake and Homer outfitted themselves with old civilian-looking clothing they'd traded for with the motley clad Southern prisoners, using rum Homer slipped out of Doc Gutnick's stash. They certainly didn't want to wear anything gray while floating down the river. Homer had secreted a supply of hardtack and salt beef in an oiled sack under his mattress. As soon as the last of the winter snow quit falling, they'd be off.

The twenty-fourth day of March 1865 arrived with a brilliant sun that rapidly melted the previous week's snow into the muddy ground. Travis gathered the other two conspirators in his office. "Jake, unless you've an objection, I say we leave tonight."

"Sounds good to me, Doc. I don't see any sign that another snow is coming. Might as well get going. I'm ready as I'll ever be. You agree, Homer?"

Homer gulped and nodded his slender head. "I'll have the food here right after dark." Taking his glasses off, he polished them nervously. This was as bad as being close to the fighting. He'd stick it out as he had always done in the past. Travis had gotten him through rough times before; he'd do it again.

The day dragged by, and as night fell, Travis waited for the others to join him in the clinic. Calling in his next senior orderly, Joe Potts, he revealed his plan. "Joe, Homer and I are slipping out tonight. We'll swim over to Quincy and then work our way down to Louisville. We'll be able to catch a train once we're into Kentuck, I reckon, and be in Tennessee by Wednesday. Don't tell anyone about our plan until then." Travis embellished his bogus plan, wanting to convince Joe of its authenticity.

Joe gasped in amazement, "But Doctor Sasser, the war's

almost done. Why try something so risky?" He looked at Travis as if he were insane. "Besides, who's gonna take care of the prisoners if you leave?"

"I have to get home quick, Joe," Travis replied. "I can't wait any longer. You'll have to take charge of the hospital and do the best you can." He paused and then told the truth. "My folks are about to lose their farm, and they need me. Now that the war's nearly over, we have to take care of ourselves."

Travis knew that the prison authorities would soon hear what he had said to Joe. There were numerous informers in the general prison population, sustained by favors and good treatment. He hoped by sending his pursuers off on a false trail, it would keep search parties from looking along the river. He also figured that since nobody knew about the boat, and when they didn't find any sign of the men around Quincy, they might think the escapees had drowned while trying to swim across the frigid water to the mainland and give up the search.

As the quarter moon dipped behind some high clouds, the three men slipped out of the back of the clinic. Careful to stay in the dark shadow cast by the log wall of the huge prison stockade, they made their way to the east end of the compound. The guards' attention was directed inward, toward the dim interior of the stockade. Travis hoped they would be undetected as long as they were quiet. As the night wind pushed even heavier clouds across the face of the moon, they dashed to the skimpy stand of trees at the easternmost tip of the island.

Luck was with them, as they reached the little cove without being discovered. They spread out and searched for the rope tied to the root Robert had described. "Here it is," Jake whispered. Struggling with the wet rope, he untied the muddy halter and tugged hard. "Jiminy, this thing is heavy. You boys lend a hand."

Straining with the effort, they couldn't pull the boat to the shore. "Jake," Travis hissed, "We'll have to get out of our clothes and pull the damn thing out of the mud."

Without waiting for a reply, he started pulling down his pants. Grumbling and with his teeth chattering under his breath, Jake shed his clothes and joined Travis in the dark, cold water. Travis gasped as the freezing water hit his bare legs. Following the rope, they felt the wooden outline of the rowboat.

Grunting with effort, they pulled it from the suction grasp of the muddy bottom. Homer pulled on the tie rope and they were able to maneuver the boat and its load of mud and water to the edge of the bank. Tipping it over, they dumped the slimy muck back into the frigid water and slid the small boat onto the slick bank.

Shivering violently, Jake and Travis hastily dried off and got back into their clothes. Travis's legs were numb and the returning warmth sent little needles of pain shooting through his body. He tried to keep his chattering teeth quiet, but it was in vain. Their clattering sounded to him loud enough to wake people across the wide river in Iowa.

"Gawd almighty, I'm cold," Jake muttered as he pulled on his ragged coat and sat on a stump to pull on his boots. "I hope we don't tip over; iffen we get our clothes wet, we'll freeze for sure."

"Not a chance, Jake," Travis chattered, "I've been rowing on rivers since I was shirttail high to my pa. We'll be safe as can be, mark my words."

To his relief, the oars were tied to the inside of the small craft, and it was ready to carry them downriver. Tossing their meager possessions in the back, they pushed the little boat out on the water, where it sat bobbing in the sluggish current. Climbing in, Travis moved to the rear and spoke. "Come on, let's get going while the moon is still behind the clouds. We've got a long way to go before daylight."

Shoving away from the bank, they rowed out to the middle of the wide river. Turning the bow downstream, Jake started to row first shift, while Homer sat in front looking for floating debris. Travis sat in the rear and guided the crude rudder.

As they drifted past the island prison, Travis looked over at the stark outline of the massive wooden barricade outlined against the dark sky. He thought of the many days he'd spent at this terrible place and the heartbreaking number of young men he'd lost to disease therein. They lay in silent rows in the dreary camp cemetery, spared by fate from the shells on the battlefield, only to fall to the unseen scourge called smallpox or the flux. He suddenly shivered; a spasmodic chill ran down his spine. He didn't know if he was just cold or afraid. He did know he wanted to be far away from Rock Island Prison, far, far away.

By daybreak, they had traveled twenty miles south of Quincy. Gliding into a bushy thicket, they pulled the boat out of the water and hid it in the weeds. "Build us a small fire, Jake," Travis ordered, blowing warm air into his cupped hands. "We need it." Grateful for the temporary warmth, they heated some coffee and then after a breakfast of hardtack and beef, rolled into their pallets and slept the day away.

After sundown, they ate again, and drank their fill from a nearby stream. By the time it was full dark, they were back on the river. Staying away from the shore, unless it was to avoid the occasional steamboat or barge, they spent the next eight nights moving steadily southward.

It was so bitterly cold that rowing was the only way to stay warm, so they traded off the chore and rowed hard as they could, thus making good time. They huddled together during the daylight hours, warming their bodies. The sparse food they had to eat did little to replenish their flagging energy.

Only once were they threatened with discovery or destruction. It was nearly dawn on the sixth day when a massive river dreadnaught loomed out of the morning mist, silently steaming downriver. Sweating hard, Travis pulled the oars as rapidly as he could while Homer steered away from the iron monstrosity. The black hull slipped past them by mere inches and the wake made their tiny craft bob and pitch like a leaf in a hurricane. As the dark mass steamed on, unaware how close it had come to ending the careers of the escapees, they sat shaken in their little boat.

Travis spoke for all of them. "Damn, that was close. We're too tired, let's call it a night and get some rest."

"I agree to that, by gum," Jake agreed. "I'm tired and cold. Let's build us a big fire and git warm, I don't care what the risk."

The morning of the ninth night was close to dawning as their boat drifted toward the banner that was draped across two poles next to the water's edge. "Welcome to the City of Belle Fontaine," it said in three-foot-high letters.

"There she be, Doc," Jake cried. "Just like Greer said. We stay on the water for a little longer; and then we should see the rock with the flag on it. Good ole Sergeant Greer. He sure steered us right."

"All right with me, as long as we find it soon," Travis replied. "No need to become careless after getting this far."

"Look Doc," Homer said. "Over there." He pointed with his finger. "A big rock with the flag painted on it. And there's a place to tie up."

The three men clamored up the slippery bank, and immediately saw the white farmhouse across the fallow wheat field. Jake muttered, "Come on, men. We may as well find out if the rest of my information is as good as what it's been up to now." Jake led the way toward the distant house.

As they walked into the farmyard, a stocky, bald man came out of the barn, a milk bucket in hand. "Howdy," he spoke as he eyed the strange trio with their muddy boots and disheveled appearance. He had a good idea of what he was looking at.

Jake answered back, "Howdy, neighbor. We're a bit lost. Looking for the Wright family farm. Is it hereabouts?"

The man replied, "They're good folks to know, fer certain. They live a long ways from here, though. Would you want to rest up a bit before going on?"

"That would be appreciated," Travis replied. "I'm Major Sasser, and these are Sergeant Jake Wheeler and Corporal Homer Waites. We've escaped from Rock Island Prison."

"Glad to meet you. I'm Jim Tosh, from Arkansas originally. I was sent up here in sixty-one to set this place up and do what I could for the cause. You boys are the first customers I've had in weeks. Must be gettin' harder to get out of them Yankee prisons."

He motioned them toward the whitewashed barn. "Let's step inside, and out of the sight of any Yankee busybody passing by. I've got a real cozy place back of the loft for you to hide in while we plan your next step."

Jake chortled with every step. "A Arkansas man, by gum. I mighta knowed this was gonna be my lucky day."

Leading the way up the hayloft ladder, Mr. Tosh showed the fugitives a sparsely furnished room, hidden behind a huge pile of stacked hay. Four cots lined the far wall and a small table and two old wooden chairs sat in the center of the room. The simple furnishings were luxury enough for the weary men.

Throwing himself down on one of the cots, Jake remarked happily, "Shucks, I'm prepared to spend a week here just resting up. I'm plumb wore out from all the rowing I done. Wake me up when the war's over."

Sitting at the small table, Travis asked Tosh, "What's the news about the war? We've been on the water for the past nine days."

Tosh shook his head. "Not too good, I'm afraid. General

Lee's still holding back Grant at Richmond, but the papers say he can't last much longer. Sherman is tearing up South Carolina just like he done to Georgia. The end is coming for the South, I'm afraid."

"Is there any news out about the three of us?"

"Not that I've heerd of," Tosh replied. "The last paper I read didn't mention any prisoner escape. I'll go into town this afternoon and see if there's anything in the latest *Saint Louis Dispatch.* You boys rest up and be quiet. I'll be back after dark. I'll bring food, and we can start plannin' for the rest of your trip. Don't leave this room until I return. Use the chamber pot there if you need to."

After the farmer left, all three men washed as best they could with the water available and fell asleep on the soft beds. They were awake and refreshed when Tosh returned with two women, one bearing a steaming pot of stew.

"This here is my wife, Emma, and this is Miss Marie LeMont, who works for the cause as a courier and information gatherer. She's been up here fer several months on a special mission."

Travis could see how the beautiful, dark-haired girl would be a natural for prying information out of lonely soldiers. He'd heard of spies obtaining information by using their female wiles to cuckold their victims. Hiding his immediate distain for any woman who would sink to such a low base, he introduced himself and his friends to the two women.

"Doctor Sasser, I was sort of thinking about sending Miss LeMont out with you. She's been up here scouting for General Sterling Price. He's planning another raid north. It might help take the pressure off Richmond if the Missouri legislature raises enough alarm. General Price is just the man to give them the shakes."

"Mr. Tosh, isn't there a better way of slipping Miss LeMont

back to our lines? We're certainly a risky bunch of companions for her." Travis frowned at the thought of having a young woman along to worry about. The trip would be hazard enough as it was.

"Ordinarily, I'd agree," the farmer admitted as he looked at the tall, young woman. "Unfortunately, the Yanks have an idea about what she's been doing in Saint Louis. They're looking for a single woman fitting her description, headed south. She could blend in with you three and not be as obvious as by herself. Once you get to Vicksburg, she'd meet her escort from Price's headquarters in Mississippi and be out of your hands."

"Doctor," the young woman broke the following silence. Her voice was soft and flavored by a distinct Louisiana accent. "I'll be as little trouble as possible. You must help me return to Vicksburg, I beg you. I have to deliver my information to General Price immediately. I have the disposition of all the troops in the Missouri command. He needs this before he strikes north."

Travis looked over at Jake and Homer, who were gulping down their stew while listening to the conversation. "What do you fellows think? You have as much to say about it as I do."

"I'd be plumb satisfied to help the lady and the cause," Jake replied.

"Me, too," seconded Homer.

"Welcome to our little band of desperadoes, Miss LeMont." Travis surrendered reluctantly.

"Please call me Marie, all of you. And thank you. I'll try very hard not to be a burden."

"Now, Doctor," Tosh interjected, "we have to prepare for the next leg of your journey. Just how do you plan to make yur way back to Texas?" Tosh got out a map and spread it on the table as he spoke.

Pointing to the dot marked Paducah, in Kentucky, Travis

tapped his finger on the map. "We have slipped into this town first, Mr. Tosh. Next, we were going to head toward Memphis and then Vicksburg, maybe on a paddle wheeler or by horseback if necessary. From there, we'll cross over the Missip to Louisiana and then on to Texas and home. Once there, we'll report for duty with the nearest unit."

"Lord's sake, Doc," Tosh exclaimed, "do you have any idea just how hard that's gonna be? There's Yankees all over that part of the country. What's gonna keep you from being policed right up by 'em?"

Pulling out the wallet of Lieutenant Colonel Chase, Travis outlined his plan. "If we pass ourselves off as Sanitary Commission inspectors, with orders like this, we should most likely be able to travel where we want. We can write up Marie as a female inspector from Washington, and she wouldn't have to hide the fact that she's a woman."

Smiling at Tosh, Travis concluded, "Can you steal some Yankee uniforms and letterhead paper from their headquarters for me to forge the orders on?"

"I should be able to get uniforms and papers, except for yours, Doctor. I have a man who buys items from deserting soldiers, and he'll have most everything you'll need but a colonel's coat."

Handing Tosh the thirty dollars, Travis replied, "Then have a tailor make me one. Also, I'll need a doctor's medical kit and horses for Jake and me. Homer and Marie will need a small wagon, if possible."

Turning to Marie, he inquired, "Do you have clothes for traveling? If not, we must find you some."

"I've got a trunk full; just exactly what a well-bred lady from Washington would want on a rugged visit to the battlegrounds," she gaily replied. "I do believe this plan is the best yet for fooling the Yanks." She concluded her remarks in an eastern accent,

"I can even sound like a Washington lady, so don't worry about me sounding like a Louisiana Creole."

Homer spoke up. "Mr. Tosh, how do you plan to obtain our horses and a wagon?"

"Same way the Yankees got 'em, son," the farmer replied. He looked at the three men with a mischievous grin. "We'll steal 'em."

Chapter 6

The next afternoon, Marie brought the hungry trio some fried chicken and biscuits, but more importantly, several blank papers with the Department of the Army letterhead on them. "Compliments of some friends over at Headquarters, Department of Missouri," she modestly explained.

"Excellent," Travis exclaimed. "Homer and I will forge orders explaining the reason for our presence in the area to any Yankee commander. Jake, hand me the orders that Doctor Chase was carrying."

Travis and Homer were soon deeply engrossed in their forgery effort. In their haste to forge the orders so necessary to their escape, the hot chicken supper was almost overlooked. "I swear," Travis remarked, "if we don't watch it, we'll be too fat to fit into our uniforms. Tell Mrs. Tosh that the food is grand."

"Thank you very much," Marie smiled. "I'm afraid that you are eating my efforts from the kitchen. Just a sample of what to expect when we're on the road."

"Doggone iffen I ain't gonna marry you afore we get to Vicksburg, you keep cooking like this," Jake exclaimed while gnawing on a plump chicken leg.

"Travis," Marie suddenly was serious. "Mr. Tosh says there are wanted posters out on me all over Saint Louis. He says the drawing isn't a very good likeness, but it means I may be a threat to you and the others." She shook her head, her dark locks swishing across her bosum. "I suppose I should have returned much sooner. My little masquerade is at an end."

"Don't fret, Marie, with these orders as an inspection team from the Sanitary Commission, you should be quite safe. You wouldn't believe the fear their visit strikes in the hearts of Union commanders. They'll be too busy trying to cover up the wretched conditions around their camps to ever take notice of us as individuals. Besides, the Yanks would never think of us trying to move south in such an unusual disguise. By the way, I'm calling you Miss Sara Livermore, who will be the niece of the founder of the commission, Mary Livermore. I don't think anyone would dare cause such an important lady trouble."

"Well, don't you think it will seem odd that a single woman is traipsing about with three soldiers?" she asked.

"Possibly," he admitted. "But what choice do we have? Unless you have another spy who wants to travel south the hard way."

"As a matter of fact I do," she answered, to his surprise. "Not really a spy, but a widow friend whom I've used from time to time, name of Irma Farris. She wants to return to Mississippi. Irma came up here in sixty-two from Natchez after her husband was killed at Shiloh. She's been living with her sister here in Saint Louis. She's willing to accompany us as my traveling companion if you'll let her."

Travis frowned. "Does she know the risks she'll be taking? I assure you they will be severe."

Marie nodded. "I explained the dangers to her, and she's willing to accept them. She understands it could help me complete my mission. Can you write her into the fake orders?"

"I don't see any problem," Travis admitted. "I'll use her real name, so she won't have to memorize a new one. You know, I sort of like this writing my own orders, after following someone else's orders for so long. I think I could enjoy being a general. Now, how does Irma spell her last name?"

When they had finished, they had composed several different letters from General Joseph Barnes, the army surgeon general, detailing Lieutenant Colonel Chase, Medical Corps, to accompany Miss Sara Livermore and party on an extended inspection of camps and forts of the Mississippi River Military District, which stretched from Cairo, Illinois, to New Orleans. He also wrote escort orders for Homer and Jake under the names of the two pay books purchased from two deserters of the Western Missouri Command garrison troops.

"Look here, Jake," he noted. "The Yankees owe you fifty-six dollars in back pay. We'll ask the first paymaster we meet to bring you current. That'll give us some spending money."

Marie interjected, "Don't worry about money, I'll have several gold coins sewn into my dress if we need cash."

"I don't suppose it will hurt," Jake replied. "We may need all the money we can get our hands on, especially if things get too hot."

They paused as Mr. Tosh clambered up the loft ladder. His pained expression was evidence of the bad news he carried. "I've been into town and picked up your uniforms. They're out in the wagon, but I bring disastrous news. General Lee has abandoned Richmond and got hisself and his troops surrounded at some place called Appomattox Court House, Virginia. The paper says he's gonna ask Grant fer terms tomorrey. It's a black day for the South."

"Damn," Jake muttered, "I never suspected that the Yanks could corner General Lee and his troops." The shocked Southerners discussed the implications of the disturbing news.

Travis broke the silence. "I don't know about the rest of you, but I don't see any recourse for us but to go on with our plan."

"I agree," Marie seconded him. "The war may go on for a long while yet, and if it does, it will be here in the West. I must get my information to General Price. It is more important than ever that his raid into Missouri be successful."

"Fine by me," Jake chimed in. Homer nodded in agreement.

"Well, it might make the next step in our project a little easier," Tosh remarked. "The Yankee commander in Saint Louis is having a victory celebration tomorrow. There'll be parades, fireworks, and parties everywhere. May be a good chance for us to get the horses and wagon we need."

"A good idea, Mr. Tosh," Travis responded. "Let's try the uniforms on. Nobody is going to notice three extra soldiers with all the festivities and excitement."

After admiring the dashing figures they made in their new Yankee blue uniforms, the four conspirators continued planning for the next day.

Travis issued final instructions. "Marie, you and Mrs. Tosh go into town before dark and visit with Irma and her sister. We'll ride in with Mr. Tosh after dark. We'll meet you at her house. I'll explain our plan for her, and you can then guide us to the Yankee camp. We'll sort of mosey in and see if we can't pick up a few things we need like horses, wagons, and weapons." He smiled at the pretty, dark-haired woman. "It ought to be real exciting."

Riding beside Tosh into Saint Louis, with Homer and Jake sitting in the rear of the wagon, dressed as Union soldiers, Travis's nervous anxiety grew with every step away from the farm. If they slipped up now, it might be fatal, or at best many years before he saw his home again. For sure, the brave Marie would face the hangman's pleasure. While he looked like a Union colonel, with his nicely tailored coat and new blue hat, he prayed that he could also sound like one if questioned by some suspicious sentry.

Reaching the home of Irma's sister, they knocked and were invited inside. Marie introduced the young widow from Vicksburg. Irma was slight and sweet, with locks of fine brown hair and freckles on her nose. She must have been widowed awfully young, Travis thought to himself. He outlined his plan for passing through the Union rear lines until they reached Vicksburg.

"I'm ready, Doctor Travis," Irma insisted. "I've spent enough time here grieving for my Andy. It's time I got back to living and doing what I can for the South. If this will help Marie and the Confederacy, then I'm happy to do my share."

"You're a brave woman, Irma, and we're fortunate to have your help." Travis smiled at her. "Marie, can you show us where the Yanks are most likely to have some horses for us?"

"I know where the Twenty-first Missouri Cavalry has their main headquarters, if that will do. They've been on active duty for a year and never left the city limits. If anybody should be slack in their vigilance, I should suspect they would. Their commander is a rummy and a slimy political hack to boot. He has given me much good information while in his cups, which I suspect he will be deeply into by now."

Travis frowned at Marie's description. He didn't like the idea of someone as nice as Marie carousing with drunken Yankee officers.

Tosh escorted Travis, Jake, Marie, Homer, and Irma through the raucous crowds of celebrating soldiers and civilian residents out on the town. Nobody paid them the slightest attention, except to salute him, or the Union colonel he was impersonating. A huge bonfire had been set in an empty lot near the waterfront. A group of drunken soldiers was busy pushing some wagons into the flames. Nobody seemed to object at the waste of good rolling stock.

"You know," Jake mused, "if we get a wagon, the Yanks will figure it was burned and not look any further for it. Keep your eyes peeled."

As they turned toward the area of the cavalry camp, an officer's carriage with several boisterous Union officers inside drew up to what was apparently a very busy sporting house. As the officers staggered inside, one shouted to the driver, "We'll be a while, Corporal Simms. Why don't you relax and wait for us over at the tavern there?" He gestured down the street and slammed the door, shutting off any reply.

Travis and his party watched as the grumbling driver tied the pair of horses to the hitching post in front of the tavern and walked inside. The carriage was exactly what they needed for their plan. It had cover, room for luggage, and was just the sort of transportation a high-ranking woman from the Sanitary Commission would use during a protracted visit to the field.

"Quick, Homer," Travis whispered, "jump into the driver's seat and drive back to the farm. Marie and Irma, you go with him. If anyone stops you, Homer, say you are on an errand for the brigade commander, and point to the ladies in the back. They'll think they're some doxies you're transporting home. Hide the carriage and horses in the barn. We'll be back before daylight, if we're lucky." Homer drove the carriage away without incident, Marie and Irma inside, out of sight. It was a good omen, and their morale improved immediately.

Continuing their walk, passing several groups of soldiers, who saluted Travis and greeted Jake as if nothing was amiss, they soon reached the headquarters of the Twenty-first Missouri Cavalry. The guard on duty at the front entrance casually waved them through without asking for a pass, and the few men who were moving about paid no attention to the three men, although one was not in uniform. They strolled over to the stables at the back of the compound. Inside were several fine-looking animals.

"Gawd Almighty, Doc," Jake whispered, "we're in the officers' stables. It's like being in a bank with no safe. Just take what we want and ride away."

Travis nodded. "Mr. Tosh, please saddle four animals and wait for us behind the stables. Jake, you come with me, and let's see if we can find some weapons."

Moving down the rows of tents, Travis kept watch while Jake ducked in the nearest opening. Grinning in satisfaction, he stepped out the back flap and showed Travis four rifles and two belts with holstered pistols. Giving him a nod and a grateful smile, the satisfied doctor motioned for Jake to rejoin Tosh.

Walking with the confident stride of a man who knows what he is doing, Travis strolled toward the wooden building marked with the sign "Brigade Hospital" on its front. Slipping through the door, he saw an orderly tilted back in a chair, asleep. The ward was dark, and no one was aware of him as he eased open the door to the surgeon's office. There on a table was what he was after, the field medical case of a military doctor.

Almost reverently, Travis opened the dark leather bag. Inside, it was filled with shiny new medical instruments and the various pills and potions required for treating field injuries and sickness. The equipment made the ones he'd lost to the Yanks in Tennessee seem pitifully second-rate. He almost felt like leaving a thank-you note to the thoughtful doctor who had filled his new kit. Smiling at the thought, he picked up the bag and slipped back out the door.

Jake and Tosh were waiting for him, shuffling about nervously. "Jake, get all the horses left in the stable out and turn them loose. I'm going to set the stable on fire. When the horses turn up missing, maybe the Yanks will think they broke loose and ran away."

Jake and Tosh complied and Travis started a blazing fire in the dry straw. Hurrying out the rear door, he climbed onto the back of a magnificent roan gelding, which came from the stable marked "Brigade Commander." With nonchalant ease, as if they hadn't a care in the world, the three men cantered down the back roads toward the Tosh farm. Behind him, he could hear the faint shouts of alarm as the burning stables and running horses took the attention of what few soldiers were available or sober enough to care.

After everyone was safely back at the farm, the elated Southerners had their own celebration. Tosh brought out some hard cider and sweet cakes that Irma had sent back with Emma Tosh.

Travis led Marie over to the carriage and admired the comfortable interior. "Marie, we should leave immediately, while the bluecoats are recovering from last night's activities. I think we should leave tomorrow morning, if you and Irma are ready."

"I'm in complete agreement with you, Travis," Jim Tosh spoke. I'll pick up Irma tomorrow morning and be back here by nine, with her ready to travel." He paused for a moment, then continued, "I'll draw a map to the ferry what gets you over the Mississip, and then the route for you to take across Illinois to Paducah. After that, you'll have to get directions from the Yanks."

"Mr. Tosh, Jim. I want you to know just how much we appreciate what you and Emma have done for us." Travis took the farmer's hand and shook it firmly. "We'd be in a hell of a fix if it weren't for you both."

"Don't say a thing, Doctor Sasser," Tosh replied. "We should be thanking you boys for all your sacrifice for the South. Emm and me are proud and happy we can do a little to help you in our own small way. I'll have food and water ready for you tomorrow morning."

"When the war's over, what are you gonna do, Mr. Tosh?" Homer inquired. "You gonna stay here, in Yankee country?"

"Me and Emm are moving out West, away from all the troubles, and I'm gonna farm and fish till it's time to meet my maker," he answered as he smiled. They shook hands all around, and the three escapees retreated to their hidden room in the hayloft.

Before noon the next day, the party was crossing the river at

Belle Fontaine toward Illinois and the road southeast toward Paducah. The orders he showed the ferry guard were accepted without question and gave Travis renewed hope their plan might succeed. That night, they stayed by the town of New Athens, nearly thirty miles from Saint Louis. The horses were first-rate animals, as was the team pulling the carriage. They had no trouble making nearly good mileage. As Marie and Irma fixed a quick meal, the men carefully inspected their new weapons.

"These here are fifty-two-caliber Spencer carbines, Doc," Jake explained. "The best rifle the Union cav has got. It's a tube-fed, seven-shot repeating rifle. See how the tube of bullets slides in the stock here? Then you just fire, cock the lever, and fire again till you run out. This here little box holds six more tubes of reloads. It's too bad my Arkansas boys didn't have 'em at Paducah; we'd still be in control there."

They also had nearly new, .44-caliber Dragoon pistols with two additional reloaded cylinders for each pistol. The cap-and-ball revolver was a big handgun, weighing nearly three pounds, but had great stopping power.

Travis felt they could stand up to any small-size force that cornered them into fighting. The goal, of course, was to avoid any conflicts of that nature.

After an early breakfast, they continued on their way. They were challenged only once, and the forged papers worked without a problem. The extra horse came in handy, as Marie liked to ride. She and Travis rode side by side and enjoyed the lovely day, warm and sweet with the smell of spring flowers heavy in the air. They were riding so close together, their legs brushed each other's from time to time. Neither made any move to increase the distance between their horses.

Travis told her a bit about his family and his days on the ranch in Texas. She listened with interest as he described attendance at Harvard College in Boston, where he studied medicine. She grimaced as he described the taunts and insults he took from the sons of radical abolitionists regarding his Southern roots. "To be honest, Marie, I don't think I ever knew more than half a dozen men who owned slaves until I joined the army. There weren't many on the ranches in east Texas."

Marie nodded. "My father had many, and we never treated a single one badly. I had one he bought me for a house servant, and the first thing I'm gonna do is set her free the first chance I get." She paused and gazed toward the high whispy, white clouds. "Although, she may already be free, I'm not certain."

They rode silently for a few moments, until Travis urged her to tell him more. He was captivated by the sound of her voice.

"Father was killed at the head of his brigade at the siege of Vicksburg. I lost my fiancé at Pea Ridge, and my only brother when the *Mishawaka* was sunk by the Yankee blockade off Galveston in January of sixty-four."

Travis nodded. *How many women of the South had the same sort of experiences,* he wondered. "Please accept my deepest condolences, Marie. Is that why you started spying for the army?" He could not hide his distaste for the idea.

She smiled at him in a sad way. She knew most men disapproved of women who used their feminine charms to spy, no matter how grateful they were to receive the information. Unfortunately, sometimes intimacy was necessary, but it had meant nothing to Marie. What she learned might save the lives of hundreds of men like those she had lost. *Men were such silly fools about it,* she thought for the hundredth time.

"Yes, I had known General Polk since he was a bishop in Louisiana before the war started. He convinced me I could help the South. I wanted to do something to even the score against the North."

Travis felt his blood start to boil as his imagination drew vivid flashes of lurid scenes with drunken, Yankee officers, cooling any ardor he felt toward her at the moment. His mood soured and Marie sensed his change in attitude. She fell silent and soon returned to the carriage to ride with Irma and Homer.

Jake and Travis trotted ahead of the others to survey the road. "Mighty fine lady there, Doc," the old man remarked, as he spit at a toad beside the roadway. "A fellow could sure do a lot worse, if you ask me."

"Jake, you old broken-down razorback, did I ask you anything at all? Besides, wait until you meet Clarissa. She's been on my mind a great deal lately. She stayed home where she belonged, and out of other men's beds. Now there is a gal worth waiting for."

Having the good sense not to pursue the conversation, Jake subsided and scanned the road ahead. It had been a long day in the saddle, but at last, there was Marionville, only a day's ride from Paducah. He dared to pray that the money was still there.

They stayed at the local training camp in Marionville where they enjoyed a bath and a warm, filling meal. The two women ensured the treatment the party of Rebel evaders received was first-class. Travis noticed with wry amusement that Homer stayed close to Irma and saw to it that she didn't want for anything he could provide for her.

"It appears that Homer has taken a shine to Mrs. Farris," Travis softly remarked to Jake as they watched Homer's careful attention to the comely young widow.

"Yep," Jake laconically answered, as he spit a brown stream of tobacco juice to the ground. "I don't reckon he's long fer the world as a bachelor." Jake scratched at the warm underside of his arm. "He could do a whole lot worse. She's one spunky woman, mark my words."

Late the next afternoon, they stood on the ferry crossing the Ohio River toward the Kentucky town of Paducah. The next step of Travis's plan was about to begin. Travis watched the brown waters of the Ohio River sluggishly flow past, feeling the nearness of Marie, standing silently, next to him. He searched for words that did not seem to want to come out of his mouth. She was an appealing vision, framed in the dying sunlight of the day, her dark hair reflecting the gold of the sun in a red-black sheen.

"I wish we could just keep on drifting down the river," he finally muttered. "It would sure save us a passel of time and effort."

Marie came out of her reverie and looked up at the tall, good-looking man beside her. She felt the stirring in her heart, and a shiver flashed its way to her fingertips. She resisted the impulse to touch this man she had met so fortuitously. His arrival meant she could accomplish her mission for General Price. Yet, he had already started to worm his way into her heart and thoughts, drawing some of the focus away from her mission.

She responded with heartfelt conviction. "We'll get there, I just know it. Your plan is a masterpiece."

"I don't know," Travis grumbled. "I'm not so sure, at least when I think too long about the odds."

"Well, don't think about it, then," Marie gaily responded. "Tell me about Texas, and your home."

"Now that's something worth talking about," Travis replied, his eyes sparkling. "Let's see, where shall I begin?"

As the ferry nosed into its landing dock, Travis mounted and led his party toward the entrance of the compound where the Union garrison was stationed. The earthen walls were on a small bluff that overlooked the river and town below.

Straightening out his coat, he returned the sentry's salute and instructed in his sternest officer's voice, "Take me to your commanding officer, soldier."

Chapter 7

The commander of the Paducah army garrison, Major Chas A. Akins, according to the small desk sign, held the disturbing orders in his hand and looked up in agitation at the tall, fit-looking lieutenant colonel from the Department of the Army Medical Corps. "Damn it, sir," he complained. "Why wasn't I sent word of this visit by army headquarters in Cincinnati?" The skinny officer's Adam's apple bobbed nervously in his scrawny neck. He appeared to be more like a harried storekeeper than a soldier. Gaunt and shallow-faced, he hardly seemed capable of commanding a team of broken-down horses, much less an army garrison.

"For the very reason that it's precisely what these do-gooders want," Travis commiserated. "They hope to surprise you boys and find fault to complain about in Washington." He favored the disturbed major with a conspiratorial look. "Don't you worry, Major. I'm here to help. I'll show the inquisitive Miss Livermore enough to satisfy her, and then be out of your hair. I'll make sure my report fails to include anything which might be detrimental to your command."

"Why, thank you, sir," the relieved Akins gushed. "I am most appreciative of your concern for the difficult job I am forced into at this forgotten outpost." He adjusted his coat and spoke with a renewed confidence in his voice. "How may I help you during your visit?"

These were the exact words Travis was hoping to hear, and

he responded. "Just give me the freedom to show the pettifogging Miss Livermore what she thinks she needs to see, and I'll soon have her convinced that this garrison is a model of modern sanitation. Any recommendations she suggests you must seize as if sent from above with sincere admonitions of prompt compliance. What you do after we leave is up to you, of course."

The overwrought Akins grabbed the advice like a thirsty man for water. He had better things to do than babysit some silly women from the Sanitary Commission. This Doctor Chase was an all-right gentleman, in his opinion.

"My thanks for your understanding, Colonel Chase." He opened his desk drawer. "Care to share a small drop of rum with me?"

Pouring two small glasses full, without waiting for a reply, he passed one to Travis and toasted him before gulping the amber liquid without pausing. Travis sipped his a bit more carefully. It tasted more like coal oil and sugar than rum, but he smacked his lips appreciatively. "That was mighty good, Major. Thank you, and to your good health."

"My pleasure, sir." Akins wiped his lips after a healthy swallow. "I seem to detect a slight accent that says you spent some time in the South. Am I right?"

"My compliments, sir," Travis replied. "I lived my first ten years in Texas with my father, who was a cotton broker. After we moved to Boston, I thought I'd lost all my Southern drawl. You have a keen ear, Major."

"Boston, you say," Major Akins laughed. "Well what do you know? That's where I'm from, at least Norwood. You know where that is, I presume? Say, did you ever go to the Old Triangle Tavern in Boston? What a wonderful place to relax and enjoy good friends."

"You mean the inn at the split of Beacon Street and Beacon Drive? I've spent many a happy evening there myself." Travis was grateful he'd spent some of his precious free time in medical school enjoying the pleasures of the city.

"That's the one," Major Akins replied. "What a coincidence that we were once almost neighbors, and now we meet in Kentucky."

The rest of the initial meeting passed without incident. Travis and the two women ate with the major and his small staff. The ladies were the object of everyone's attention and had easily convinced the bored soldiers in the backwater post that they were true blue Yankees from Washington, DC. Travis hoped that Jake and Homer were as successful at the enlisted mess where they were guests. Jake was no problem, and if Homer didn't say much, then their ruse should succeed.

The small VIP guest quarters were assigned to the ladies, and Travis took the room of the post doctor, who was away resupplying his medical stores, and most likely, his liquor cabinet. According to Major Akins, the post doctor spent most of his days and nights quietly drunk. "At least he's no trouble," was how he put it.

The next day was spent looking over the post facilities, and surprisingly, it appeared that contrary to his first impression, Major Akins had done a fairly impressive job of keeping the small post disease-free. The small dispensary was under stocked and not as clean as Travis would have liked it and the post doctor was indeed more interested in drinking than healing. However, the post mess hall was reasonably clean and sanitary, primarily because additional kitchen help was plentiful from the post sergeant major. The veteran NCO used the assignment as a kitchen helper as a form of punishment for petty offenses. The food was as well protected as possible from flies and rodents, and the head cook seemed to take some pride in his efforts.

Following lunch, Travis and Marie reviewed the medical log while Homer and Jake inspected the latrine facilities. The ditch that conveyed the foul effluent out to the edge of the river where it was discharged was far too small. This meant it probably overflowed every time it rained. Travis and Marie escorted Major Akins to the site after evening supper, explaining the need for a bigger ditch and why. The Union officer gave a slight wink toward Travis and swore he would immediately start a construction project to improve the channel.

"By the way, Major Akins," Marie spoke as they walked back toward the guest quarters, "I would like to look at the other facilities in the area tomorrow, if you don't mind."

"Not at all my dear Miss Livermore," the Union major responded. "I'll assign an escort to guide you over to the south post first thing in the morning."

"Don't bother, Major Akins," Travis spoke up. "My senior NCO has been in this part of the country before. He can guide us and free your men for the many important duties you must have for them." Smiling at his host, he continued, "I need to have some time with Miss Livermore to discuss her report to Washington. One which I can assure you, is going to comment most favorably on the excellent sanitary conditions of your command."

Major Akins nodded, a satisfied smile on his face, and continued to walk with Travis, enumerating the many burdens he had to endure in commanding a garrison so far from the front. It was a relief to say good night to him and call their little group of conspirators together.

"Homer, you and Irma will have to spend tomorrow inspecting the medical supplies while Jake accompanies Marie and me to the south post. We'll be gone most of the day, so stay busy and be careful who you talk with."

"We will, sir," Homer replied, "but when are we getting out of here? I'm not comfortable around so many blue bellies."

Travis and Jake exchanged glances. "If we're lucky, Homer,

we'll be on our way day after tomorrow. However we'll probably have to repeat our little performance again a time or two before we make it far enough south to cut and run for Texas."

"That's all right with me," Homer admitted, "I just don't want to stay too long in one place. It pushes our luck, if you ask me. I'm always afraid I'll say *y'all* or something that makes some Yankee suspicious about where I come from. Besides, Irma is a-scared the Yanks will get ahold of her."

Travis patted Homer's shoulder. "You're doing admirably: I'm very proud of you both. Just stay in control and watch what you say a little longer." Travis smiled confidently at the two and then bid them and Marie good night. "Jake, let's take a walk around the camp before we turn in."

"Well, Jake, what say we take a look-see tomorrow for your Yankee money and see if our luck is good." Travis spoke softly as they strolled around the earthen berm that formed the post's outer defenses.

"Just what I was hoping you'd say, Doc," Jake replied. "I'm nervous as a cat in a doghouse waiting until you was ready to go fur it." Jake stopped at the corner of the wall and sat down on a rain barrel beside the dirt wall. "How do you suppose we can get over to the cave?"

Travis leaned against the wall, and gazed out over the slow-moving Ohio River to his front. "I've got Major Akins's permission to visit an outpost on the south side of the town. We'll go there first and then stop at the cave on our way back. After all this time, can you still find it?"

"I recollect I could find it in the dark with my eyes closed," the old man boasted. "I've gone there a thousand times in my mind since we first started talkin' about gettin' the money and goin' back South."

"We'll have Marie with us Jake," Travis remarked. "Do you have any problem with her finding out what we're up to?"

"Nope, Doc. Do you?"

Travis shook his head. "I suppose not. However, the fewer we let in on the secret, the better, don't you think? Who knows, we may be able to get it without arousing her interest. I'll not lie to her, though."

"Let's worry about it later, Doc." Jake stretched and yawned. "I'm fer bed and let tomorrow bring what it will. Night, Doc. See you after breakfast."

The next morning's weather was ideal for Travis's plan. He awoke to a dreary sky covered with dark, gray clouds along with intermittent, cold rain. There wouldn't be anybody out and about unless duty required it and thus less chance of unexpected encounters while at the cave.

Travis, Marie, and Jake rode out of the post under wet rain slickers, hats pulled low over their foreheads against the cold raindrops. Marie wanted to ride, so they had left the carriage behind. Travis admired the spunk of his lovely companion.

Major Akins had given Travis clear directions to the small outpost and they arrived without incident. The outpost commander, a young captain, was expecting them and dutifully showed his important guests around the small compound. Travis and Marie made enough notes and suggestions on sanitary improvements to satisfy their host and departed after a simple noon meal with the disinterested garrison soldiers.

They left the post just as a major downpour hit the area and they quickly disappeared from the view of any soldier at the outpost. Jake stopped at the first crossroad and pointed to the east. "Turn here, Doc, and watch fer the Tennessee River channel."

"Wait." Marie stopped her horse. "I'm sure we go straight here to get back to the fort."

"Jake and I want to take a little detour, Marie." Travis motioned Jake on. "We'll get back to the post a different way.

You'll not want to go in without us, so come along for the ride."

At the river, Jake turned north and soon pointed out a limestone outcrop that overlooked the rolling hills. The heavy downpour forced them to pay close attention as the slick path led them to a massive cave on the bottom face of the bluff. Many people had used it as a refuge over the years and had left numerous blackened remnants of fires near the entrance to its dark interior.

Swinging down from his soaked horse, Jake started to gather up some sticks. "Let's light a fire and get warm and dry before we go back to town."

"I certainly can't understand why we are stopping in this cold cave when town is just a couple of miles ahead," Marie grumbled.

Travis climbed off his roan and held his hands up to help Marie. "We won't stay long. A little warmth might be just what the doctor ordered." He helped Marie find a seat on a rocky ledge, and then hurried to find additional wood for Jake's tiny fire.

"Well," Marie admitted as she stood close to the cheery warmth of the blaze, "it is nice to dry out a bit, but my hair is going to smell like wood smoke if I don't wash it tonight."

"You can use that as an excuse to avoid spending any time with Major Akins, tonight. I think he's developed a serious crush on you," Travis responded. "It doesn't matter as we're getting out of here tomorrow morning. The next stop will be the fort at Dyersburg, two days south, and then only two more days to Memphis."

After warming themselves and drying their damp clothing by the flames, Travis glanced at Jake, and seeing his nod of agreement, gathered the horses and led them to the entrance of the cave. "May I help you to the saddle, Miss LeMott, or rather, Miss Livermore? It's time to be on our way."

"Why thank you kindly, Doctor Chase, Yankee extraordinaire," the laughing Marie responded.

As he led her out of the cave, he saw Jake standing on his saddle near the back wall. Marie saw his gaze and glanced back as well. She stopped her horse at the foot of the trail. When Jake rode up, a smile was plastered all over his furry face.

"Jake," she inquired, "what were you searching for back there?"

"Why, Miss Marie," he stalled as he tried to suppress his grin, "what are you talking about? I was jus a'looking to see if anything were there."

"From the dusty saddlebags you have on your horse, I'd say your search was a success. What did you find?"

Marie looked intently at the old scout. Jake glanced at Travis, a question in his eyes.

"All right, Jake." Travis nodded to Jake. "Why don't you tell Miss Eagle Eyes about our little treasure hunt?"

Jake related his story to Marie. "What an extraordinary story, Jake." She smiled at the happy sergeant. "How much money do you think you have?"

"I'll bet we've got better'n ten thousand Yankee greenbacks," he replied.

"It will help a lot of people in Texas when we get home," Travis said with satisfaction. "We'll be happy to share it with you when we get to Vicksburg, Marie. As well as with Irma and Homer, of course."

"My God, no, Travis. This money must go to the Confederate headquarters in Meridian. It's needed by the South to continue the war."

"Marie," Travis emphatically replied. "There is no more war to continue. There's no South, no more Confederacy. The only thing we have anymore is our family. That's the only loyalty that's important now. I'll use this money to save my family's ranch from carpetbagging Yankees. I'll help other ranchers to save their land. We'll use this money to stop those Yankee thieves from stealing land they never worked nor bled for."

Marie sat straighter in her saddle and firmly replied, "You're wrong, Doctor. This money is needed by General Price to continue the fight. You must turn it over to him. I am sorry, but I must insist." Marie swung her horse's nose toward the fort and gave him a jab with her spurs. She rode ahead of the two men, her back stiff as a board.

"Dang," Jake exclaimed. "She's right put out over our intentions, ain't she, Doc?"

"Be that as it may, Jake," Travis muttered. "This money isn't going to finance any more bloodletting if I can help it. We'll just have to convince her our way is best."

The post was in sight before Marie spoke again. "Doctor Sasser, you must see that I am right. Give the money to me so I can pass it on to General Price. Please, don't even think of taking it for yourself; I am sorry, but you must do as I say."

"Marie," Travis answered as gently as he could. "It's not for me, but for ranchers who will lose everything to tax thieves if I don't help them. People who have given their sons and husbands, their money and livestock, and sweat to help the Confederacy. Now that the war is over, they need our help."

"No, Travis, our cause comes first. It is your duty to the South to help it continue the war until the Yankees quit. Can't you see?"

Angrily, Travis snapped back. "Can't you see, Marie LeMott, there is no country left to help! Lee has surrendered. President Davis is on the run. All we have going forward is one another. I'm not gonna argue with you about it."

In sullen silence, the three riders rode through the open gate of the fort. After a warm bath and a hot meal, Travis reported to Major Akins. "A first-class facility, Major. I don't see any reason to linger here any longer. My report will speak very favorably of your careful attention to the sanitary condition of your command. I'll ensure that Miss Livermore's report is equally as complimentary. I believe we'll be under way tomorrow to visit Fort Penny at Dyersburg. I'll count on you not to alert them of our coming."

He saw the conspiratorial gleam in Major Akins's eyes. If Travis gave the commander at Fort Penny a poor report, then Akins would be ahead in the race for a better assignment.

"Don't worry, Colonel," Major Akins smirked. "I'll forget I ever saw you."

The next morning, as the sun rose above the river, the little group of Southerners rode south out of Paducah. Hidden deep in Travis's clothing case were nearly twelve thousand dollars in new Yankee greenbacks. In the wagon sat a very frustrated and disturbed, young, female spy, trying to decide what to do.

"Jake," Travis remarked as they rode side by side in front of the carriage, "I didn't think I'd feel any reservation about using the damn money. Things never seem to figure out easy like in the old days."

Jake spat at a circling horsefly, barely missing his horse's ear. "Couldn't agree more, Doc. We just have to play the cards as they fall and hope fer the best. Git along there hoss, time's a'wasting."

Chapter 8

The road they followed that warm, spring day was well traveled. A surprisingly large amount of traffic, both military and civilian, was transiting between the forts at Paducah and Dyersburg. The forged papers Travis carried passed inspection from two checkpoints, to his relief. He removed the women from the carriage when stopped by the roving details of military police looking for deserters. Their cheery smiles and attractive appearance distracted the police patrols from too thorough an inspection of the forged passes. It appeared they might be able to carry out their ruse all the way to Vicksburg.

"I reckon Miss Marie is pretty burned up about the money," Jake remarked after the third attempt by Travis to convince her to ride with him met with failure. "Want me to explain to her again just what we have in mind?"

"I'm afraid it's a waste of time, Jake," Travis muttered. "That hardheaded Cajun has decided we're a couple of no-good looters, and she's not about to change her mind."

"Let her cool off a mite, Doc," Jake counseled. "No need to push her into saying or doing something rash."

"All right by me," Travis snapped peevishly. "Let her pout all the way to Vicksburg." However, the ride seemed longer and more tedious without her company. He looked back at the silent woman riding in the carriage with Irma Farris. Her eyes were riveted on him and Jake. They camped that evening near the town of Fulton, on the state line between Kentucky and Tennessee. Homer and Irma obviously enjoyed the pleasant spring evening. The couple drew closer together with each passing day. The youthful Homer appeared more mature, as his feelings for the sweet, young widow grew. The rest of the party sat in stoic silence around the campfire until time to turn in for the night. Travis covered a wide yawn with the back of his hand and bid a good night to Marie. She merely grunted something unintelligible in return.

Over breakfast coffee, Travis spoke to Homer while Marie sat silently, sipping her hot brew and listening. "Of course, Jake and I will give both you and Irma a share when we reach the safety of Texas," Travis promised. Jake nodded his agreement.

"Thank you, sir," Homer modestly answered. "I know that Irma has nothing left for her. Her place was shelled and burned during the siege of Vicksburg. As for me, I'll do what you think best, Doctor Sasser." Homer returned to sit beside Irma, talking to her softly.

Travis turned his attention to Marie, sitting silently, looking absently into the sputtering campfire. "The same holds for you, Marie. You can take some of the money and rebuild your family home, or give it to the wounded veterans or whatever you want."

All Travis got for his offer was a frosty glare and a vigorous shake of her head. "No, thank you, sir. I don't cotton to taking money the South needs to continue this war and using it for my personal gain."

"What do I have to do to convince you that this damned war is over? There'll be no army to use the money for even if we wanted to give it to 'em."

Marie sniffed in disgust and walked to the small tent Jake and Homer had erected for her and Irma to sleep in.

"Damned stubborn wench," Travis muttered under his breath. He spent the rest of the morning grumbling and mumbling words too low for Jake to hear. The old man smiled at the two young folks and kept his counsel to himself. *Them two oughta marry, sure as shootin'*, he mused as he shared the silence with his troubled companion.

That evening, they rode into the small outpost called Fort Penny, halfway to Memphis. The place was obviously immersed in a deep gloom. Presenting himself to the commander, Captain Dillon, he inquired, "Why the long faces on everyone, Captain? Has some disaster befallen our forces?"

"Haven't you heard, sir? Some Rebel scum named John Wilkes Booth killed the president last night while he was at Ford's Theater, in Washington. I fear we're doomed without our glorious commander-in-chief. It is a black time in our history." The young officer, who was short and blond, with pale-blue eyes, was visibly distraught.

"My God," Travis replied, truly shocked by the announcement. "What could anyone be thinking of, killing President Lincoln? It is indeed madness. Is there anything I can do to assist you during this time of disaster?"

"Thank you, sir, but no, I am able to meet the responsibilities of this sad time. Thank you for your kind offer. The commander, Army of the Ohio, has declared three days of mourning and stand-down from duty. Your inspection will have to wait until the nineteenth."

Escorting his guests to the simple visitors' quarters at one end of the post, Captain Dillon suddenly blurted out, "Miss Livermore, you're from Washington, right? I suppose you've met President Lincoln many times."

As Marie sputtered an affirmation, "Why, um, of course, Captain, why do you ask?" She looked in desperation to Travis. He could only nod his head in support.

"We will be having a memorial service day after tomorrow, and I'd like for you to present a eulogy for our beloved president. You don't mind, do you?"

Gulping in confusion and surprise, Marie responded, "My privilege, Captain. It would be an honor."

As soon as they were alone, she turned to Travis and Jake. "Well," she snapped nervously. "What am I going to do? I have no idea what to say."

"Lord sakes, don't ask me." Jake shrugged his shoulders. "I don't know nothing about Lincoln 'cept he's a black Republican and drove the South to war."

"All right, let's use our heads here and not panic." Travis scratched his jaw and motioned the other four to sit down at the small table in his room. "I'm sure nobody here has ever even seen Lincoln, much less met him. Marie, think about what you've read about him. I'll work with you tomorrow and together we can come up with a short speech which will satisfy our patriotic hosts."

"I can help you as well," Irma chimed in. "I've read many of the newspaper accounts of Mr. Lincoln while staying with my sister. We should be able to come up with several good things for you to say, Marie. Don't let it worry you."

Marie turned her determined gaze upon Travis. "This ought to convince you, Doctor Sasser, just how important it is that we turn the money you have over to General Price and his Confederate forces. The North will be doing all it can to punish the South for this crime." Marie pleaded her case with passion. "We have to continue the struggle."

"Just the opposite, I'm afraid," he quickly responded. "The last thing the South should do is to fight on. It will just give the Yankees an additional reason for completely destroying what's left of our land."

"Damn it, sir, you are as stubborn as any pig-eyed mule I've ever met." Marie's eyes burned with fiery indignation. There was shocked silence at the use of such a word by a woman.

Travis swallowed and tried to defuse the intensity of her

ardor. He looked deep into her dark eyes. "That's just what I'm trying to prevent, Marie. The stubborn attitude that put the South into this terrible war must not be encouraged to continue any longer. If I send the money to General Price, that same stubbornness will be the cause of more boys being killed, and for nothing. It is not going to change the outcome of the war, and I don't intend to see one more man hurt, if I can help it."

Standing and putting both hands on the tabletop, she looked at her antagonist in righteous anger. "I must tell you here and now, that it is my duty to inform any Southern troops we meet that you have contraband monies that belong to the South." Speaking sarcastically, she looked at the men. "Good night, gentlemen. Come on, Irma, let's retire to our room and let these so-called *gentlemen* discuss how they are going to spend their ill-gotten gains." She spun on her heel and swept from the room, Irma trailing behind, after a quick, longing look at Homer.

"Dad gum, but she's got her dander up, Doc." Jake whistled in admiration. "I sure hope you two don't come to blows a'for we get across the Mississip to Texas."

"Jake, you're no help at all," Travis wearily replied, rubbing his eyes. "Let's grab some shut-eye and hope tomorrow is a better day."

"It'll fer certain be a interestin' one, I calculate."

The next day, they focused on writing a speech honoring the slain president and his life. Everyone contributed what little they knew or had read about the slain president. "Oh, dear," Marie complained around noon, "I swear to do a better job of reading the papers from now on if I ever get out of this mess."

Marie took the information she had gathered and retired to her room to write the coming day's eulogy. Irma went with her, leaving the three men to wander about the post, killing time until supper.

The fort was draped with black crepe. Every building had

some symbol of mourning attached to it. The post soldiers were practicing the memorial parade scheduled for the next afternoon. The road seemed devoid of military traffic.

"The post commander said the entire Union army is standing down for three days of mourning," Travis told his comrades. "It's almost too bad we don't have any army left. What a time to go on the offensive."

"From what I gathered listening to everyone this morning, Mr. Lincoln was a wonderful person," Homer remarked. "The South needs his spirit of compassion more than ever. I wonder if the new president will be as forgiving?"

"I have my doubts," Travis replied. "I heard about Vice President Johnson while he was military governor of Tennessee. He was hard on Southern sympathizers. The South may be much worse off with him as president. I wonder what that Booth fellow was hoping to accomplish, anyway. What he's done has hurt our country and her future badly, damn him."

"Do you think we can get away tomorrow after the memorial parade, Doc?" Jake inquired.

"Not a chance. We're stuck here until two days after tomorrow, like it or not. We'll hurry on to Memphis and then hope we can get passage on a military steamer to Vicksburg. We still have to act like Sanitary Commission inspectors or risk arousing somebody's suspicion."

The next day was solemnly spent. The main activity was in the afternoon under a bright, warm spring sun. The full complement of troops first marched past a reviewing stand where Travis and the two women were guests, along with several prominent civilians from local towns. After the review, several local preachers gave short sermons. Captain Dillon spoke of the job yet not completed of whipping the Rebel armies in the West, and then he introduced Marie.

"Officers and ladies, distinguished guests, troops, I have the distinct pleasure to introduce Miss Sara Livermore, niece of the founder of the Sanitary Commission, and personal acquaintance of our martyred commander-in-chief. She is among us on an inspection tour directly from Washington. I give you Miss Livermore of the US Sanitary Commission."

Marie stood before the multitude. She wore her most somber dress, which she and Irma had liberally draped in black silk bunting.

"Thank you, Captain Dillon. Ladies and gentlemen, officers and soldiers of the Republic, we have most cruelly lost a giant from our bosom. Torn from our midst by the foul hand of a coward who hid his evil behind the cloak of patriotism to the South. Our President was a giant, indeed, in thought, in action, in word, and in compassion. We must give up our beloved dead to the most merciful God above, but we can keep his ideals, and his hope for the speedy reunion of our war-torn land, with love and compassion for those brave people in the South who loved the man as they loved their own leaders."

She paused, letting her eyes sweep over the silent congregation. "This great American, who led our country through the dark days of war to this time of victory and peace, has left our sight, but not our hearts, not our memories, and not ever in our forgiveness of wrong. Remember the noble giant who was Lincoln, and live and treat others as he would have asked you himself, had he been able. Mourn him as you would one who has been ripped from you by the savage beast. You have that right. You may mourn only those you were privileged to love, as we loved our president. Rest in peace, dear President Lincoln. Our cause marches onward, 'For we have seen the glory of the coming of the Lord.' "

Cheers erupted from the assembled crowd, and Travis saw, to his amazement, numerous men and women openly crying. Captain Dillon dismissed the troops, and soon a mob of people engulfed the stand to shake Marie's hand, and that of anyone near her. The speech and her powerful delivery had captivated everyone present. Travis smiled at her as she was inundated by well-wishers, all issuing loud cries of praise and congratulations.

A civilian stepped to his side. "A wonderful eulogy, sir, I must say, simply wonderful. No wonder she is so successful in the Sanitary Commission work. You can be sure that people beyond here will read what she has said this day." The speaker held out his hand to Travis. "Robert Connert, your servant sir, reporter for the *Memphis Daily Journal.*"

Travis could barely sputter his forged name he was so surprised. "I am Lieutenant Colonel Chase, Medical Corps, and Miss Livermore's escort. What are you doing so far from home, Mr. Connert?"

"Oh, I was up here already doing a piece on a local boy who is stationed here, and got caught in the stand-down. I'll be telegraphing this to my paper for publication this very evening. Excuse me, I see an opportunity to speak to Miss Livermore. Would you be so kind as to make the introduction for me?"

Travis took the eager reporter over to Marie and made the introduction. He stayed by her side protectively, as she fended the reporter's questions, but she was experienced beyond most young women and maintained her cover story without any slipup. Travis smiled his encouragement and admiration every time he caught her eye.

The rest of the afternoon and evening's activities were crowded with eager well-wishers and lonely officers eager to make a good impression on the poised and beautiful Marie. It was almost midnight before any of the escapees could speak alone.

"Gracious, Miss Marie," Jake exclaimed, "you sure caused quite a stir with that speech makin' of yours. I shore am proud of you." He glanced at Travis. "Right, Doc?"

"I couldn't agree more, Jake," Travis answered. "The entire post is hers for the asking."

"What about that reporter fellow from Memphis?" Marie worried her hands together, as she relaxed her guard for the first time all day.

"I wouldn't be too concerned about him, Marie," Travis spoke with more assurance than he felt. "I doubt if his incidental story gets too much space in the Memphis paper, with all the news about the funeral in Washington and so on."

"Still and all," Homer interjected, "if her story gets anyone interested in the niece of Mary Livermore, we could be riding straight into a trap at Memphis."

"We have no alternative," Travis concluded. "We're committed to the story that we're on a sanitary inspection tour. We can't quit now. I just hope we can bluff our way through Memphis in a hurry."

The following day they accompanied the fort's commander in a quick inspection of the sanitary facilities. Even though Travis was only using the cover as a Sanitary Commission inspector, he couldn't pass up the opportunity of making some suggestions that would improve the fort's sewer system. He hoped they would reduce the chance of disease and sickness among the soldiers, blue bellies though they were.

"Captain Dillon," Travis spoke in his most self-important voice. "We appreciate your hospitality and assistance during our inspection. I'll make certain my report mentions your name most positively."

"Why, thank you, sir," Dillon gushed. "I'm happy that I could please you and Miss Livermore. I hope you have a pleasant trip down to Memphis. You'll meet Colonel Kincaid, the area commander. Please give him my compliments."

At sunrise the next morning, Travis led his small party out of the post gates and down the road toward Memphis, one step closer to home. They continued their journey confidently assured that no Yankee soldier who met or passed them would discover their ruse; so confident were they of their disguise. Two days later they rode into Memphis and reported to the district commander, Colonel Kincaid. "A pleasure, Colonel Chase. And where is the delightful Miss Livermore whom I've been reading so much about in the paper?"

Chapter 9

"Colonel Kincaid," Marie curtsied as Travis completed the introduction. "I am honored to meet you, sir. Do you know my aunt Mary?" Marie's voice gave no indication of the terror she was struggling to suppress.

"No, my dear," the bewhiskered and florid-faced officer replied, "but your moving eulogy to our late president has captured the imagination of everyone in town, since it was printed in yesterday's paper." The aged colonel stroked his silver mustache, his rummy eyes devouring every line of Marie's trim form.

"Believe me, sir," she responded, "it wasn't my idea to seek fame from my farewell to dear Mr. Lincoln. I hope there won't be a lot of fuss made over it. I would much rather complete my inspection and depart without fanfare."

"Not much chance of that I'm afraid, my dear," the Yankee colonel replied. "The reporter who you met up at Fort Penny, Mr. Connert, I think his name is, has asked to interview you upon your arrival. He wants to write about how your commission is involved in safeguarding the health of our brave fighting boys. I know you want to get that information out. Also, the ladies of the Union Support League have asked to hold a ball in your honor Saturday night. I took the liberty of accepting for you."

"Thank you, Colonel. You are too kind. Of course, I'll be honored to meet the ladies of the league." Dabbing at her temples with her hankie, Marie pardoned herself. "If you would be so kind as to direct me to my quarters, I would like to freshen up from the ride. The dust was quite impossible, I must say."

"Of course, of course," the officious colonel replied. "Please consider yourself as my guest for dinner. Please include Miss Ferris and your escort officer, Lieutenant Colonel Chase."

"Lordy," Travis grumbled as they followed the post runner over to the guest quarters. "Who would have thought that a short speech at Fort Penny would threaten us so close to getting home?"

Marie shrugged her shoulders. "Nothing we can do about it now. We'll have to put up a brave front and slip out of here as soon as the ball is over. We'll be just like little mice, hurrying home before dawn."

For the next two days, they thoroughly inspected the various camps and forts that comprised the Memphis Military District. Travis made numerous suggestions, especially directed at the prisoners' holding compound, which was still the filthy cattle lot, just as it was when he'd gone through nearly eighteen months earlier. He insisted that the provost marshal's troops clean and repair the shamefully maintained buildings. He felt a perverse pleasure in finding additional deficiencies no matter how his former captors tried to please him. The regard in which Colonel Kincaid held Miss Livermore helped ensure grudging but prompt cooperation from all the subordinate commanders.

Every evening, Marie tactfully eluded the persistent colonel's ardent overtures trying desperately not to offend the man who was old enough to be her father. She admitted to Irma that it was all she could do to keep a straight face at times. "I declare, Irma, if I was of a mind I could obtain every secret the old coot possesses. He's like a bull in rut and would say or do anything to get me alone in his bedroom." She smiled at Irma's shocked expression. "You know what silly fools men can make of themselves when their blood gets to boiling."

"You listen to me, Marie," Irma firmly admonished. "You stay away from that nonsense until we can get outta here. Homer says we'll have smooth sailing once we leave this place."

"You really like Homer, don't you, honey?" Marie smiled at her companion. "Looks like you have him pretty well hooked and ready to haul in."

"Maybe so," Irma laughed. "But first I've got to get him away from any Yankee soldiers, so you just take care around that red-nosed fool, Colonel Kincaid."

The evening of the ball was warm and pleasant, and the home of the hostess was filled with officers and their ladies, as well as numerous Yankee sympathizers, civilian administrators, and their wives or painted lady friends. The home was in a lovely, elite section of Memphis, high above the river. Travis hadn't seen such a colorful assembly since his days in Boston. The band was properly constrained in their selection of music, and the buffet table was laden with delectable food displayed on silver platters. It was obvious that the master of the house had made a tidy profit from the war. Travis wondered if he had once shown the same devotion to the Confederacy as he was currently showing to the Union.

Marie was definitely the center of attention; everyone wanted to speak to the celebrated niece of Mary Livermore of Washington. Two complimentary articles in the local newspaper had done much to locally increase her fame. The crush of people around the tall, dark-haired woman never slackened unless she was dancing. As a result, Marie spent a good deal of time on the floor with several partners, mostly young officers or businessmen.

Travis saw his chance. Moving to her side at the beginning of a slow waltz, he asked, "May I have the pleasure, Miss Livermore?"

"Very well, Colonel Chase," she replied, playing his game. "I'd be honored." Slipping her hand in Travis's arm, they walked onto the dance floor. Soon they were encased among the swirling couples, able to speak without being overheard.

"Is everything all right?" he inquired.

"Certainly, it is," she answered. "Don't forget, I know how to conduct myself while among the enemy."

"Just watch what you say." They moved slowly around the dance floor as if a single person. "Some people here may know something about Washington or Mary Livermore that we don't. By the way, you dance marvelously." Travis smiled warmly at the woman in his arms. She was light as a feather on her feet.

"Thank you, Colonel, so do you." Marie's smile was bright as a sunbeam, to Travis's eyes.

"Marie," Travis stumbled to find the right words. "I want us to be friends, in fact, to be the very best of friends. I admire your bravery and your intelligence. Especially, I am grateful for your help. We would never have made it this far without you."

"Nonsense," she responded carefully, not wanting to encourage him. "I'm grateful to you for helping me escape from Saint Louis. The information I have will help General Price in planning his raid."

"Ladies and gentlemen," the florid-faced Colonel Kincaid interrupted the dance. "I have wonderful news. I have just been informed that General Sherman has accepted the surrender of Confederate forces in North Carolina. Our forces are in pursuit of the Confederate president, that scoundrel Jeff Davis, down in Georgia. The war is very much closer to being over."

A loud cheer broke over the assembly of revelers. The babble of excited voices discussing the news washed over the crowd, and everyone moved over to the punch and food to discuss the event.

Colonel Kincaid rushed up to Marie and took her hand.

"Great news, my dear, don't you agree?"

"Why, yes, my dear Colonel Kincaid. The war must surely be over. The only Rebel army still fighting is General Price down in Mississippi."

"Don't worry about Price," Kincaid blustered. "We'll have him strung up on the wall shortly. He's probably trying to send word to us as we speak, that he's ready to quit and surrender. Mark my words, the war is done. Our job is nearly finished. Won't you share a dance with me? If you'll excuse us, Doctor Chase."

Travis watched the young and beautiful spy dancing with the pompous, old colonel and smiled. The smitten fool didn't appreciate what a vixen he held. How she molded in his arms as they danced together rolled across his memory. His loyalty to Clarissa suddenly imposed itself in his brain. He measured her against the woman he was watching. Both were beautiful, but Marie was so, so self-assured, he guessed was the best way to describe her. Clarissa was soft and seemed much more helpless and dependent. As he thought about it, he was not so sure which attribute was the more appealing.

Travis watched as a messenger from the colonel's headquarters rushed up to the dancing couple and give Kincaid a written message. The colonel's florid face grew grim and he looked his way, as he escorted Marie off the floor. Travis moved to the couple's side. "Something wrong, sir?"

"Yes, I'm afraid so," the older man replied worriedly. "A steamboat full of repatriated Union war prisoners has just exploded near Fort Pillow, on Old Hen Island, about ten miles north of the city. The post commander wired that there are many casualties and that he needs medical help. Would you take your people up immediately, and I'll send the rest of my medical staff as soon as I can get them gathered and equipped for emergency treatment."

"Of course, sir," Travis replied. "I'll leave immediately with all my party. Will you give me a note to your post quartermaster so that we can draw some emergency supplies to take with us." Silently, he cursed the bad fortune to his plans. Nothing could be done but respond to the call. Men needed his skill, and that was that.

The old riverboat *Sultan* had paddled by the bright lights of Memphis only an hour earlier. Twenty years old when the war had started, the side-wheeler had been pressed into Union service and made many, many trips up and down the Mississippi and Ohio Rivers. The old boat had carried livestock, supplies, and soldiers from the North to the South. On the return trip, it had hauled wounded soldiers back to the North and taken captured Rebel soldiers to their prisoner-of-war camps.

For this voyage, the boat was packed with nearly two thousand Union prisoners recently freed from Andersonville and Meridian, Mississippi, Confederate prisoner-of-war camps. The men were uniformly malnourished and weak. Many were sick and lame from poorly treated wounds. The orders were to get the men to the big Union hospital at Louisville immediately. The boat's captain had shouted at the chief engineer that he was falling behind schedule, and they must increase the revolutions to ten knots. The engineer had shouted at the boiler chief, and the chief had screamed at the stokers and wipers. "More steam, more speed, hurry up, damn your hides."

The main boiler was entering its fifteenth year of service. The pipes that carried steam and water through the fire were nearly completely blocked with scale. The system was running hotter than normal, and the added pressure only compounded the danger. Suddenly, a piece of scale broke free and flowed into the main cooling pipe, almost completely plugging the interior. The cooling water flow dropped to a trickle, and steam pressure began to climb at an alarming rate. The steam gauge quickly climbed well into the red zone, but since the stoker was cooling off, enjoying the night air, while the wiper was getting a drink of water, no crewman was available to catch the error.

The iron-plate walls of the boiler ruptured with the force of a hundred cannon shells going off at once. The blast tore through the wooden decks of the boat as if they were made of paper. The old wood split and broke in two like matchsticks. Many men died never knowing what had happened. They were the lucky ones. Many more were burned and broken, and then left in the cold water to drown when the mortally damaged steamboat sank. Hundreds of injured men tried to scramble out of the cold waters of the mighty river and hold onto life until rescuers could find them.

Travis and the rest of his party arrived to find a scene of uncontrolled chaos. Burned and wounded men were piling up like cordwood at the farmhouse that was nearest to the explosion. Concerned people were trying to do what they could, but no one seemed to be in charge, and the two doctors there were clearly overwhelmed by the task confronting them.

Travis used his rank to take charge of the situation. He was experienced in the handling of mass casualties. Soon, he had Homer directing the wounded to various areas of the yard. The most critical were placed together, and then the less serious at another location and then so on until all were allotted a place according to the necessity of treatment required in saving them. Even the obviously dying were afforded a spot where they were placed, manned by a calm preacher and two older women parishioners, who comforted them as they made their last earthly journey. Jake took charge of the enlisted helpers and directed them in setting up a hospital.

Marie and Irma served as nurses to those examined and treated by the doctors. As morning arrived, other women from the area joined in the caretaking. Travis and the other two doctors worked for thirty-six hours straight, bandaging burns, setting broken limbs, and sewing up the various lacerations caused by flying steel and wood.

Near the end of his first day, Travis started to work on a young man who had both a broken leg and a nasty burn on his back. The man was in obvious agony, but gritted his teeth to the pain and only moaned a little as Travis cleaned the burned skin off his back and set the broken leg. Several additional medical staff had arrived from Memphis, and Travis could see that the worst was over by then. He was as tired as he had ever been in his life, he thought. He'd never worked on so many men at one time, even in the worst battles.

"Thanks, Doctor, I appreciate your attention to my injuries," the young soldier spoke as the weary doctor finished wrapping his broken leg. "I'm Lieutenant Joe Glenn Richardson, Michigan Ninth Volunteers. Been in Andersonville since the Rebs caught me near Atlanta in sixty-four. What's your name?"

Travis was so tired, he never even thought of the alias under which he was traveling. He simply answered, "I'm Travis Sasser, from Nacogdoches, Texas."

The young officer grimaced in pain. "A Texan working for the Union. What do you know? I've got a brother serving on occupation duty in Texas. He says it's a nice place. I'll mention your name to Ben in my next letter. Well, here I go, I reckon." As the orderlies lifted the young soldier in his litter, he grasped Travis by the hand. "Thanks again, Doc."

Travis quickly forgot the exchange as the next few hours swiftly slipped by in a hectic effort to treat the many survivors of the tragedy. Nearly twelve hundred men died that terrible night, almost as many as Travis had lost during the long weeks of the smallpox epidemic at Rock Island. He pitied the next man who tried to recruit him for a war. That foolish fellow was in for a bloody nose and more. As the medical effort slowed,

Travis went to find Marie; then he planned to sleep as long as he could.

He found both women in the barn, moving among the many cots filled with treated men, doing what they could to relieve their suffering. He motioned her outside and walked with her over to the pole fence at the corral. "Is everything all right here?" he inquired. "I've been so busy in the operating room, I've neglected the recovery area." He folded his arms on the top pole of the corral and looked over the still-busy scene.

"Yes, thank you, we've got most men bandaged and have plenty of opium for their pain," she answered. "You look exhausted. Why don't you take my bed? It's the first room at the top of the stairs over there in the main house. I'll come get you if any more injured come in."

She had seen the extraordinary effort he expended as Travis worked to relieve the suffering of the men. His brown hair curled over his forehead and made him seem years younger, even in his weariness. She'd overheard the other doctors talking about the skill and ability of this young doctor. The black smudges under his eyes showed just how long he'd been at work without rest.

"Seems as if you're quite the hero," she smiled. "Colonel Kincaid was here this afternoon, and everyone said you were the main reason more men hadn't died. He looked in on Irma and me, and then you, before he rode back to Memphis. You never even looked up from your work at the operating table."

"Great, that's just what I need," Travis yawned. "That old fart's approval. What I do need is to get some sleep if I can. I'll take you up on your kind offer. Call me if you need me for anything."

He smiled at the bright black eyes looking into his and walked over to the house. Seeing Homer, busy helping a young soldier, he called out where he would be for the next few hours. Homer nodded and stayed at his task. The doctor knew the slight medical orderly was all business when it came to treating injured soldiers.

Travis sighed and settled into the soft pillow of Marie's bed. Just before he fell into an exhausted sleep, he noticed the lingering fragrance of her body. It sent a tingle of pleasure through his entire body. With that pleasant thought, he fell into a deep and restful sleep.

The next couple of days were less stressful, as they completed the emergency treatment of the *Sultan*'s survivors and shipped them off to hospitals better able to take care of them. Travis watched the young officer named Richardson, the one to whom he'd revealed his name, being loaded on an ambulance. He hoped his slip of the tongue didn't make its way back to Colonel Kincaid before he was away for Vicksburg.

Travis and the others cleaned up and departed for Memphis late that afternoon. The trip back seemed one of leisurely meandering compared to the frantic rush that dark night three days prior. They rode into the post just as the evening sun was painting the western sky a panorama of blushing pinks and orange. High clouds were edged with bright, rose-colored accents to their dark gray mass. The night was destined to be dark and cloudy.

Travis dropped the carriage and his horse, along with Jake, at the stables, while Homer and the ladies went into the guest quarters. He strolled over to the headquarters building to report in to Colonel Kincaid. He wanted to extend his personal praise for the work done by the two doctors sent to help him.

He reported to the colonel and provided a brief outline of the activities at the temporary hospital. Kincaid nodded and fingered a telegram laying on his desk. "Colonel Chase, can you give me a written report of what you saw and did? There will be an investigation and your observations will be helpful. I'll send a recorder to take your statement and you can use the room next door. Afterwards, I'll treat you to a drink at the officers' billets."

Travis nodded his acceptance and moved toward the door. "By the way"—Kincaid picked up the telegram and waved it in his hand—"I just received this telegram from an acquaintance in army headquarters, Cincinnati. He says that Mary Livermore doesn't have any family except her husband. Maybe you'd better bring Miss Livermore over as soon as you're through with your report. I need an explanation of this." He frowned as he reread the message. "Perhaps she is a distant kin and just prefers to call herself a niece."

A cold chill ran through Travis. He'd not have much time to figure a way out of this predicament. Nodding, faking a frown of puzzlement, he agreed. "I'm certain there's a simple explanation. I'll finish your report and bring Miss Livermore over for you to question. With her help, you'll be able to get to the bottom of it, I'm sure."

Hurrying from the room, he picked up the waiting enlisted secretary and went into the room next to the colonel's. He could hear the low mutter of the post adjutant and Colonel Kincaid talking through the walls. Turning to the young man who was to record his report, he smiled. "I'm going out for a few minutes, Private. Please wait for me here until I return."

"Yes, sir," the young soldier replied and settled more comfortably into his chair.

Travis eased out of the building and walked swiftly to the guest quarters at the far end of the fort. Grabbing Jake by the arm, he moved on to Marie's room.

"Someone's asking questions about Marie," he quickly explained. "We've got a few minutes' head start. Pack your things and get over to the barn. Irma, you and Homer stand on the porch and watch for soldiers. If you see any Yanks coming, warn us. As soon as you see the carriage leave the post, walk out and we'll pick you up at the corner. Move. We don't have much time. Jake, you come with me."

Jake, Marie, and Travis grabbed their gear and hurried to the stables. After saddling the horses and hitching up the wagon, Travis helped Marie into the carriage. Swinging up on the driver's seat, Jake drove the team through the gate, Travis behind leading the extra horses.

"I'm taking this lady over to the hotel fer supper," Jake remarked to the disinterested sentry, who passed them through the post gate.

Soon Homer and Irma strolled out the gate as if on an evening stroll, albeit carrying their luggage made that seem unlikely. At the corner, they jumped into the carriage and the evaders rode into the darkness.

As they rode out the levee road, past the docks at the south end of town, Travis saw a riverboat obviously preparing to steam south. "Wait here for me," he ordered. This was the ideal the time to try his idea.

Riding over to the dock, he asked to speak with the captain. A lanky man with a shaggy beard and dark greasy hair ambled over to him, his only badge of rank a dirty captain's hat. Travis carelessly saluted and spoke earnestly. "Sir, you may be able to help me with a problem."

"What might that be, Colonel?" the scruffy skipper replied. His shifty eyes and pinched face spoke volumes about his character. He gnawed at a dirty toothpick with yellowed teeth.

"I am tasked to escort these ladies to Vicksburg and don't relish the cold nights on the trail, as well as the chance of encounters with Rebel bushwhackers. If I were to make it worth your while, would you consider allowing us to take a somewhat unauthorized passage on your boat?"

"Well, the old tub's leased to the government anyhow, so if

fifty dollars was to come my way, I guess it could be arranged."

"Done, sir, and my thanks." Travis motioned his party to the dock. "Please load the carriage and horses on board, Jake, while I conclude my business with our kind captain." Digging into his bag, he pulled out the money from his hidden stash. Shortly after nine, the paddleboat eased out into the current and started south down the mighty Mississippi River toward Vicksburg. Assembling his companions in the only furnished cabin, Travis told them what had happened at Colonel Kincaid's office.

"The captain won't hear about any of this until after we've left the boat, so I think we've given the Yanks the slip. Stay alert, and don't leave the cabin except when necessary. I'll stay as close to our host as possible so I can keep my eye on him."

The next twenty-four hours seemed to drag by, but finally they were just a few miles from Vicksburg. Travis stood at the rail with Marie, watching the brown waters churned up by the massive wooden paddle wheel.

"You know," he remarked to Marie, "I don't have the faintest idea where you live. Do you even have a place to return to after this is all over?"

"Yes, my family home is at Bawcomville, just south of Monroe. You nearly pass it when you travel to Texas. I'll be headed east though, to General Price." She paused and then blurted out, "Have you changed your mind about the money you are taking from the Southern cause?"

"No, you stubborn woman, I haven't. Do you want a share?"

"Not even a little bit, Doctor Sasser. You take the money. I can't stop you, but you'll wish you never had, once you get home and think about it."

Homer and Irma came toward them. Stopping, the young orderly spoke with a rush. "Sir, Irma is coming with me if that is all right. She doesn't have anything in Natchez except a house, and it may be gone, thanks to the Union bombardment of the city. We plan to get married once we reach Texas and safety."

"Wonderful," Travis exclaimed. "My very best to you both. Of course, I don't have any objections." He shook Homer's hand and smiled at the beaming Irma.

"Marie," Travis asked of his companion, "do you have knowledge of anybody we could see in Monroe who would trade us a wagon for our Yankee carriage?"

Marie finished hugging Irma and nodded. "I'll write you a message for one of my contacts who should be able to help you. His name is Durmon, and he runs a livery in Monroe. How are you going to get across the river from Vicksburg?"

"Easy; I'm going to persuade the captain to land us on the Louisiana side right now. Come on, Homer, let's find Jake and skedaddle this old paddle bucket."

After explaining his intention to the old man, they moved to the bridge. "Captain," Travis informed the riverboat's skipper, "we've decided to disembark there on the Louisiana side." Travis pointed at a flat bank ahead.

"No way am I going to." The captain felt the hard barrel of Travis's revolver poking him in the short ribs. "That is, whatever you want. Helmsman, steer for the west bank ahead. Slow to stop and prepare to disembark passengers."

As they watched the boat steam around the river, Travis remarked, "The captain won't want to say anything about taking unauthorized passengers aboard, so we should be free from pursuit for the time being, anyway." Digging into his kit, he took some paper that he'd taken from the office of Colonel Kincaid. He carefully wrote orders detailing himself and the others as escort for Mrs. Irma Farris to Nacogdoches, Texas.

"Marie, will you be all right if we leave you here?" Irma questioned as they slogged through the soft black mud to higher ground.

The dark pants and shirt she wore made Marie almost invisible in the darkness. "Yes, I'll swim my horse over to Mississippi before daylight and then ride east until I reach General Price. Don't worry about me. I've done this many times."

As they parted in the darkness, Travis felt a deep pang of loss rush through him. He'd miss her dark beauty and the stimulating discussions over which they had spent many interesting hours. He shook her offered hand and wished he could figure some way to justify kissing her inviting lips. She hugged Irma and the other two men, but only glanced at Travis with a silent, imploring look. He prayed for the safe completion to her self-imposed mission.

As her horse's hootbeats faded in the inky darkness, Travis spoke. "Come on, folks, let's travel. We need to be in Monroe tomorrow morning, and then we're just four days from God's country. I can hear Texas calling us clear from here."

Chapter 10

"You know somethin', Doc?" Jake stirred the breakfast fire with a stick. Sparks flew up, and then drifted slowly away with the light morning breeze. "I shore do miss her now that she's gone, even iffen it's only been a day." Jake spit into the hot coals. "I hope she got across the river safely and didn't get picked up by some Yankee patrol."

Travis threw the remaining dregs of his coffee into the fire and climbed to his feet. "I feel the same damned way, old friend. I suppose we'll never know what happens to her from here on out. Probably, that's the way she wants it. Hell, come on, we've got to get to Monroe by dark."

"Homer, you and Irma ready to travel?" Travis called to the pair, who were loading the camping supplies into the carriage boot.

"Yes, sir," Homer called back. "Lead off; me and Irm will be right behind." He smiled shyly at Irma, loving affection written all over his boyish face.

Twice, before noon, they met small Union army patrols riding east toward the river behind them. "Take care, Colonel Chase," the young officer in charge of one patrol cautioned. "We've been getting reports of stragglers and deserters from the Reb army waylaying passersby. Many of those held up have been killed as well as robbed."

Travis thanked him for the warning. He directed Homer to pull the carriage to the side of the road and give way to the

Yankee patrol. "That's the last thing we need," he mumbled to Jake while the mounted patrol rode by. "Stopped by deserting Confederate soldiers and shot as Yankees."

The sun was almost directly overhead when three men stepped out in front of them, blocking the road. The armed strangers were clad in faded, patched pants and sweat-stained shirts, crusted with filth. The tallest of the three was barefoot, his blackened feet showing a long absence from water. His greasy beard and matted hair matched that of his shorter companions. Two of them held well-used rifles with scarred stocks and rusted barrels. Their leader, stocky and short, with a vivid red scar that bisected his left eyebrow and ran down his cheek to a bearded chin, carried two pistols. All had their guns pointed at Jake and Travis, before either had any opportunity to react.

"Well, lookie here, boys," the scar-faced one drawled. " 'Pears like we done caught us a fancy Yankee officer and his party. And would you look at this, the bastard has his whore right along with him. Clyde, you and Billy Ray keep them two covered. I'm gonna introduce myself to the little lady."

He walked past Travis and Jake to the carriage, where Irma sat beside Homer, fear stiffening her posture. Travis looked at the two men to his front. The tall, skinny man with the dirty feet couldn't keep his eyes off the scene behind them, but the smaller one was watching Travis and Jake suspiciously, his rifle not wavering an inch.

"Don't you twitch a muscle, Yankee," he snarled. "I'll put this here minié ball right twix yer brisket, iffen you do."

The scar-faced leader stomped up to the side of the carriage. "You there," he said, pointing his pistol at Homer. "Climb off and go stand by yer friends." He waved his pistol toward Travis and Jake.

Irma put her hand on Homer's arm before the flustered

Homer could give any reply to the leering outlaw. "Do what he says, Homer. I'll be all right. Go on, before he hurts someone."

"Yea, sonny." The scarred man grinned at Homer's enraged expression. "Do as the little gal says, and ya might get to see the sun go down." Looking over at his two henchmen, he instructed them. "Get their guns and tie 'em up. I'm gonna get me a little loving from this here Yankee's fancy whore."

He started to climb on the seat where Irma sat silently. As his head came level with her waist, she jerked a small derringer out of her purse and shot him through his left eye. The impact threw him off the wheel he'd been standing on, and he landed with a loud thump on his back in the middle of the road. His heels drummed in the dust, kicking up a spray of dust, which gently settled back on his worn, dirty shoes.

"Hey," the smallest outlaw shouted. The tall drink of a man just gaped in stunned amazement.

Travis threw himself off his roan, landing with a bone-jarring crash on his side. A fired bullet cut the air where he sat an instant earlier. He drew his Colt revolver and shot the rifle-toting gunman in the throat. The wounded outlaw sat down hard, holding his hands over his bloody neck, gagging on blood and trying to scream through the gore in his mouth. Travis saw the barefooted man staggering back into the brush by the side of the road, Jake's Bowie knife sticking out of his chest. Jake jumped off his horse and walked over to the dying outlaw and pulled his knife out of the now-still body. "Mine's done fur, Doc. What about yours?"

By the time Travis reached the man he'd shot, the small outlaw had toppled over, blood all over his face and chest, quite dead.

"He's a goner, too. Homer, what about scar-face?"

Homer had rushed back to Irma, who sat holding the smoking derringer in her hand, looking down at the dead highwayman she'd just shot, abject horror on her face.

"He's dead, Major. Irma, honey, are you all right?"

She nodded and allowed Homer to help her off the carriage seat. Walking over to the side of the road, she sat down under a tree. "If you all don't mind, I need to take a few minutes before we continue."

Travis nodded. "We all can use some time to recover. By God, Irma, that's some brave thing you just did." He smiled his admiration at the pale-faced woman.

"I'll second that sentiment," Jake added. "You gave us the chance we needed to get the jump on these other two skunks afore they did us in, permanent-like. Yer one fine gal, Miz Irma."

Homer held Irma's hand, tightly, shuddering at what might have happened. "You sure took care of him, honey. I didn't even know you had that little gun in your purse. What a wonderful, brave woman you are."

"Thanks, dear," she modestly replied. "I've carried it ever since I left Vicksburg. My brother-in-law taught me how to use it. I just wanted to stop him before he hurt someone. I'm thankful it worked out right for us."

Travis and Jake gathered up the dead bodies and dragged them off into the brush. "The ants'll take care of them fur us," Jake intoned. "Save us taking the time to bury 'em."

The inspection of the robbers' pockets yielded a nice watch, probably stolen from an earlier victim, and twenty dollars in gold. The two .36-caliber pistols carried by the scar-faced leader were the only other items worth having. The rest Jake threw in the brush with the bodies.

"I don't see no sign of horses, so I guess they was afoot," Jake observed. "They most likely got a camp around here about, but we don't have time to search it out." He admired his new watch, and said, "It's nearly one twenty. We best get on to Monroe afore we miss the afternoon."

They rode into the town about three hours later. Stopping at the main hotel, Travis registered everyone, paying with the gold he'd taken from the robbers. As soon as he'd washed his face and hands and put his valise under his bed, he and Jake headed down the stairs to the saloon, which opened off the hotel lobby.

The bartender, who was tall and nearly bald, suspiciously eyed the neatly dressed Yankee officer as he stepped to the bar. The only other customer was a sleeping drunk slumped over a table, his face in the crook of his arm.

Travis nodded to the barkeep. "Give me a small beer." As the barkeep slid the foam-topped glass in front of him, Travis asked, "I wonder, do you happen to know a Mr. Durmon?"

"I guess you mean Roscoe Durmon, the owner of the livery stable, Colonel. It's down at the end of the street. Turn right two blocks." He went back to his tub of soapy water and dirty glasses, ignoring Travis, who sipped his beer in solitary silence. Leaving two bits on the bar, Travis and Jake went off to locate their contact. He was ready to shed himself of his Yankee disguise and return to his home in Texas.

Jake and Travis strolled down the street, as if they had nothing to do but take in the local scene. The livery was at the end of the street, with a corral holding several horses beside it. The inside of the old livery smelled of horses and hay, like any of a thousand others. A closed door at the far side proclaimed itself as the entrance to the office.

Travis knocked on the office door, and entered at the invitation. "Sir, are you Mr. Roscoe Durmon?" he inquired of the gentleman sitting at a scarred, worn desk.

The gray-haired man looked at the two Yankee soldiers, and tightness quickly spread over his bewhiskered face. "Yes. What can I do for you?"

Travis spoke the secret code given him by Marie. "The cause is just. Rally to the flag."

The older man's mouth dropped and he slowly got up and walked over to his coat, hanging on a nail next to the potbellied stove in the corner of the room. When he turned, he had a small revolver in his hand. "Now then," he said, menace in his voice. "Where did you Yankee bastards hear that phrase? Quick, afore I blow your brains out."

"Easy, Mr. Durmon," Travis quickly spoke. "I'm Major Travis Sasser, Hood's Texas Volunteers. This is Sergeant Jake Wheeler, Forrest's cavalry. Both of us escaped from the Union prison at Rock Island, Illinois, and are trying to return to our homes in Texas. We met up with Miss Marie LeMont in Saint Louis and helped her reach Vicksburg. She said you might be able to lend us a hand."

"I suppose the little red-haired vixen was fine the last time you saw her?" Durmon looked expectantly at Travis.

Travis smiled. "The lady has hair black as crow's feathers, and black eyes to match. But yes, she was fine, as long as you don't get in the way of what she's set her mind to do."

Durmon chuckled at the response. "I'll be damned, a body never knows what the wind will blow in. I reckon you boys is the real thing." He scratched his gray-streaked beard, a puzzled look on his face. "Why are you all sneaking around now that the war's over? Just turn yourself in to the nearest Yankee camp and take the oath of allegiance to the Union. They'll let you go right after that."

Travis shook his head. "No, thanks, Mr. Durmon. We've slipped through too many Yankee hands to take a chance on the goodness of any Yankee pardon at the moment. We'll just ease on back to Texas and then worry about how we settle up." He told Durmon the story of their escape and trip through the Union lines, leaving out the story about Jake's money.

Durmon slapped his thigh at the almost implausible tale of fooling the Yankee soldiers. "What can I do to help you boys?"

He grinned at the two escapees.

"We need to rid ourselves of this Yankee officer's carriage, purchase a buckboard, and obtain a bill of sale for the horses we swiped from the Union cavalry. Also, we need to buy saddles. Ours are obviously Union issue." Travis looked over at Jake, who nodded in agreement.

"Don't furget," Jake added, "we need civilian clothes for us."

"Certainly," Durmon answered. "I have just the goods you want, and I've got plenty of fake bills of sale for Union horses. Where are they? I'll need to see them so's I can describe them in the bill of sale."

Jake took the stable attendant with him to gather the carriage and horses, while Travis picked out saddles for himself and Jake from the several Durmon had for sale. They made plans to meet the next morning at sunrise, to exchange their uniforms for civilian clothing. "I'll have all your papers ready for you then," Durmon promised.

As Travis and Jake walked back to their hotel, they noticed several groups of soldiers walking around. "We'd better stay in our rooms, and slip out of town as quietly as possible tomorrow," Travis observed.

Before they entered their room at the hotel, Travis knocked on Homer's door, to tell him of the morrow's plan. The young orderly answered the door, clothed in just his pants, after a short delay. He was blushing red as a beet, and Travis recognized the outline of a person under the covers of the hotel's brass bed. Smiling at his friend's obvious embarrassment, Travis explained the plan and asked, "Will you get word to Irma, so she is ready to go at sunrise?" Homer nodded, blushing even more furiously, and Travis walked on to his room, a happy grin on his face. No need to worry about those two tonight.

Thank goodness it wouldn't be long until he saw Clarissa. The need for some tender loving was a raging fire within him and needed quenching.

The morning sun was starting to burn away the night mist when the four travelers slipped into the livery. Durmon was waiting with clothing for the men and authentic-looking bills of sale for the horses. They hitched up the two carriage horses to an old but sturdy buckboard Durmon had obtained for them. Travis and Jake saddled their mounts with their newly purchased saddles. Travis offered fifty dollars in greenbacks to Durmon.

"Go ahead, take it," Jake urged at the man's reluctance. "We've got it, and you've earned it."

"Thanks, boys," Durmon replied. "Good Yankee money is hard to come by these days. Here, I've gathered some supplies for you to eat on the way." He handed a filled sack of foodstuffs to Irma and smiled at his fellow conspirators. "Now, beat it outta of here before the Yankee soldiers get wise to ya. Stop by if y'all ever ride this way again. I'd like to hear the rest of the story. Ride careful now." He opened the stable doors and after scanning the area, motioned the party out.

They rode away from Monroe, no longer liable to be shot as spies if discovered by the Union soldiers. It was an unexpected relief to all of them. Tension dissolved as the miles slipped by and they moved on toward Texas and home.

Travis was tempted to push the others hard, but admitted to himself that there was no reason to exhaust the horses so close to their destination. The Angelino River finally lay before them, with the Diamond S ranch in the hazy distance. All that was left was a short ride across the ford and up the gentle hill that sloped down to the river. Travis forced back a lump in his throat. It had been four long years since he'd ridden away with Hood's soldiers to fight the "quick little war" against the black-hearted Yankees. What would his home be like today?

CHAPTER 11

Travis nervously tried to swallow the lump that filled his throat as he led his friends down the front drive leading to the main house. For the past hour, since he'd first sighted the distant homestead through the morning haze, his anticipation had grown with each step his black horse took. The warmth of happier times rushed through his mind, washing over the bitter memories of the war.

Their longtime Mexican cook, Paco Velez, weathered and aged like well-used leather, sat outside the main kitchen, which was built on the north side of the house. He appeared to be peeling potatoes, away from the stuffiness inside the busy kitchen. Paco looked up at the sound of the riders, but his aged eyesight prevented him from recognizing any of the visitors. They didn't appear threatening, so he returned to his chore.

Travis carefully looked around the ranch yard before climbing off his horse, drinking in the familiar and welcomed scene. The corrals were empty of horses, save one old, gray mare, who nickered at the new animals headed her way. The barn and outbuildings looked a bit run-down and in need of care. Nothing paint and some sweat couldn't fix, but Travis frowned, puzzled at the sight. His father had never allowed this sort of sloppy maintenance of the ranch buildings before. Only a huge garden beyond the chicken coop seemed to be cared for. The even, rows of leafy green vegetables were already yielding a harvest.

Travis led the horses toward the main house. He swung off and walked up the three steps onto the front veranda. He stopped and turned to look south, over the undulating land where the ranch's cattle had always roamed. Not a single brown speck was visible, something Travis could not recall in all the time he'd lived on the ranch. He pushed opened the heavy wooden door of the sprawling adobe main house and walked into the cool dimness of the home of his youth.

The library was off to his right, as he stepped through the door. He saw his mother bending over a seated form and turned toward her. She heard the sound of his boots and looked up. For a moment, their eyes locked in silent recognition, and then she gasped and opened her arms as she surged toward him.

"Oh, my God. It's my boy. Travis, my boy, is it really you?" She swept into his arms, and he lost himself in the warm softness of her familiar embrace. Her hair smelled of the aloe soap she made from cactus plants, and her cheek was warm and wet with tears of happiness. She hugged him tight to her bosom while uttering his name over and over.

As his mother released him, he saw a frail man sitting in a rocker. It was his father, although the memory Travis carried of him, strong and robust, did not match what he saw. The limp white hair hung down the sides of his father's head in wisps, and the proud mustache was yellow-white and ragged. A drop of drool ran from the corner of his twisted mouth and fell on a frozen arm, the clawlike hand immobile and thin. Only the eyes displayed the fire of the man Travis carried in his memory. They glistened in silent agony and joy as the old man struggled to say something, but only a muffled gurgle issued from his slack mouth.

"Look, Tom, it's our son come home from the war." Travis's mother led him toward the seated form. Travis reached out and took his father's left hand, which extended shakily toward him.

"Howdy, Pa. I'm happy to see you again." Travis looked at his mother, a question in his eyes.

"Oh, Father can hear you fine, son. He has a hard time making any sounds, but he knows you're here. Don't you, Tom?"

The crippled man shifted his eyes back and forth between the two people in front of him and tried to speak. The effort was painful to witness, as the damaged man struggled to make his body obey his mind. Finally, a grunt came out and he turned to his youngest son. A tear welled up and slipped down the sun-weathered face. Travis hugged his father tenderly and stood up, wiping away the sudden moisture in his own eyes.

"I've brought company." Calling out to his friends to come in, he introduced them to both his parents. "I'll show them to the guest rooms and let them freshen up from the trip, Ma. I'll be right down." Travis escorted his friends to their rooms in the west wing. As soon as they were settled, he came back to the den where his folks were waiting.

"Where're the household servants?" he asked. "The place seems almost deserted."

His mother looked down in embarrassment. "We had to let all the help go a couple of years ago. We ran out of money, so most of the vaqueros left and returned to Mexico. All that's left is Paco and his wife, Lupe. She's down with the rheumatism most of the time, so she's not much help. Then there's his grandson Pepe, who's ten. The cowboys all left for the army except for old Pete and Ollie Parkhurst, who was too crippled to join. They're out in the east range today, looking for strays, along with Vernon."

Travis grinned in anticipation. "It sure seems strange, Vernon back from New Orleans and me home as well. I'm eager to see him."

His mother looked at him, concern in her eyes. "You know he lost his left arm at Vicksburg, don't you?"

"Yep, you told me in the only letter that reached me from you while I was in the prison camp," Travis replied. "But that doesn't matter, as long as we're all together again."

His mother shook her head sadly. "It's really changed him, son. Vernon thinks he's a useless cripple and won't do much except mope around and feel sorry for himself. I sent him off with the boys just to get him out of the house. Maybe now that you're back, he'll snap out of it."

Travis nodded in understanding. "We'll have him back on his feet again, Ma. Don't you fret over it. Let's talk about Pa? Tell me all that you've learned from his doctors."

Travis and his mother walked over to the window facing the south range. "He had a bad stroke, about four months ago, when the Yankee carpetbaggers came and told him a tax was coming due in July and it would be twenty-two hundred dollars. We don't have any money, just some requisition vouchers for our horses and cows the Confederate army confiscators took." She returned to her husband's side and held his trembling right hand, which was beginning to shake itself off his lap.

"Hell," Travis exploded, "that's ten times what the taxes ever were before the war. What rancher can afford that sort of thing?"

"No one can," his mother answered. "That's exactly what the land-grabbers want. They got the military governor to set the tax rate too high, and then their hired thugs buy the best ranches when the owners default. We surprised them last year, using the gold pesos your father had hidden away in the smokehouse. This year, we're sunk. Tom was sure that now the war was over, the legislature would take over the revenue department, and reduce the tax rate, but nothing has happened so far. The state legislature is powerless to stop them until the military turns over control of the state back to the citizens. When Tom found out how much they wanted, he got so mad that I'm certain it caused his stroke. I don't know what we're going to do, son."

"We'll be just fine, Ma," Travis replied. "I've come home with plenty of Yankee cash. The only thing is, how best to use it." He looked out of the glass window toward the range. "Why didn't you sell some of the cattle to the Yanks?"

"Not enough help to gather a herd. Besides, where would we take them? While the war was goin', the Yanks wouldn't let a person travel anywhere without a pass. At least that's changed since the surrender of Lee. I heard last week that travel restrictions had been lifted as long as a body takes the oath of allegiance."

"I'll think on it while we get settled in. We raise cows, and the Union army needs to feed its soldiers. They'd pay with good money, too, if we can figger out a way to get the critters to them." He paused and smiled at his mother's solemn face. "For the time being, let's catch up on our visiting. I've been away a long time. How's Molly? And June? How 'bout their husbands?"

"The girls are well. So's Alex. He got home three months ago. June is in El Paso with Raymond. He's been sick a lot since he got back from the Yankee prison, so they went out to his folks. Maybe the air is drier there, and it'll ease the consumption in his lungs."

They visited until Homer and Irma came down from upstairs, the dust of the trip washed off their faces and brushed from their clothes. Soon, the two women were in the kitchen planning the homecoming meal, comfortable in each other's presence. It was easy to see that Ma and Irma were going to get on fine. His mother sent Pepe over inviting Molly and her husband for supper. Their small ranch was just downriver five miles from the Diamond S.

Big Tom was asleep in his rocker, so Travis and Jake walked outside and measured the wear and tear on the outbuildings and barn. Homer decided to stick close to Irma. There was needed repair on nearly every structure. It was evident that there had been a lot of neglect visited on the ranch in the last three years.

"Riders coming in, Doc." Jake once again proved the keenness of his eyesight.

"Probably my brother Vernon and the hands. Ma said he'd be back for supper."

Vernon and two cowboys trotted into the barnyard and swung off their saddles. Only then did the oldest son of Big Tom recognize his little brother.

"Jesus, it's Travis, come home from the Yankee prison. Damn, it's good to see you, little brother." He rushed over and threw his arm around Travis's shoulder.

"Hello, Vernon," Travis replied while he carefully hugged his older brother back. "It's great to see you. It's been way too long. I swear, you're looking more like Pa every time I see you."

Vernon turned toward the two men with him. "Pete, Ollie, look what the coyotes drug in while we were out."

The two cowboys heartily welcomed Travis back home. After all were introduced to Jake, they headed to the bunkhouse to wash up for supper. Vernon struggled out of his shirt and dipped his hand into the soapy water. He washed his face and the reddened stump of his left arm and dried himself on the clean rag hanging on a nail by the washbowl.

"See how the good doctors in Vicksburg took care of me." He waved the stump toward Travis.

"It looks like they did a pretty decent job, Vernon. What kind of wound did you have?"

"It was just hanging by a shred. Can you believe it? One of my own cannons blew up in my face. Killed every man in the section, and damn near tore off my arm. Made right in the Confederate arsenal at Birmingham. Rotten bad luck. The Yanks and us had been trading shell fire for weeks and not a scratch in my whole battery, and then one of our own cannon nearly wipes everyone out."

He wiggled back into his shirt. "I would just as soon they'd let me die as to whack off my arm, damn butchers."

"Not me," Travis answered. "I'm going to need you while we figger out what to do to save the ranch. Besides"—he smiled at his brother—"I'll bet half the gals in New Orleans would be heartbroken if you didn't show up there shortly."

"Yea," Jake chimed in. "As long as the shell didn't clip yur dingus, you'll always be able to keep the womenfolk happy with yur company. Don't need no arm fur that."

Just then, Molly and her husband, Alex Collins, rode up in a battered, old wagon. "Travis, darling, it is you. Oh, it's so good to see you here, safe and sound." She jumped off without waiting for her husband to help her down and rushed into Travis's open arms. Alex was not far behind, pumping Travis's hand like he never wanted to stop.

Travis felt a wonderful sense of happiness at his homecoming. "It's good to be back, Molly. I sure did miss you all."

After the hugs and introduction to Jake, the hungry bunch trooped into the main house for fried chicken, mashed sweet taters, and fresh green beans. To top it off, there was spring-cooled buttermilk from the smokehouse out back. To the hungry Travis and his friends, it tasted like the most delicious meal they'd ever eaten and they ate as if they had not eaten in days.

"Ma"—Travis finally quit and pushed his plate away—"that was some fine food. It was worth coming a long way for." Jake instantly agreed, while reaching for another sourdough biscuit. It wasn't long before the table was stripped of any edible food or drink. As Irma, Molly, and Mrs. Sasser cleared the table, Travis wheeled Big Tom into the family room and waited while Alex poured everyone homemade blackberry wine in the silver-rimmed crystal goblets used only for parties in the old days.

When everybody had settled on the horsehair couches and

chairs, Travis opened the family meeting by telling them that he had nearly five thousand dollars to pay the taxes and rebuild the ranch. "Don't ask where the money came from," he cautioned. "It's here for us to use, and that's enough. Jake has the same, as an ace in the hole, and Homer and Irma have two thousand for use in their new life." He looked at the seated pair, who were holding hands and listening quietly. "Have you two decided what you're gonna do?"

Homer shyly smiled at Irma and replied. "Yes, sir, we're going to get married as quick as possible. Then I'm going to open a store in Austin. I figger I can sell patent medicine, apothecary supplies, and do some dentist work. I got pretty good at it while I was in the army. Me and Irma would be pleased to have you be with us when we say our wedding vows. As soon as we can find a preacher, that is."

"I'll ride in to Nacogdoches tomorrow," Travis volunteered. "I'll have the local reverend out here at noon day after tomorrow. That soon enough for you two?" He smiled to himself. That would give him an excuse to see Clarissa as well.

Irma and Homer were thrilled with the answer. The women immediately excused themselves and began working on plans for the wedding while Travis directed the men's discussion toward the problems of the ranch.

"As you are aware, I have some Yankee money, so we can pay the taxes on the ranch this year. I'll also have enough to hire some good men so we can get this place fixed up. How about you, Alex? Do you need tax money?"

"Yep," Molly's sandy-haired husband replied. "But it's not as bad as your folks. We were assessed only three hundred dollars."

"Odd," Travis noted. "Even though your spread isn't as big as the Diamond S, that still seems awful low in comparison."

"It is," Vernon interjected. "The damned carpetbaggers pick out the spreads they want and set the taxes extra high, to make sure they get a default. When they get all the big spreads, they'll most likely move on the smaller ones like Alex and Molly's."

"How do the skunks do this here default buying?" Jake asked.

Vernon sipped his wine and glanced over at Big Tom, who seemed to be following every word. "They've set up a land office in Nacogdoches, with a local man running it. The money is from outsiders, Yankees for sure. No Southern man would have the gall or the cash to do this big a deal."

"Who's running it from around here? I wouldn't think anyone would do that to his neighbors?" Travis asked.

"That little weasel, Jeremy Asherton," Vernon replied with venom in his voice.

"You don't mean that fat little Jeremy who used to run around bragging what a big shot he was going to be someday? Too bad a Yankee minié ball didn't take some of the starch out of him." Travis shook his head at the thought of the obnoxious, greedy young man whom he remembered as the town brat when he was growing up.

"Hell," Vernon answered, "he didn't get near a fight. His pa bought him out of the draft every time his name came up. He's married now to some snooty gal and has a fat little brat of a son who looks just like him. Jeremy's as treacherous as a rattlesnake, smiling at you like a friend while trying to stab a bayonet in your back."

Travis couldn't believe what he was hearing. "I never had much truck with Jeremy, but I never thought he would turn against his neighbors."

"Explain how this tax buyout works," Jake interrupted.

Vernon pointed his arm toward the big map of the area pinned on the wall behind Big Tom's scarred, wooden desk. "They have a tax commissioner, appointed by the Yankee army, in charge of each county in the state. This tax commissioner sets the taxes, and the blue bellies, mostly colored occupation troops, make sure you pay or get thrown off the land. Then, an auction is held, and since none of us has any money, the land-grabbers buy the ranch for the back taxes. So far, they've picked up a dozen good-sized ranches in this area. We're 'bout the only ones, 'cept for the widow Gunther, who've escaped their greedy hands. She's probably as strapped as we are and will lose her place come July first."

Travis nodded and instructed Vernon, "The first thing tomorrow, you and Jake ride over and talk to her. Tell her we'll lend her the money to pay her taxes, if she's interested in our help." Travis turned to Jake. "She's a feisty old gal who may just shoot your pants off before you can say a word edgewise, so mind your manners."

"Just how old?" Jake questioned. He had a devilish look in his eyes.

"She's not old, Jake," Vernon interjected. "I don't think Ruby has reached forty yet. Her two youngest girls are still at home and neither is more 'n fifteen. The oldest girl ran off before the war with a drummer and Ruby's only son fell at Murfreesboro in sixty-two." He smiled benevolently at Jake. "Her husband died near ten years ago, so she seems harder than she really is. Taking care of a ranch by herself and all."

Jake just nodded and smiled.

Travis figured the crafty mountain man would have the widow Gunther on their side before tomorrow's sun was set.

Travis and the men continued to discuss the best way to save the ranches. They decided to take the tax money directly to Austin and pay the ranch's assessment there. That way there was not much chance that anything would happen to the money before it got credited to their account.

"You fellows will need to sign the oath of allegiance to the federal government as well," Vernon remarked. "That means you're a citizen again. Suppose you could do that in Austin as well."

Travis agreed. "A good idea. That will make us legal again. I'll go to town tomorrow and ask the preacher to come out here Friday afternoon." Travis could hardly contain his excitement at the thought of seeing Clarissa again. "Alex, you and Vernon try and find some men for us to hire. I want to gather up a herd as quickly as possible." A daring plan had suddenly revealed itself to him.

"What on earth for?" Vernon interrupted. "We don't have a single order for beef. Besides, I don't know how many we even have, they've strayed so bad."

"Don't worry," Alex interjected. "They's a bunch more than you think out in the scrub country."

"I'll explain when I get back from Austin. Just you fellows gather a big herd as quick as you can. Add Mrs. Gunther's cows to the herd as well, if she'll let you, Jake."

Travis slept in his own bed that night with the audacious plan whirling around in his brain. But it would have to wait until he'd seen Clarissa, by gosh. First things first.

Chapter 12

Travis awoke before dawn, habits of the early morning roll-call at the prisoner-of-war stockade firmly ingrained in his routine. He wandered outside, to enjoy the sunrise with Colonel, the name he had given to the handsome black he had stolen from the cavalry barn in Saint Louis. With just a touch of humor, he wondered if some Yankee officer was still searching for the magnificent horse. Hopefully, with the fake bill of sale provided him by Mr. Durmon, back in Monroe, he would never have to give the animal up. He'd developed an attachment to the horse, and Colonel seemed to return the affection.

Jake was already up and leaning against the corral fence, sipping some chickery coffee he'd taken from the big, fire-scarred pot Pepe kept warm on the kitchen stove. He nodded toward Travis and sipped from his tin cup.

"Morning, Jake," Travis greeted his friend as he moved beside him. The black horse strolled over to see if there might be a treat for him. Travis rubbed the horse's nose and fed him the two lumps of hard sugar he'd swiped from Pepe's pantry. "I suppose you slept soundly, Jake." He grinned at his older friend. "Seems to me that you always could grab a few winks no matter where you lay down. That feather bed you were on last night must have seemed like floating on a cloud."

"Yep," Jake replied. "I suppose I'd a'heard a twister iffen one had come through durin' the night, but that's about all." Jake took a sip and looked silently over the landscape for a moment.

"This here is some fine land, fer a fact."

In silent admiration, they watched the simmering gold orb slowly lift itself off the low rolling range to the east and cast its brilliance over the land. "It sure feels good to be free and home again," Travis remarked softly. He observed the early morning activity around the chow hall. Ollie and Pete came out of the bunkhouse and splashed cool water from the washbowl over their sleepy faces. Shortly, they were moving up to the kitchen to grab a hearty helping of biscuits, bacon, and eggs before heading off to their morning chores. Travis was anxious to get into town. He desperately needed to see Clarisse. Did she still care? Was she waiting for his return like she had promised?

"Well," Jake sighed, "I'd better make my way to the table afore those two jaspers what work fer ya eat all the grub. After I talk to the widder lady, I think I'll spend the day looking over the land. I want to have a feel fer the lay of things afore it starts to get active around here. I'll be back in plenty o'time fer the evening meal."

"Go ahead," Travis answered. "I'll take the women into town along with Homer." He paused and then confided in his friend. "I want to find Clarissa. I need to see her after all this time away. By gum, I'll invite her to the wedding. It'll give me a chance to introduce her to my family. That is, if she still wants to meet 'em." He smiled at his inspiration as he watched Jake amble toward the dining room.

Travis went back inside after a few more strokes of Colonel's silky-soft nose. His mother was stirring around in the kitchen with Molly and Irma. The entire family gathered for a hearty breakfast and then scattered to complete the morning's chores before they left for town.

Travis gave his mother and Molly fifty dollars each. "Be careful and don't flash this around," he admonished them. "We don't want it known that the Diamond S has Yankee greenbacks."

The two women looked at the money with an almost hungry, awe-stuck gaze. It had been a long time since either had any money to spend on themselves. He repeated the same warning to Irma and Homer, and they nodded their understanding.

He put a pair of twenty-dollar bills in his own pocket and soon was leading everyone out of the front gate. Homer and the women were in the two-seat buggy that had been gathering dust in the saddle shed since the Confederate army had seized the ranch's horses over two years earlier. The pair of fine horses that had pulled the officer's carriage from Saint Louis to Texas looked grand hitched to the rig. It reminded Travis of Marie and her beautiful black eyes. He hoped she was alive and well.

Nacogdoches was twenty-two miles southeast of the Diamond S and back across the Angelina River. As they splashed across the shallow ford, Travis's thoughts turned to Clarissa and her golden beauty. Her features had blurred in his memory, but not the intense feelings she aroused in him. Soon, he'd have her in his arms again, and things would be right between them. It had to be, he hoped. He whistled a Rebel marching song as they trotted toward town.

They passed the brush-shielded turnoff to Parson's Creek where he and Clarissa had spent their last moments together nearly three and a half years earlier, just before they reached the edge of town. It still appeared to be lightly traveled, with grass growing up among the ruts of buggies that had entered from time to time. *"Probably still a lover's rendezvous,"* Travis mused.

The ranch and farm community of Nacogdoches hadn't changed much. The stores were a bit shabbier, and a couple had been boarded over by their departed owners, as money was probably scarce for most folks who lived around the area. The buildings and sidewalks along Main Street were built three feet above the ground, to provide a safe walkway from the occasional springtime overflows of the Angelina River.

The high sidewalks had been the source of numerous drunken accidents, when a tipsy cowboy or townsman stepped off the walk and fell flat on his face in the street. Each building had a three-step stairway from the dirt street to the sidewalk entrance of the store. Travis stopped at Miss Martha's Dress Shop and helped the womenfolk out of the buggy.

"I'll meet you all at the General Store after Homer and I call on Reverend Jenkins," he called. Molly hurriedly nodded as they rushed into the store. "Come on, Homer," he laughed. "The women will be a couple of hours shopping or perhaps more. We may as well line up the preacher while we wait."

It didn't take long to obtain the old preacher's agreement, especially when Travis mentioned there would be a fee involved for the ceremony, and a celebration feast afterwards. "Honored to be there, my boy," the Reverend Jenkins solemnly intoned.

Travis could see that the preacher already had a nip of the alcohol-laced cough medicine he favored for his perpetually sore throat. "It comes from the hell fire shouting he does every Sunday," Travis assured Homer as they walked away from the parsonage. "Don't worry, he'll be sober enough to hitch you and Irma. He wouldn't want to miss a free meal and some spending money."

Homer grinned shyly and led the way toward the General Store. "I need to buy some decent clothes myself," he remarked. "Where do you think the best place is to buy pants?"

"Come on." Travis slapped his shoulder. "I'll be your personal guide to all the shops in town. You'll need new boots, a hat, shirt, the works. We'll finish at the Emporium, which is the best place for pants and shirts. Clarissa's pa owns it; I'll ask for her while you're shopping."

As they made their way around the town, buying and being

served with vigor by the cash-hungry owners, Travis saw a sign over the building where the former saddle shop was once located.

"East Texas Land and Livestock Company" was emblazoned in bright red letters. "That must be the land-grabbing company Vernon told us about. I'll have to stop by there on my way out of town just to see what's inside." Homer barely glanced at the place, so intent was he on finishing his shopping and returning to his Irma.

They walked through the open door of the Emporium and soon had the attentive clerk rushing about showing Homer pants and shirts of various colors and design. Travis bought some denim shirts and pants to use while working at the ranch. They each purchased a new suit for the wedding. Travis noticed Clarissa's father desending from his upstairs office, curious to see what the commotion was all about.

"Mr. Watkins." Travis strode over and shook the surprised man's hand. "It's good to see you again, sir. I'm Travis Sasser. We met the night of the Christmas dance, over three years ago. Can you tell me where Clarissa is?"

The agitated shopkeeper rubbed his muttonchops-whiskered cheek and muttered, "Ah yes, Captain Sasser, wasn't it? Happy to see you back from the war. No, I don't have any idea where Clair's at this moment. I suggest you don't bother her anyway. In fact I suggest you leave her alone. Things have changed since you've been gone."

"I think I'll leave that decision to Clarissa, Mr. Watkins. Would you call her for me?"

"I have no idea where she is. Please, you stay away from her. It's best for everyone."

Travis was about to give the pompous old store owner a piece of his mind when Molly and his mother stuck their head in the door and called for Travis and Homer to hurry over to the general store. "Come on, we need some advice about what to buy for the wedding cake," Molly said. As they walked out the door, she offered an explanation for her odd request, "We don't do business there anymore. Mr. Watkins is part and parcel of the land-grabbers and hasn't given us any credit for over a year."

Travis was deeply disturbed by the abrupt way Watkins had talked to him about Clarissa, and now he understood why. Well, that would change, as soon as he and Watkins's lovely daughter announced their engagement. He glanced back. Watkins was standing at the top of the stairs, a worried frown plainly visible on his bewhiskered face.

After filling the buggy with the newly purchased food and clothing, Travis looked again at the building under the blue sign. "Homer, if you'll stop off at the leather shop across the street, you should be able to find a nice belt and holster for one of those Navy thirty-sixes we took from the outlaws in Louisiana. I do believe I'd like to stop in at the East Texas Land and Livestock Company and pay my respects."

"Oh, Travis, please be careful," his mother worriedly interjected. "Don't start trouble on your first day home."

"Don't worry, Ma, I'll be on my best behavior. I just want to have a look at the new enemy, since we're all Yanks again."

He moved easily across the rutted, dusty street and climbed the three steps to the sidewalk outside the land office. As he entered the office, he noticed an unshaved man wearing a pistol slung low on his hip, leaning up against the far wall. Travis could see he was being sized up by the scowling pistolero and just as quickly dismissed as no threat to the establishment.

At the rear, behind a glass partition, the chubby face of Jeremy Asherton looked up at him and gaped in surprise. Then Jeremy's face broke into an exaggerated smile. Travis could see that the smile never reached Jeremy's eyes. Jeremy wasn't grotesquely fat, but for this time and circumstance, he seemed so. It was obvious he'd not suffered any privation of food or comfort during the war. He bustled through the door and rushed to pump Travis's hand.

"Well, well," he beamed, "here's the brave Doctor Sasser, safe and home from the war. Happy to see you again, Travis. How's your poor, unfortunate father?"

Travis reluctantly took the offered hand. "Thanks, he's doing better every day. You seem to be doing fine since I saw you last, Jeremy."

"I try, I try," Jeremy beamed. "There's a lot of opportunity for the man with vision and the guts to try. I expect to be a mighty influential man in Texas someday."

"Don't forget money, and a sympathetic tax commissioner," Travis dryly replied.

Asherton laughed, "Yes, there's that, too. I hear you've been spending a few greenbacks since you arrived."

Travis raised his eyebrow. Jeremy had some quick informants, it appeared. "Thanks to a generous Yankee soldier who named me in his will," Travis answered. He could see the faint wave of relief that flowed quickly across Jeremy's beady eyes at his next statement. "We may need a lot more soon, unless I can reason with the tax assessor. I guess you've heard that it's unreasonably high. I don't suppose that's any surprise to you though, is it?"

"Not a thing I can do, I'm afraid," Jeremy smoothly answered. "The military government appoints the assessors. I just represent a consortium of Eastern investors who are trying to set up a big operation in this area."

"Well, Jeremy," Travis drawled as he started toward the door, "I'll bet you find it mighty profitable to be in bed with these strangers when it comes time to destroy the lives of your friends and neighbors."

"I just do my job," Asherton whined. "I can't help it if folks didn't save any money for their taxes. A person's got to take care of himself and his family first, don't forget."

"Right," Travis snarled. "Don't you forget it, either." He stomped past the silent man who had been watching the exchange between Travis and Jeremy from the outer office.

As Travis shut the door, the taciturn gun hand looked at the frowning face of Asherton. His contempt for the porcine, little man who paid him to be the company enforcer and protector was scarcely concealed. "Think that hombre may try and stink up your operation, boss."

Jeremy watched the retreating form and snapped, "I doubt it. However, if so, that's what you get paid for, Ace. Could be you'll have to start earning the money I've been spending on you." He took satisfaction at the flush of anger on the gunman's face.

Travis swung into his saddle and led the way out of town, hot anger rising up in his craw. The peculiar way Mr. Watkins had responded to his question about Clarissa and the smooth oiliness of Jeremy had his temper near the boiling point.

As they rounded the bend of the road, Travis looked at the turnoff to Parson's Creek, where he and Clarissa had spent the most wonderful afternoon of his life. He made a quick decision. "Homer, take the womenfolk on back to the ranch. I'm gonna swing off here and visit a place where I can think in peace. Ma, I'll be along later."

He waved the others along and turned down the hidden path. Low willow trees and scrub brush lined the route, and it wasn't long until he was hidden from the road. Then the clearing came into view. It was just as it had been so many months ago. The creek was running with a throaty gurgle, and birds were singing in the trees. He climbed off Colonel, tying him to a bush near a lush stand of green grass. He sat down on a fallen tree trunk and gazed at the twinkling water.

The sound of an approaching horse and buggy interrupted his musings. With an irritated oath at the disturbing intruder, he watched an expensive rig bounce down the rutted path. The driver was a woman, dressed in pale blue with a dark-blue bonnet. With a lurch in his heart, he realized it was Clarissa. Rushing to the side of the buggy, he helped her down from the seat and took her in his arms. "Clarissa, how did you know I was here?"

She eagerly returned his kiss and gushed, "Darling, I just heard you were back and at Papa's store. I took a chance and drove here, hoping you'd stop off on the way back to your ranch." She raised her face to his again, seeking another kiss. Then, grabbing a blanket from the seat, she led the bedazzled Travis to the grassy plot by the log. Carefully, she spread it on the ground and sat down, allowing Travis an easy view of her feet, encased in white leather button-top shoes and a good deal of her calf as well.

He sat beside her and taking her in his arms tried to tell her of his life since their last good-bye, while taking the opportunity to kiss her again and again. Their passion grew hotter, and before he knew it, she had her soft hand gently stroking his groin, and he was blindly groping at her breasts, his mouth covering hers. Suddenly, she broke away, and gasped, "Darling, we're wasting time. Here, help me with my buttons. I want to get out of this dress."

In barely an instant, she was clad only in her chemise and pulling the shirt from his body. He quickly stripped off his pants and in frenzied lust and desire, possessed her. Their union was as intense as any coupling of stallion and mare, and almost as quick. Travis wasn't through however, and immediately slowed his passion to a more gentle and sustained motion. Clarissa rocked and moaned beneath him and joined him in a shattering finish, which left both gasping and soaked with sweat.

Without pause, Travis continued to love the woman he'd been waiting so long to see. She answered him in kind, her long legs tightly wrapped around his hips, her skillful hands increasing his pleasure. Only after a third blinding finality did he carefully roll off of her and prop himself on his elbow. Looking down at his beloved Clarissa, he traced his finger through the sweaty valley between her milky-white breasts, toward the golden fuzz below her stomach.

"My God, lover," she gasped. "I didn't think your hitching post was ever going to give up. What a wonderful homecoming surprise you have given me."

"I suppose there's nothing for me to do but make an honest woman of you as quickly as possible," he remarked gently. Breathlessly, he waited for her response.

The briefest of frowns crossed her lovely face. "Darling, didn't you get my letter? I wrote you about it nearly two years ago."

A cold fist rose up in Travis's gut. "No, Clarissa. What letter? I haven't heard from you but once since I left after Christmas of sixty-two."

"Why, silly boy," she laughed nervously. "I married Jeremy Asherton two years ago last July. We had a son last October." She pouted and continued. "You were gone, and I didn't hear from you at all. Honestly, I didn't even know if you were alive or dead. Papa was after me to marry Jeremy, and anyway, it won't matter to us."

She grabbed his arm and gave him a dazzling smile. "You can set up an office in town, and I'll come over as often as I can. We can go away on trips from time to time, and Jeremy has to go around to the ranches he runs nearly every week. We'll have a lot of time to spend together." Her voice went faster and faster as she saw the look of dismay on Travis's face.

Stunned and feeling nauseous, as if he'd been punched in the stomach, he jerked his hand back and got to his feet. Clarissa lay there, unashamed in her nakedness, babbling on about how they could work her dirty scheme on her husband. He looked more closely at the nearly naked form before him. The signs of childbirth were there if he'd only taken time to notice. Travis turned and walked into the cool water of the creek. He knelt and washed the sweat and stains of their union from his body and, after a few silent minutes, returned to his clothing. "That's why you didn't answer my letter, isn't it?"

Clarissa was talking almost hysterically, trying to convince him to join in the adulterous plan she had concocted. "Really, Travis," she cried. "You can't blame me. I couldn't write. The Confederate mail returns any letter it can't deliver. I was afraid to write. My father or Jeremy might have seen it. But don't worry, we can have the best of both worlds if you'll just listen to reason. Darling, please be realistic about this." She scrambled to get into her clothes as he finished dressing. Without another word, he grimly climbed on Colonel and spurred the animal out of the glen, leaving the half-dressed woman behind, shouting at him.

"Fool. You pious bastard. You'll come back to me, on your knees. Travis, darling, wait for me. Please listen to me." Her voice faded as Travis spurred Colonel down the dusty road toward the Diamond S. His body was numb and his head ached like he'd been hit with an ax handle. He blindly let the horse follow the road back to the ranch, before even taking notice of where he was.

He turned the horse toward home and splashed across the shallow ford. For the first time since he left Clarissa's side, he spoke. "Damn you, Jeremy Asherton. You've stolen the last thing you'll ever take from me or my family."

Chapter 13

By the time Travis returned to the ranch house, the shock of Clarissa's callous betrayal to both him and her new husband was beginning to wear off. It was replaced by a quiet rage at the bitter trick she played on him, her family, and Jeremy Asherton. He remembered the bitter young soldiers who had received letters from home with the devastating announcement that a new love had replaced them in some callous girl's heart.

The story was all too familiar. The girl back home, growing tired of being alone, takes up with a local who'd avoided the war in some way. Sometimes, her family had pushed like Clarissa's did, and sometimes the girl was just too anxious for marriage to wait for the absent soldier. Often, he'd told the despondent soldier that he was lucky to be rid of such an unfaithful woman and that he'd find a better girl than he'd lost. Now the boot was on his foot, and it was a mighty uncomfortable fit.

He smiled grimly at the memory of those bitter looks he'd received in return. The young men might as well have said, "What do you know about it anyway? You don't have to live with the pain I'm feeling." As the ranch house came into view, he remarked out loud, "Well, boys, now I do know how it feels, and it's not one damn bit pleasant, is it?"

As he had ridden up, he had waved at his father, sitting in the old rocker, his gaze focused across the grassy field toward the river, but had received no response. Young Pepe sat silently nearby on the front step, waiting to help his patron if needed. The boy was industriously whittling on a stick with his prized pocketknife. He had been assigned by Travis's mother to watch the weakened man. Travis decided to take the both of them on a ride. No telling when his father had been away from the house.

"Pepe, let's take the patron on a ride in the buggy. Run get it hitched up, please."

"Sí, Señor Travis." As soon as the young servant led the horse and carriage out of the barn, Travis helped his father to his feet.

"Pepe, you ride next to the patron."

"Sí. I weel ride in the fine buggy like a grande." He clamored on and sat waiting for Travis and Big Tom to get on, looking around imperiously.

Travis assisted Big Tom as his crippled father worked his way onto the front seat and put the reins in the old man's good hand. "Hold the reins, Pa, while I tell Ma where we're going." He stepped inside the cool of the house and shouted up toward the rooms on the second floor. "Ma, I'm gonna take Pa for a ride in the buggy."

His mother immediately stepped out of the master bedroom, a new dress in her hands, and pins in her mouth. She was already adjusting one of her newly purchased dresses. "Do you think you should, son? Doctor Miller said he wasn't to get worked up."

"Don't worry," Travis replied. "We'll take the road down to the south range and back. I'll take Pepe with us and turn back if Pa becomes too tired." With that, he stepped outside and climbed up beside his father. The old man's eyes seemed to be alert and to reflect an interest in what was happening. Pepe squirmed on the seat, sitting haughtily, as he supposed a grand jefe would sit.

Homer walked out of the house and inquired, "Want me to tag along to help you, Doctor Sasser?"

"No thanks, Homer. Pepe and I will handle it fine. Why don't you take the opportunity to look at my medical books in the library? Read any you desire. We'll be back before supper." He snapped the reins, and the team smartly pulled the buggy out of the yard and down the dirt road toward the rolling meadows of the south range.

The fields were blooming from the late spring rains, and color was abundant. The wagon cast a moving shadow on the wildflowers and green grass as it moved along the rutted road. Travis talked to his father about the war, his escape from the Yankee prison, and the ranch. The old man couldn't respond, but Travis sensed that his father was attentive and understood what he was saying.

From time to time, they came upon a number of brownish red cattle, munching the wild grass around some mesquite bushes or darting into some gully at their approach. "The cowboys are going to have their hands full rounding up these critters," he told the silent man beside him. For an instant the trace of a smile appeared on the twisted mouth of the crippled rancher. The old man managed a grunt of affirmation.

The rest of the afternoon, Travis drove the buggy around the south range, clear to the far end of the ranch boundaries before returning for supper. Travis talked and his crippled father grunted in reply. Eventually, the subject turned to Clarissa and how she'd betrayed him. After he had finished venting his feelings with his father, he felt he could handle the small talk of the family at the dinner table.

The afternoon out with his younger son boosted Big Tom's morale. As they returned to the ranch house, his eyes seemed brighter and he struggled to make legible sounds. The old man fell peacefully asleep in his favorite rocker once inside the ranch house. Before dark, Vernon stomped in, spitting and snorting from the dust he'd eaten while in the saddle all day.

"I took Jake over to talk with the widow Gunther," he stated. "Then while he was palavering with her, I rode on over to the Randolphs' spread. The two older boys will be here Monday, eager to earn some hard cash. I met Jesus Mendez on the road and sent word by him for any of the Mexicans in Naggi-docsh who wanted to work to show up as well. We'll probably get four or five vaqueros in the next couple of days who need work." He paused and looked around. "Jake not back yet?"

"Nope," Travis answered. "I sure hope he didn't rile the widow and have her shoot his backside off." They laughed and went on in to eat.

Alex rode in as they filled their plates with food. "I scouted around the range with Ollie and Pete. I'm sure there's better than two thousand head of our cattle scattered about the ranch. I've got another three hundred, and Mrs. Gunther, probably that or more." He looked at Travis expectantly. "So, what do you want to do?"

"Gather a herd and have them ready for the trail. Jake and I are going to Austin with the tax money, and as soon as we get back, we're gonna drive them to a market, somewhere." Travis looked at his mother and Vernon. "Is that all right with you?"

"Whatever you say, dear. I'll leave it up to you boys to decide what to do," his mother replied.

"Well," Vernon jumped in. "How do you plan to sell them? I haven't heard of any buyers comin' this way lookin' for beef."

"That's just it, big brother," Travis responded. "The North has to be hurting for beef. The Yankee army has a bunch of troops to feed, and Texas hasn't been sending any beef up to market since the war started."

Vernon groused, "I can tell you, I wouldn't give a pig's fanny for any of this if the cotton market wasn't busted up so bad." Vern ignored the frown from his mother and continued. "I sure wish I was back in New Orleans, brokering cotton, instead of playing nursemaid to a bunch of stinky, half-wild cows."

Vernon continued to grouse about the sorry state of the cotton business. "There's hundreds of empty cotton barges lining the wharfs at New Orleans that used to carry thousands of bales of cotton up to Saint Louie, or Louisville, or Cincinnati. I wonder if they'll ever be filled again?"

The answer hit Travis like a lightning bolt. "Vernon, 'bout how many cows could a person put in a cotton barge?"

Vernon's eyes widened as he calculated in his mind. "Why two, three hundred easy. Why do you ask?"

"Suppose I sent you on ahead to New Orleans. Could you line up some empty barges and a paddle wheeler or two to push 'em?"

"I reckon so. What would you do with 'em after you got 'em all loaded on the barges, anyway?"

Travis looked around the table at the inquisitive faces of his family. Each person was imagining the sight of cattle on barges in the middle of the Mississippi. "Just as soon as I take care of the tax situation, Alex and I'll drive the herd to the Vicksburg crossing and meet you there. Then, I'll go upstream with half, and you go downstream with the rest. I'm betting that we can sell all we have to the army posts along the river. Vicksburg, Natchez, Baton Rouge, New Orleans, Memphis, Cairo, New Madrid. Hell, there are more forts than that even. We'll be able to get twenty or twenty-five dollars apiece for 'em, maybe more."

"Oh, Travis," Molly cried out. "That would mean enough money to save our places, no matter how high the taxes get. Can you do it?"

"Can we, Vern?" Travis passed the question to his brother, who had a thoughtful look on his face.

"Damn, sorry, Ma," he exclaimed. "It might just work. For sure, the shipping people will be eager to rent their cotton barges. They're just sitting on the river, rotting from inactivity.

If you can sell cows to the Yanks, then so can I. Yes, by God, we'll make it work. That is, if we can get the herd to the river at Vicksburg."

Molly spoke up, "Alex and I will throw in our cattle. Count on it. Right, Alex?" Travis looked at his sister's husband, who nodded enthusiastically.

They continued to discuss the plan and finished eating. Homer and Irma stayed mostly silent, and as soon as possible, politely excused themselves to take a walk in the cooling shadows of the evening. Vernon and Travis stepped out on the porch and talked over the roundup plans with Ollie and Pete. Well after dark, Jake rode up, whistling a tuneless melody.

"Howdy, Jake," Vern called. "I was afraid the Gunther women had taken you hostage or something."

"Naw," the old scout replied. "I did stay fur supper though, so's I could continue to charm Martha and her gals." He chuckled at some private memory.

"Why durn if that don't beat all," Ollie said. "I don't think airy another man has set at their table since Rufe Gunther died, ten year ago."

"Well, she was a bit testy at first, but my natural charm soon turned the day. By the way, Doc, she's in to the hip pockets with us. She says iffen we'll take her herd to sell, she'll give 'em to us at half the market selling price, the rest to be our drivin' fee fur gettin' 'em there."

He paused and smiled again at the dumfounded look on Ollie's face. Ollie had tried to become friendly with the widow on several occasions, only to be soundly rebuffed. "I told her that we'd pay her taxes fur her before we do anything else. I'll handle that out of my share iffen you don't mind, Doc. She says she'll pay back out of the money from the cattle drive."

Jake looked at Ollie. "Ollie, how did her man die, d'you know?"

"Shore do, since I was the one what found him," Ollie answered. "It was because he was such a hard-drinkin' man. I never knowed a fella what could drink so much, so fast. Folks always thought it was because Mrs. Gunther was a touch sharp-tongued and all. Anyhow, it was the first day of January fifty-six, I think. I was coming back from town, and there he was, passed out plumb in the middle of Naggi-doch ford. Facedown and drowned dead, in four inches of water. His backside was dry as a bone and he was drowned. Can you beat that?"

Ollie looked at his receptive audience and continued. "Well, I toted him over to Mrs. Gunther's and tried to help, but she just shooed me away like I was some pesky ole fly and that was that. I reckon she and the girls must have dug the grave themselves, 'cause when they planted him two days later, it was done dug. Nobody's been able to get close to her since, 'cept you, Jake. How the hell did you do it?"

"Just a good ole Arkansas boy and the gals all know it, I reckon. Anyhow, I'll be going over tomorrow to invite 'em to the wedding, iffen that's all right by you and Homer," Jake answered confidently.

Travis agreed and Ollie just shook his head. "I'll be durned if I can figger out womenfolk. They sure never acted like they was interested in having me around, and now look at you. Practically one of the family in less than a day. I'll swan." Ollie stomped off to rub down his horse and sulk at the idea that the widow Gunther would choose some broke-down old mountain man over him.

Travis asked Alex, Jake, and Vernon to take a walk with him down by the bend in the river. Almost without thinking, Travis led the way to where he and his brother used to swim when they were youngsters. It was as he'd remembered it, with the fallen tree they'd used as a bench, right by the bank. The four men sat on the fallen log and watched the rippling water, while

Travis outlined his plans.

"As soon as the wedding is over, Jake and I will escort the newlyweds to Austin. We'll pay the taxes there, to avoid any mistake that might cost us the ranch. We'll take the oath of allegiance there, and I'll try and get a letter from the territorial army commander introducing us as a legitimate cattle sales company. While we're gone, Vern, you and Alex start to gather a herd. We want to keep it quiet if we can, so nobody gets suspicious and decides to interfere with us. Alex, you go around to the neighbors and ask if they're interested in putting in with us. Offer them the same deal Jake got for us, half the market price, with a five-dollar-a-cow advance to carry them while we're gone."

Everyone agreed to the plan and continued to discuss it until time for bed, reviewing the fine points to make certain nothing had been overlooked. The four men walked back to the ranch satisfied that selling the cattle to army forts along the river was the best chance to foil the land-grabbers. Travis slept soundly, not a single visit in his dreams by the two-timing Clarissa.

The next day was devoted to the preparations for the wedding. Alex brought in a small heifer, which was prepared by Paco and placed over the barbecue pit. By the time the Reverend Jenkins, Jake, the widow Gunther and her two daughters arrived, the savory aroma of an old-fashioned Texas barbecue drifted across the yard. Molly and Mrs. Sasser had fitted Irma in a pale-green dress trimmed with lots of white lace. She made a beautiful bride standing beside the shyly proud Homer in his new suit.

Old Reverend Jenkins didn't waste any time tying the knot for the two beaming lovers. As soon as he said, "Man and wife. You may kiss the bride," he headed right for the little bar that Paco had set up next to the table. Soon he was gulping the free liquor and talking a blue streak with Jake and Mrs. Gunther.

Travis had enjoyed meeting her and her daughters again. The two girls had grown into young women since he'd last seen them. All the Gunther women seemed quite taken with Jake, and it was plain to see that he was on a short string already, as far as Mrs. Gunther was concerned. The old mountain man seemed to enjoy the female attention, so Travis was happy for his friend.

Molly and Irma went off to pack the goods Irma had recently acquired for her trip to Austin. Homer joined Travis and Vern on the porch, where they watched the sun dropping over the low foothills to the west. "Irma and me will be ready to leave first thing tomorrow morning if you want," he gravely told Travis.

"No need to hurry, old son," Vern answered. "If you're on the trail by ten, you'll still make Austin in four days easy. Go ahead and sleep in a tad tomorrow. After all, it's your wedding night."

Homer blushed and gave a wry grin. "We're a bit ahead of that, I'm afraid. Still, if it's all right with you, Doctor Sasser?"

"Sure." Travis smiled at his studious friend. "Take your time, and don't worry. We'll get you lovebirds to Austin right on schedule. Come on, let's go have some barbecue and quench our thirst in the cold applejack that Alex brought to the festivities."

The next morning, the newlyweds were happily surprised to find an almost-new buggy and team of horses waiting for them. Travis had purchased them from Vern as a wedding present for his friends. By midday, the party was well on its way toward Waco, where they would turn south to Austin. The four days passed quietly, with the miles falling behind them in monotonous regularity. On the evening of the fourth day, the lights of the Texas capital could be seen twinkling in the dusk. By the time they'd arrived and secured a room at the Capital Inn and seen to the horses, it was late enough to only have a quick meal and then turn in for the night. Tomorrow would be an eventful day for the former Yankee prisoners of war.

Chapter 14

After an early breakfast in the hotel cafe, Travis, Homer, and Jake stepped out on the already-busy boardwalk of the main street of Austin. At first glance, Austin seemed more alive than Nacogdoches. Numerous shopkeepers were busy setting up displays for passersby to inspect or sweeping the dust from the worn boardwalk in front of their businesses. The stores carried a larger and more varied array of goods than any other Southern town Travis had seen since returning to Texas.

He decided that since Yankee soldiers had garrisoned Austin for over a year now, maybe it had become acclimated to the presence of blue-clad soldiers. Personally, he felt a bit unnerved by so many of his former enemies strolling around the city, rifles slung over their shoulders. The mostly black Yankee soldiers seemed to glare at everyone, as if daring anyone to start trouble. It would take some getting used to the new way of life. Travis and Jake accompanied Homer to the office of the lawyer, Regent Johnson, who was handling the estate of his mother. The seedy-looking lawyer hurriedly gathered the necessary papers for Homer's signature in order to probate the will.

By the time the will was read and the probate of Homer's small inheritance completed, it was noon. Homer now was the legal owner of the modest house and a one-room store his mother had used as a dress shop. "I'll be using it as my dentist and apothecary store," he informed the lawyer, who shrugged his thin shoulders as if to dismiss the thought. Realizing that he might be offending a potential client, Johnson quickly added, "The town needs a good apothecary. If you can stay in business while folks sort of get back on their feet, you should do very well." He harrumphed, "I regret that my bill as executor will take most of the cash money your fine mother left you."

Homer nodded stiffly, gathered up his deeds of ownership, and took his leave. As the three friends walked back to the hotel to eat lunch with Irma, he remarked, "Thank heavens for the start-up money you gave us, Doctor Sasser. And you too, Jake. If we didn't have that, we'd be out in the cold without a blanket. Where does that old rooster come off thinking we'd have any money to keep going? Sure didn't stop him from taking his pay right off the top, did it?"

"You be sure to keep the source of your money to yourself, Homer," Travis warned. "The Yanks would sure take it all back if they knew it was once theirs."

Homer chuckled, "Don't worry, as far as anyone here is concerned, it's an inheritance from a rich uncle who died back in Ohio."

After lunch, they accompanied the two newlyweds to the little cottage that Homer had inherited and did what they could to get the newlyweds settled in. Soon Irma was off to the store to buy the basics needed to furbish a home, while Homer decided to visit the local doctors, to find out where he could order the various drugs and potions needed to supply his apothecary shop.

Travis and Jake continued down the street toward the Capitol building. "I'll bet Homer is a successful shopkeeper before the year is out," he remarked to Jake.

"Yep," Jake answered. "I reckon the two of 'em are off to as good a start as most any returning soldier could expect." He spit into the dust beside the wooden sidewalk. "Where to, Doc?" The old bandy rooster hitched up his dusty pants. "Ready to take on them Yankee blue bellies?"

Travis chuckled. "Almost, my feisty friend. First we've gotta locate the representative from Naggi-doch County, the right honorable Randolph Cutter, and find out how we go about paying our taxes. He's been a longtime friend of Pa's and should steer us straight." Travis turned into the courtyard of the nearly finished Capitol building. "Then we go meet the Yankee occupation army commander, and see if he'll give us a letter allowing us to drive our cattle to army forts along the Mississippi."

At the office of Representative Cutter, the florid-faced man with snow-white chin whiskers, bounced out to grab Travis's hand and in a booming voice that marked him as a politician, greeted the son of one of his best political contributors. "Travis Sasser, my boy, how are you? How are your fine ma and poor sick pa?" He barely allowed Travis a chance to answer before he continued. "I've been meaning to get out and visit, but the time just goes by so fast these days. What can I do for you? Here, come on into my office. Have a seat. Care for a spot of liquid refreshment to cut the dust?" Spotting Jake, he thrust out his hand. "Randolph Cutter, at your service." He smoothed the wisps of white fringe around the bald crown of his head.

Seating himself behind his scarred desk, he glanced at his pocket watch and folded his hands over his potbelly. Having made his point about the value of his time, he beamed at Travis.

In the lowest voice possible for him, he inquired, "What can I do for you, son?"

Travis almost answered, "You can quit calling me son, you old reprobate," but held his tongue. "Mr. Cutter, I suppose you know that the tax assessment for our place is due the first of July?"

"Yes, my boy, and a sorry time it is, the way those Yankee carpetbaggers have come down here and started stealing ranches from hardworking Texas folks. I'm afraid I can't do much this year. The legislature has its hands tied by the Provisional Occupation Force. They appoint the tax assessors, not us. If you can get by this year, I'm certain the scoundrels will be thrown out by next year." Cutter's face grew progressively redder as he spoke. "Damned skunks think they've got the bull by the tail. We'll see how they like it when this great state of Texas gets to rule itself again."

"I hope it's soon, sir," Travis replied. "What I want to do is pay the taxes here in Austin, so there's no chance the money won't be credited to our assessment before the due date. I don't want to have any land-grabbers buying our place for delinquent taxes. I'll also pay my sister's taxes, and the widow Gunther's while I'm here."

Cutter's eyes widened. "Where'd you get the money to do all that, my boy?"

Travis smiled grimly. "Let's just say a rich uncle from Maine remembered me in his will."

Cutter laughed, "Damn, it'll be my pleasure to turn the tables on those coyotes for a change." He grew solemn and looked hard at his guests. "Those boys'll not like having their plans disrupted like this. You all take care how you handle yourselves, you hear?"

"Speakin' o' that," Jake interjected, "how do we git our oath taken so's we ain't Rebels no more?"

"Lord's sake, you mean you two haven't been sworn back into the Union yet? Don't you realize that you've got to carry the oath around with you and show it to any Yankee soldier who asks to see it? Otherwise, they can arrest you as Rebel soldiers who haven't surrendered yet. Here, take this note over to the Yankee fort south of town and ask General Kelso to swear you in. He owes me a favor or two."

He wrote a message on paper with a feathered quill and

brought it around to Travis. "Did you bring the tax assessment notice with you?" He accepted the papers from Travis and motioned them to follow him. "Let's get on over to the treasurer's office and git you paid up before he closes shop. Then you boys hightail it over to the fort and git yourselves legal."

The tax money was deposited with the clerk in the treasurer's office. His eyes widened at the sight of the roll of greenbacks that Travis pulled out. He happily wrote up several receipts for the tax assessment bill, and both Travis and Jake put copies in their shirt pockets, wrapped in soft oilskin. The homesteads were safe for another two years, as long as one of them made it back to the ranch.

They strolled over to the livery and saddled their horses for the short trip to the army post located on the far side of town. The livery owner was forking hay up to the storage loft, but stopped to chew the fat with the two strangers. "You boys just back from the war?"

Jake nodded and swung onto his dark gray. Travis decided to lead Colonel until they were out of the barn, in case the bright sun spooked the animal.

"Those are two fine horses you fellows have there. Care to sell them? I'll give you twenty dollars apiece fur 'em."

Jake sputtered in shock. "What'd you mean, twenty dollars apiece? These here animals are worth a hundred or more each. You some sort of crazy man?"

The livery owner shook his head. "Nope. It's just that money's so tight today that everything's going on the cheap. That's the best I can do. What say?"

"These horses ain't fer sale, no matter what the price," Jake snarled as he trotted out of the barn. "Twenty dollars, my furry ass. Come on, Doc, afore I do somethin' rash."

They rode in silence to the front gate of the fort, digesting the words of the livery owner. Travis asked for an appointment with General Kelso. He showed the lieutenant adjutant the note from Representative Cutter.

"The general's gone down to Houston, reviewing some new occupation troops," the adjutant informed them. "Major Richardson is in command during his absence."

"Then would you please give him this note from Representative Cutter?" Travis asked.

The young officer nodded and left the office while the two men waited with a soldier clerk as their only company. Shortly, he returned and motioned them to the door he'd just exited. "Major Richardson will see you now."

Major Richardson was standing by his desk when they entered. He had the note from Cutter in his hand, and a page of a letter as well. "Gentlemen, I'm Major Richardson. Which one of you is Doctor Sasser?"

Travis stepped forward. "I'm Doctor Sasser, and this is my friend, Jake Wheeler. Can we get our oaths taken here?"

Major Richardson shook his head affirmatively. "Doctor Sasser, do you have a brother serving in the Union army?"

"No, my only brother was wounded at Vicksburg with the New Orleans Grays. Why do you ask?"

"I just received a letter from my younger brother, Joe, telling about the fine job a Doctor Sasser did on him after he was hurt in a steamship explosion at Fort Pillow, in Tennessee. I don't understand. Was that you, by any chance?"

A cold chill ran through Travis, and he glanced at Jake to see if he was ready to run, should the situation require it. "Yes, I remember your brother. He mentioned he had a brother in Texas on occupation duty. How is he doing? I remember he had a nasty broken leg and a bad burn on his back."

"Joe's doing fine, according to his letter. He also says you're the reason, thanks to your skill as a doctor. What I'm trying to figure out is how a Rebel who needs to take the oath of allegiance was working as a Union surgeon, taking care of wounded Union soldiers."

Travis held up his hands in mock surrender. "Major, the story of how I came to be where I could help your brother is a long one. I'll be happy to tell you tonight all about it over supper, if you'll be my guest. I can assure you that no Union soldier was hurt by my little deception. I swear that to you on my oath as a doctor."

Major Richardson frowned, not sure what to make of the statement. "All right, Doctor Sasser, I'll accept your invitation. Since my brother says you saved his life, I am in your debt. If you'll swear no Union soldiers were hurt by your deception, I'll let it slide. I suppose I can't do anything else."

"I swear to you, Major. No Union soldier or civilian was hurt by my little charade."

"All right, let's give you the oath of allegiance, so I can get my desk cleaned off by Retreat. I'm in the mood for a juicy steak over at the Stevens' Dinner House, especially since you're buying."

Travis and Jake left the fort newly sworn citizens of the Union and headed back to the Capitol Inn. They dropped the horses off at the livery and walked down the crowded main street of Austin, appropriately named Capital Avenue. They stopped off at the first clothing store and bought some more clothes for the trail and then headed toward the hotel. Jake suddenly stopped and looked in the window of the Perkins Gun Shop.

"Come on, Doc," he blurted. "Let's git rid of this army leather we're toting and buy a decent gun belt and holster. My treat. This here Yankee money is about to burn a hole in my pocket."

While the clerk was showing Travis leather holsters and pistol belts, Jake walked over to the glass-covered rifle racks. "Look here," he called to the owner. "What kind of rifle is this?"

The gun shop owner opened the case. "It's the new forty-four-caliber, lever-action Henry repeater. Just got in four yesterday. Shoots the center-fired brass cartridge, latest thing in firearms. Are you aware," he remarked, looking at Jake's Colt .44, "that I can machine your pistol there to take the same bullet, so's you'd only have to carry one size cartridge to reload."

"Hot damn," Jake shouted. "I'll take two, one fer me and one fer you, Doc. Now, give the man yer pistol so's he can fix it fer us." The two men left the store with two new rifles in saddle holsters and the promise of their rechambered pistols and new, leather gun belts by the next evening.

"Damnation," Jake crowed in satisfaction, "it sure air nice to have money when you want to git somethin'."

Major Richardson was waiting for them when they arrived at the restaurant, dressed in his blue uniform. He listened with interest when Jake described the new rifles they'd just purchased. "Think what weapons like that would have done to massed infantry attacking entrenched defenders."

"Hell, Major," Jake chimed in. "It was bad enough facin' you Yanks with yur single-shot rifles. I hope I never see such a sight agin', believe me."

"I hate to ask where you fellows got new new army-issue Colt forty-fours," continued Richardson. "Most likely found them beside the road on the way home?" The wry expression on his face indicated he knew better than that.

"You're exactly kerrect," Jake answered. He then told of the three Confederate deserters they had encountered, and the fine Navy .36's that Homer and Vernon took possession of. "There's guns all over the place, now that's the war's done. We just picked up a few off the pile."

Major Richardson nodded his head and started in on his well-done steak. "All right, I'm sorry I asked. Please, tell me the story that I've been waiting for all afternoon."

While finishing their meal, Travis told the enthralled major about his and Jake's escape and the trip back to Texas. He omitted Marie's true reason for accompanying him, finding the stolen payroll, and quickly glossed over the stealing of the horses, but gave a mostly factual account of the saga that he and Jake had experienced.

Richardson laughed at the conclusion. "Damn, you scalawags, it's a good thing I swore you in before I heard this tale. I'd most likely put you in the post stockade if I'd heard it first." He shook his head at the absurdity of it. "Right through the Union lines with two women. What a story this'll be should I ever have the nerve to tell it, in twenty years or so."

Travis joined in his guest's laughter. "All I beg of you is that you don't tell about it before then," he replied. "I don't suppose the Yankee army would want us back in prison since the war's over, but I don't care to find out." Then he described his plan for selling their cattle to forts along the Mississippi River. "What do you think?" he asked his guest.

"Makes a lot of sense to me," Richardson responded. "I imagine the troops would love to have a meal of fresh beef instead of canned meat once in a while. I'm not sure that you could get money from the fort commanders, though. Most probably don't have that amount of cash in their discretionary funds. I suggest you offer to take vouchers payable here in Austin by the regional army paymaster. I'll be able to help you get them processed. An additional bonus to you is the amount the post commanders spend that way will be more than if they were paying out of their cash funds."

Travis nodded at the major's logic. "Would you give me a written introduction explaining my purpose to the fort commanders?" He explained how he was going to transport the cattle up and down the river from Vicksburg.

"I don't suppose it would hurt to have a written introduction from General Kelso to show around. I'll have him sign a letter of introduction as soon as he returns tomorrow afternoon. Stop by about dusk, and I'll introduce you and have your letter. First, let's get some drinkin' whiskey to top off this fine meal that you bought me."

By the time Travis and Jake took their leave of Austin, Homer, Irma, and Major Richardson, they had the necessary papers to stop the tax assessor from stealing their land, and the necessary papers to sell their cattle. They rode out of town, the receding forms of Homer and Irma waving good-bye fading behind them, and headed back up the trail toward home. Homer tried to convince his friend and mentor to stay in Austin and open a doctor's office, but Travis declined.

"I'm sort of worn out on medicine for the moment," Travis explained to his ex-orderly. "I guess I saw too much suffering during the war. Maybe later, I'll feel more like practicing medicine again. All I can think about is getting the ranch back on its feet and enjoying the life I've missed these last three plus years." Homer hid his disappointment, and wished them well.

Their trip was as uneventful as the one to Austin, with one exception. On the second day, they met a couple of wranglers, heading twenty-five prime horses north along the Trinity River.

They waited for them to catch up at the ford where they had just crossed the meandering, little river. "Howdy, boys," Jake greeted the two men as they pushed the string of horses to where he and Travis waited in the shade of a stand of cottonwoods. "Looks like you two got your hands full. I'm Jake Wheeler, and this here's Travis Sasser of the Diamond S up by Naggi-doch. Where you boys bound?"

"Howdy," the lead rider answered. "I'm Jasper Skoggins, and this is my cousin, Leroy. We're taking these animals north to Dallas, hoping to sell 'em to the army for hard cash." He climbed down and wet his kerchief in the water and wiped his face.

"Nice-looking animals," Travis remarked. "How did you keep them away from the Confederate supply impounders during the war?"

"They got most of our herd," Jasper answered. "I was away with the army, so Leroy hid a couple dozen over in Mexico at our head vaquero's sister's ranch until the war was over. These here horses are all we've got in the world to pay the taxes on our place and stay alive until we can get built up agin."

Travis nodded his head in agreement. "I know the feelin' boys. I wonder if you'd be willing to sell them to me, and even work for me a couple of months or so. For hard cash, I mean."

"I might," Jasper replied. "Jus what was you plannin' to do? Me an Leroy ain't into robbin' or such."

Quickly, under the cool shade of the trees, Travis outlined his plan to drive a herd of cattle to the Mississippi. "What did you expect to get for the horses from the army?"

"Hell, we was hoping to take home twenty dollars each," Jasper responded. "There wasn't no guarantee that we would git a dad-blamed dollar fer 'em." Jasper scratched his bearded chin and did some quick calculations. "I'll take one hundred down, and three fifty more when you sell yer cattle, and work on the drive at a dollar a day, if you'll have me. Leroy the same, right, cousin?" The silent Leroy simply nodded his agreement.

Travis agreed to the terms and counted out the cash for the down payment on the herd. He'd need them to mount his drovers for the drive and was happy to purchase them. The fact that the animals were well broken was an added bonus.

Jasper requested that he be allowed to return to his home with the money, leaving Leroy to help drive the horses on to the Diamond S with Jake and Travis. "I'll be there as soon as I can after droppin' off this here money. My wife has to have some hard cash to keep the place going till I get back. Leroy'll be happy to start work immediately. Thanks, Mr. Sasser. I'll be seein' ya in about a week." He trotted his pony down the road to the south, while the others continued on to the ranch, pushing their herd of new horses for the coming trail drive.

Their homecoming was a warm welcome, enhanced by the removal of the strain associated with losing their ranch to the tax thieves. Jake rode on over to the widow Gunther's, to give her the tax receipt and to ensure that the gathering of her cattle was underway.

"All them gals need is the firm hand of a smart fella like me to keep 'em outta trouble," he proclaimed as he left. "I'll check in tomorrow to see how you're doin', and let you know what their roundup tally is." He rode off, waving to Vernon and Alex, who were just coming in, the dust from the roundup covering their faces and clothes.

Travis leaned back in the rocker on the front porch, a satisfied sigh issuing from his throat. His plan was coming together as he envisioned it. Now, he had to hope they could keep it quiet until it was too late for anyone or anything to mess up his carefully laid plans.

Chapter 15

"Yo, Travis," Vernon hollered as he rode a well-lathered, sorrel gelding into the front yard. "How did things go in Austin?" He looked toward the corral. "Where'd all these horses come from?"

Travis waved at his older brother and Alex. The enthusiasm in Vernon's face reflected the steady emergence from the depression he had suffered since he had lost his arm.

"Things went off without a hitch. I picked the animals up on the way back, since we needed some extra ponies for the remuda. We can't have a drive without plenty of spare horses. I'll introduce you to the horse wrangler, name of Leroy, after supper. He'll join us on the drive along with his cousin, Jasper. Jasper's taking the money I paid him for the horses to his family, before the tax assessors steal his place. He'll be here next week. How's the roundup coming along?"

"Pretty good," Alex answered. "There's more range stock out there than we thought. Every day we find two, three hundred, and still haven't run out of places to look." He looked at Vern for confirmation. "I reckon we have close to fifteen to eighteen hundred gathered on the south range, maybe more."

"That or more," Vern agreed. "We'll have a fair-sized herd to sell by the time we're done. How'd things go with the tax collectors? No more problems, I hope."

Before Travis could answer, Molly called for them to get ready for supper. As Travis and Vernon washed up, Pepe drove the buckboard out of the yard with the crew's meal, sitting proudly on the seat of the wagon, as if it were the finest buckboard, and he was a grand jefe.

As they ate, Travis related the events of his trip, the meeting with Representative Cutter and Major Richardson, then meeting the Skogginses and their horses. With a dramatic flourish, he laid the receipt for the tax assessment on the table. Everyone looked reverently at the piece of paper that saved their home. Expressions of relief were evident on every face.

"Irma and Homer all settled in?" Molly asked. "I sure liked her and hope to get in to Austin and visit them someday."

Travis described the cheerful little house his friends inherited and how Irma was feathering her nest. He showed them the letters from General Kelso. "This'll make our job even easier," he pointed out to Vernon. "I feel certain we'll have no trouble getting an appointment with the post commanders we visit. Then we'll have to convince them of the benefits of buying some fresh beef."

He looked over at Alex. "How much longer do you think until we can leave? The sooner we're on our way, the better I'll like it."

Alex rubbed his chin as he thought. "Well, I suppose we'll have two thousand or more gathered by the end of the week, and branded by a week from Wednesday. I'll drive over three hundred head from our place on Sunday, and we can tell the widow Gunther to have her cattle here by then as well. She's still got a few vaqueros working for her, so she's probably got 'em all branded and ready to go."

Travis nodded in satisfaction. "Fine, let's plan on leaving Friday a week. Vern, I want us to keep a tally on any cows we get that are branded by our neighbors, and we'll make good when we return. Those that are branded by the East Texas Land Company, run off into the brush. We'll not do them any favors. Agreed?"

"Fine by me," Vern responded. "It's more than they deserve.

Alex bobbed his head in agreement.

"Were you able to gather a drive crew?" Travis asked his brother-in-law.

"Yep," Alex replied. "Got some of the best hands around, especially when I offered hard cash wages." He paused, "Some of the fellas need money right away, so I promised them an advance soon as you came back from Austin."

Travis nodded but cautioned, "Fine by me, but make sure they understand to keep quiet about how they came by it. We don't want it known that we're able to pay cash money. The land-grabbers might try to move against us before we're ready." He looked at his family members. "I don't think we should show the tax bill receipt until the last moment. That'll keep them unaware that we're out of their clutches until next assessment. Cutter says the legislature will be in control by then, and we'll most likely be rid of the skunks."

Mrs. Sasser looked at her youngest son with concern. "What if they show up while you're away with the herd?"

"I expect to be back before the deadline, but if they come while we're gone, show them the receipt, tell them another one is being held for safekeeping with Representative Cutter in Austin, and order them to git." He smiled at his sister's grim expression.

"That ought to put a knot in their tails, at least until they can check out your story, and we'll surely be home by then with enough money to last us for years."

Travis excused himself to tell his father the details of his trip. The old man seemed to understand what Travis was saying and mumbled in agreement. As evening approached, Alex rode back out to the gathered herd. Vernon stayed back to guide Travis out in the morning. The two Sasser brothers walked out to lean on the corral fence and watch the sun set behind the low hills to the west. The clear azure sky slowly turned purple and gold while they enjoyed the cool evening breeze off the river.

"If we pull this off, Travis, I think I'm gonna stay in New Orleans," Vernon announced suddenly. "I'm not happy here and with what you can spare of my share of the drive, I'll have enough to make a fresh start again. One of these days, cotton will start to sell and I'll be back in the brokerage business. Don't tell Ma, though, 'cause I don't want her to worry about it while we're gone."

Travis looked at his older brother. "All right, Vern, if that's what you want," he answered. "I'm not sure what I'm gonna do. Ma needs help with the place, since Pa's been laid up, but I may want to get away myself one of these days. For the time being, saving the ranch is all I'm concerned about."

Vern toyed with a piece of straw he used for a toothpick. "Well, little brother, you know how much you always wanted to be a doctor. I sure hope you don't quit medicine forever. You know Texas needs good sawbones."

"I don't suspect I will, Vern. However, I saw so much suffering durin' the war, and was able to help those poor boys so little, I feel empty inside at the moment and don't even want to think about working as a doctor again. Maybe later. I don't know."

The next morning, they rode out of the corral just as the sun poked its rosy rim over the river. Travis experienced a sense of times past, before the war, when he and his father would head out to ride the range. Those were happy times, memorable ones, and he spent the hour it took to reach the assembled herd recalling them.

Alex had already assigned some of the men to scour the brush for mavericks, while another crew was busy roping and branding those already recovered. Travis thought back to that summer long ago, when his father, Vern, and he had planted the mesquite bushes to form the cattle pens. The enclosures were coming in mighty handy during the roundup. Alex introduced the new men to Travis. Most he remembered from the time before he'd gone away to college. Travis shook hands with Larry Randolph and his younger brother Skeeter, from the Dawkins spread further south. The two lanky cowboys with loose strands of unruly, dark hair and droopy mustaches told him how they'd been let go when Charlie Dawkins lost his ranch the previous fall, a victim of the land-grabbers.

"We've been on the grub line since then," Skeeter remarked. "Working for beans and a bunk can get old in a hurry. Alex says you got hard money fer wages, that right?"

Travis acknowledged the statement. "I'll pay everybody a partial on Saturday night."

"That'll be fine by me. We've got some provisions to buy afore we go anywhere, right, Larry?" His look-alike brother grinned and nodded in agreement.

Jesus Gomez brought over two former vaqueros from the ranch, who'd been working on the far side of Nacogdoches at a small spread. Pedro and Xavier shyly greeted Travis, before returning to their job at the branding fire.

"Joe Quinn is out in the brush with Pete and Ollie," Alex informed Travis. "Joe says his boy, Logan, is home from Virginny and will be over to join us as soon as he gets to town and buys some riding gear. Right now, Logan doesn't have a saddle, and Joe needs for you to advance some money so he can get one. I'll be sure and tell him to stay quiet as to where he got the money from."

The remainder of the week, Travis rode the bushy low hills, weeding out cows and long-horned steers from the cover they sought to hide in and driving them over to the holding pens. Alex had the men turn loose any mothers still with their calves so there would be stock for the future. The sounds of braying cattle, shouting cowboys, and galloping hoofbeats of working cow ponies echoed across the range.

Paco drove the chow wagon out every night and stayed until morning, cooking hot meals for the tired men. They ate dried corn and jerky for lunch or did without. It was hot, dusty, grimy work, and every evening the men gratefully washed in the cooling waters of the Angelina River, which formed the west boundary of the ranch. Nights were too short, and soon it was time to climb into the saddle for another day of dodging thorny brush and roping hardheaded cattle.

Saturday, Travis paid the men a month's wages in advance and released them to visit town. "Remember," he cautioned, "don't tell anyone where you got this money, and don't say anything about making a cattle drive. If any man gets drunk and flaps his tongue, he'll have the rest of us to deal with, all madder'n a wet bobcat."

After paying the men, Travis rode back to the ranch house with Vernon. Alex had left the day before to drive the cattle from his place over to the gathered herd. Jake had promised to arrive with five hundred head from the widow Gunther's on Monday, along with three of her hands, whom she wanted to join the drive.

"Let's go into town with Ma," Vernon suggested. "Old Pepe has to get the rest of his grub for the drive, and I'd like a cool beer from the Long Horn before I start eating trail dust as a regular diet."

"Fine by me," Travis replied. "I hope none of the boys start blabbing where they picked up their spending cash. We're so close now, I'd sure hate to run afoul of the land-grabbers."

"Sooner or later, we're gonna have to have a showdown with the bastards, I suppose," Vernon surmised.

They kicked their horses into a trot, anxious to return to the ranch house. After cleaning up, they accompanied their mother and Paco on the supply wagon as they all headed to town. They were in a relaxed frame of mind when they reached Nacogdoches. Their mother and Paco went on over to the General Store to buy supplies, while Travis and Vernon entered the Long Horn Tavern and had a cool beer.

As they leaned against the bar, idly sipping their drink and talking in low tones about the drive, Travis glanced in the spotted mirror hung behind the busy barkeep. "Vern," he whispered, "see that unshaven fellow with the pinto vest over by the faro table. He's looking daggers at my back."

"Yeah, I see him," Vern answered, glancing out of the corner of his eyes. "So what?"

"I saw him hanging around the land office when I went in the other day. He's probably one of the pistoleros Jeremy has hired to back up his hand. Remember what he looks like in case he shows up and I'm not around."

They finished their beers and walked out of the bar, sobered at the thought of what was facing them if their plans became known prematurely. They saw Paco loading the wagon with supplies, along with Mr. Fisher, the storeowner, and hurried over to help.

"Howdy, boys," Mr. Fisher panted as he swung a fifty-pound sack of flour onto the bed of the wagon. "Glad to see you both again. Lend a hand with this molasses barrel, would you?"

They helped finish loading the supplies and watched their mother pay the old shopkeeper. "Thanks to you, Mrs. Sasser. I'm sure pleased to get my hands on hard money again." He looked over at the two men. "It's all over town that the Diamond S has money, boys. You be sure to watch yourselves, in case it falls on the wrong ears. Thanks again and give my regards to your pa."

"Damn," Travis muttered as they rode out of town. "I knew the news would spread as soon as we started spending cash money." He noticed Mr. Watkins, Clarissa's father, standing on his front door stoop motioning surreptitiously at him as they rode past. "Vern, you take Ma on home, I'm gonna stop at Watkins's place a minute."

"Be careful, Travis," Vernon cautioned. "He's part of the other side."

"I know; I'll be all right. You go on with the others. I'll be along directly."

He turned Colonel toward the store and stopped at the hitching rail. "Hello, Mr. Watkins, what can I do for you?"

"Nothing, except stay away from my daughter," was the terse reply. The angry storekeeper glared at Travis. "Having said that however, Clarissa insists that she has to talk with you, and if I didn't get you, she'd go out on the street and stop you. I couldn't have that, in front of the whole town. She's in the back room, so please see her and don't stay a second longer than necessary. Remember, I'll be out here, so watch yourself."

Travis ignored the implied insult and walked back through the store to the room indicated, his heart beating faster at the thought of seeing Clarissa. Angry at his weakness, he told himself not to make a fool of himself again. He opened the door and saw her waiting beside the stacks of cloth goods stored in the room. Carefully, he closed the door and walked over to her, suspicion etched on his face.

"Hello, darling. I'm glad you shut the door. I would hate for anyone to see us together." She moved forward and offered up her face for his kiss.

Travis gently pushed her back and tersely acknowledged her greeting. "What did you want to see me about, Clarissa?"

"Oh, Travis," she peevishly snapped. "Are you still mad because I didn't pine away here while you were off playing war hero? Darling, don't be childish. I've explained what happened and that it doesn't matter a whit to what we feel between us. I'll do anything you say, meet you anywhere or anyplace. What more do you want?"

"What is it you want, Clarissa?" Travis asked again. He was determined not to yield to her shameless offer. "I have to get back to the ranch."

"Well," she pouted at him. "I just wanted to tell you that I overheard Jeremy talking with his man, Ace Hurley. They think something funny is going on at your place. Ace is to find out what and report back. I don't know if you realize it, but Jeremy is the head of a very powerful organization in this area, and he gets what he wants. Be careful and don't cross him, Travis, my dear. We can have each other and he'll never know the difference. But stay away from that Ace. He's a killer. Let's talk about when can I see you again and where?"

"Clarissa, I don't plan to ever see you again, except in passing on the street. If you think I'll be a part of your adulteress scheme, you're mistaken. Thank you for the warning about your husband, but I don't care what he tries, I'm gonna save my family's ranch and beat him at his own game. Please excuse me, I've got to rejoin my family for the ride home."

"You pious fool," Clarissa hissed at him. "You'll soon come begging for me and I'll have to decide if I even want you in my arms. I don't care about your stupid ranch. I want you and I'll have you. Go on, go back to your smelly old cows. You'll be back, beggin' me to hold you, just you wait and see."

Travis walked out of the store, his back stiff with anger. He saw Mr. Watkins standing where he had last seen him, the top of the stairs, glaring at him in the same angry way.

He mounted Colonel and rode after his family. He was certain that Jeremy would soon discover what the Diamond S was doing, and then trouble was sure to follow. They had to get the drive started as soon as possible. The further away he could get from Asherton and his bullies, the better. He saw the wagon ahead of him as he passed the turnoff into the little glade where he'd last been with Clarissa, and spurred the big horse to catch up. Plans had to be finalized right away and the drive started. He was determined to beat the odds against him and start the drive undiscovered.

He and Alex pushed the men hard, and by Thursday, a day early, the herd was branded and ready to trail. He gave the men Friday to prepare, and set Saturday morning as the day of departure. Jasper Skoggins showed up Thursday night and signed on as well as the three men from the Gunther spread. Travis had as good a crew as could be hoped for on such short notice. He packed his gear and the next morning before sunrise bade farewell to his mother and Molly. His sister kissed him and Vernon before saying a long good-bye to Alex. The two women stood on the porch along with the seated Big Tom and watched their men ride away.

The drive would start on the sun's appearance, and the future of their family was riding with them.

Chapter 16

Jake showed up just about the time Travis finished convincing himself to give up and start without him. The old man rode beside a horse and buggy, which the widow Gunther drove with her customary independence.

Jake waved, a wide grin on his grizzled face. "Howdy, Doc. I brought Miz Gunther with me. Just to show"—he winked at Travis—"I was fer a fact going on a cattle drive and not just a'runnin' off to some saloon." Jake turned his face to the smiling woman and favored her with a wink as well.

Travis rode over to greet the self-reliant woman his family had been neighbors with for so long. After a few pleasantries were exchanged, he outlined his plan to sell the cattle to army forts along the Mississippi River. "How many critters do you think you've got thar?" she asked in her curiously low, gravely voice.

Travis looked over the milling, dusty mass of longhorns. "Alex says we've at least twenty-two hundred head of Diamond S, three hundred of his AM brand and five hundred of yours. I'm hoping to get to the river with at least ninety percent of them. I'll keep a tally, so we can settle up when we get back."

"Don't fret, honey. Jake'll make sure things work out right fer me. You boys jus be careful and get through. And hurry home, darlin'," she shouted at Jake who was clearly the new man in her life. "Me and the gals'll be waiting fer ya."

Jake waved his hat as she turned her buggy back the way

she'd come. "Bye, sweetie. I'll be thinkin' o'ya the whole way."

"Damn if I can figger it out," Ollie grumbled while Miz Gunther's buggy faded into the dusty haze kicked up by the milling herd. "What does she see in a broken-down, old banty rooster like you, when I was here all along?"

"Sonny," Jake cackled, "it's all in the presentin." He rode over to the wagon and threw his bedroll to Paco.

Ollie just scratched his head and stared at the old scout with puzzlement. For the next few days, the men discussed and debated the cryptic meaning of Jake's words. It was as good a topic of conversation as most a working cowboy could talk about on the trail.

Travis rode over to where Alex was cinching the saddle of his horse. "Alex, would you assemble the men? I'd like to say a few words before we start." The curious cowboys gathered around the breakfast fire and waited for the news that had been the prime topic of conversation since the roundup started. Where were they going with three thousand head of cattle?

Travis stood before the assembled men and motioned for silence. The men were dressed for the trail, all in canvas or cord pants covered with well-scarred chaps and faded shirts, most a far cry from their original color. Every man had a bright kerchief loosely tied around his sun-bronzed neck and a stained, ten-gallon hat perched on his head. Trusty leather boots and gun belts showing the wear of time and hard use completed the necessities for a working cowboy.

Travis self-consciously rubbed his hands on his shiny black leather stovepipe chaps. His new clothes cost more money than most of these men had seen in a year.

"Men," he began, "I want you to be aware up front that we're gonna try something different this drive. If we succeed, there'll be a month's bonus in it for you." The crew murmured in anticipation of such an event. "We're gonna drive these beeves to Vicksburg, on the Mississippi River."

"Jeeces, Travis," Ollie interrupted. "There ain't no stockyards thar. What'll we do with 'em once't we git thar?"

"We're gonna put every last cow on barges and float 'em to where we can sell 'em. New Orleans, Saint Louis, wherever we have to take 'em." Jake smiled at the shocked faces that greeted his reply.

"Well, I swan," was all the usually verbose Ollie could mutter. "I do believe I've heard everthing now."

Travis continued, "Alex is the trail boss and will give the orders. I'm not sure but that we'll have some unwanted company before we get to the river, so be alert. Vernon, will you be the scout, at least until we reach Shreveport? After that, it'll be right along the road across Louisiana to Vicksburg. You can cut off there and head for New Orleans to get the barges. Jake, I've got a bad feeling that the gunnies working for the land-grabbers may be after us. Would you be willing to watch our rear? Maybe we'll get lucky and see 'em coming. If you do, report to me, quick. Maybe we can give them a surprise or two first."

"Sure, Doc." Jake hitched his bony shoulders resolutely. "Let me have Leroy fer company, and we'll keep a eagle eye on yur backside, jus' like I did fer Genn'al Forrest, during the war. There'll be no way anybody'll even git close to ya without me knowin' it."

"Why would a hard-talking cooter like you want to take Leroy with you?" Vernon asked. "I don't think he's said ten words since he signed on."

"I enjoy the way he listens to me," Jake answered stroking his shaggy mustache with his fingers. The stoic Leroy followed Jake toward the horses. "I'll stop by now and then, Doc, but mostly we'll be behind y'all. Just keep on a'moving, and don't fret about us. Come on, pard," he spoke to his taciturn companion as they rode away from the herd. "Did I ever tell you about the time I wintered on the Yellowstone River? Why the snow was so high . . ."

Travis smiled, but felt a sense of relief secure that the rear cover was in Jake's capable hands. Nodding to Alex, he passed the command to the acknowledged trail boss during the coming drive. "Give us your instructions, Alex. Let's get these cows to the Mississippi River. They're gonna make history."

In short order, Alex had made the trail assignments, and the men moved away from the fire. Alex rode to the point of the assembled herd and looked back. Everything was ready. The cattle milled about, restless and nervous, as if they too were waiting for the word to start the drive. Alex stood in his stirrups and waved his hat in a big swooping arc. "Move'em out," he shouted. He flicked the end of his reins at an old, mossy-backed, big-horned cow that had assumed a place at the head of the flowing mass of cattle. "Let's go, you ugly bitch. Show us the way. Git a'goin'."

Like a ripple across a pond, the herd slowly started to move in the direction desired and the cowboys settled in to keeping the half-wild cattle contained within the shifting confines of the moving herd. When one dashed for the scrub brush, a horse and rider would immediately cut away after it, hazing it back to the herd. Vernon moved out toward the northeast, moving cross-country directly toward Shreveport, five days away. Paco waited until the dust of the herd had settled a bit before he snapped the reins of the team pulling the wagon filled with food and gear for the men. Included among the gear was the treasured doctor's bag taken from the hospital in Saint Louis, placed there by Travis's ma, along with all the spare medicine she had at the ranch house.

The undulating brown mass moved across the land, stirring up a cloud of dust, which hung heavy in the morning air. Plaintive bellows of lost yearlings looking for their mothers or a steer snorting in distress over breathing the dust from the animal to its front masked the sound of hoofs on the earth. Sweat already was running down Travis's back, and dirt seeped into every pore of his body. "I'll promise you," he called over to Alex, at the other side of the twenty or so cows that made up the lead element of the herd. "The next time I offer to go on a cattle drive, you have my permission to kick me right where I sit in the saddle."

Alex laughed and glanced up at the sky. "Travis, my boy, you ain't seen nothin' yet. We're gonna have wet weather for a spell, unless I miss my guess." He galloped back to chase some reluctant mossy-back cow back to the herd. Travis looked at the billowing white clouds, tinted with gray along their bottoms. "God almighty, what next?" he groaned.

The storm held off until late afternoon, but then hit with a vengeance. Solid sheets of rain fell on the drenched men and their animal charges. Their only salvation was the fact that the cows were tired after a day of moving, and didn't seem inclined to stampede. Alex kept the men on the trail until it was pitch black. The cowboys silently gulped down a cold meal of jerky and corn fritters and wearily moved to their soggy bedrolls or reluctantly back on their horses to circle the herd during the night.

"As long as it don't start to lightnin', we should be all right," Alex remarked to Travis. "You best try and get some sleep. I'll be wanting you to relieve me in four hours." He jumped in his saddle and trotted off, as if being a nursemaid to a herd of miserable cows in a torrential rainstorm was an everyday occurrence. Travis groaned as his body ached from a long day in the saddle and spread his ground cloth under the wagon, hoping it would provide some measure of protection from the downpour.

Two days of hard work and wet misery followed. The rains

fell as if competing with the Biblical flood Travis's ma read to him when he was a child. The waterlogged men did their work, ate what Pepe put on their plates, tried in vain to find a dry place to sleep, and cursed the day they took up the cattle business. Their oilskin slickers became an implement of torture rather than one of convenience, trapping wet sweat and seeping moisture. The men rode in silence, endured their misery with grumpy patience, slept little, and ate sodden food. Pepe did his best to have a hot meal at the day's end, but it was invariably waterlogged before the men could gulp it down.

On the second afternoon, Logan Quinn's pony slipped in the mud and fell, throwing the young man out of the saddle, breaking his wrist. Travis did his first doctoring since he'd returned to Texas. Logan insisted he could still work with his arm in a splint, and returned to the herd as soon as Travis was finished. The second night, Skeeter Randolph walked into the brush barefoot to take a leak, and stepped on a pear cactus. Travis spent an hour in the back of the wagon, digging the spines out of Skeeter's foot by lantern light.

Jake rode in just before dark the next afternoon, right after they'd pushed the sullen cattle across the Big Sandy River, which was the halfway point to Shreveport. "All clear, Doc," he cheerfully reported. "If they're on our trail, they're a good ways behind us." He wrinkled his nose. "Whew, do these critters stink! Smells like you've been stomping in the manure pile."

"You're right, Jake," Travis wearily answered. "I'm beginning to remember why I was so interested in becoming a doctor in the first place. A person has to be loco to enjoy raising cattle." He raised an eyebrow and chided his friend. "You and Leroy have it made, all right. Just lie around all day and watch the rain fall. I'll probably have to trim your wages, or the workin' cowboys will have a fit."

Jake laughed and threw the bag of supplies he'd received

from Paco on the back of the pinto he was riding. "Just wait till we have to hold off a horde of bad guys before you set our wages. See ya, Doc. Jasper," Jake hollered across the fire, "Leroy says he's fine and learning a lot from me."

"Well," Jasper shouted back at the retreating form of the wiry scout. "I'll bet that's all he's had time to say, you old windbag."

While they ate the supper of beans and bacon slopped on their tin plates by Paco, another group of wet, sullen men made a fateful decision.

The morning Alex led the herd across the Angelino River and off the Diamond S land, Ace Hurley burst into Jeremy Asherton's office. Jeremy was in a black mood and it showed. He'd finally summoned enough courage to ask Clarissa why she'd spoken to Travis Sasser the previous Saturday evening. Her old man, who hoped to be a bigger part of the land company that Jeremy bossed, had mentioned it to him Sunday after the noon meal.

"They just talked, but I don't know what about," he informed his curious son-in-law. "I think she was sort of taken by him before she met you. You oughta ask her, in case she's mentioned our plans to the Sassers."

Jeremy had thought to himself, *What do you mean our plans, you old fool. My plans, my decision, not yours.* But, he nodded to the old man and held his tongue. He wanted to keep the peace with the beautiful woman he'd married. Clair was as contrary as a bobcat, when she was crossed. She'd made it plain when they were first married: her father was very important to her, so he was important to Jeremy.

Last night, she had mentioned his work, and he'd seized on the opportunity to ask about Sasser. "I heard you spoke to him last Saturday. What about?"

Clarissa stopped feeding Jonah and looked at him quickly. Her eyes narrowed and her brows squinched together like they did when she was getting really angry about something. "Where'd you hear that?"

"Your pa told me about it the other day. What'd you talk to Sasser for?"

"Listen, Jeremy, I'll talk to who I damn well please, and I don't like you spying on me. I'll tell Father the same thing. I never get to talk to folks anymore. They stay away from me since you started grabbing all the ranches in the valley. So don't tell me who to speak to. And don't bother coming into my room tonight. I've got a splitting headache, and I'll still have it every night this week." She slammed down the dish of food and grabbing Jonah from his high chair, angrily stomped out of the room.

Jeremy was silently furious with her petulance and suspicious of her overreaction to his question. He always knew when she was on the defensive. *What did she and Sasser have to talk about, anyway? Was he the one?* Jeremy wondered. He'd not been so smitten on his wedding night not to notice that he wasn't the first man for her, even though she'd tried to convince him he was. Damn that smarty-pants doctor. He'd always hated Travis Sasser and his snooty, older brother. They'd never tried to be his friend when they were young. He'd given them every opportunity, but they'd snubbed him like he was some common, dirt farmer's son instead of the son of the richest man in Nacogdoches.

He was still brooding over his wife's outburst when Ace rushed in with the bad news. "Boss, the Diamond S bunch has put together a herd of cattle and started 'em off to market."

"God damn it," Jeremy roared. "Just what I need, right before the tax bill comes due. When'd they leave?"

"This morning," Ace replied. "One of my boys who has a Mex gal down in chili-town heard a couple of vaqueros talking about it Saturday night. He told me that they was saying that they'd gathered a herd and they'd be leaving soon. I swung by on my way out to look over the Tomkins place. The herd was there last night, I could hear 'em bawling, and they was gone this morning when I rode by about eight. I could still see dust in the air from the herd."

Jeremy considered the ramifications of the news. "They must hope to sell the cows for enough to pay the tax bill. Hell, even if they can find a buyer in Fort Worth, they'll have to hurry to get home with the money before July first."

He looked at the unshaven Hurley with a thoughtful expression. "How many hands would you say Sasser has to help him with a drive?"

Ace studied the ceiling for an instant. "He's got his one-armed brother, probably the brother-in-law, the two crippled cowboys from the Diamond S, maybe one or two Mex vaqueros. The old man's a slobbering idiot, you know. I figger six or seven, tops."

Jeremy decided. "Ace, gather up a dozen or so of the men. We'll scatter the herd before they reach the next town. By the time they round 'em up, they won't be able to get 'em sold and return with the money in time to meet the tax deadline." Asherton looked smugly at the tintype photo of Clarissa on his desk. "I'll come along with you. We'll make short work of Mister Travis, Doctor Smartass, Sasser. Be ready to ride by dark. We'll loop north around the herd, and hit 'em after they cross the Neches River. That's rough country up there. It'll take 'em weeks to gather a herd again if we do a good job of scatterin' 'em."

Jeremy led his band of toughs out of town just as the rain started. The men grumbled, but everyone consoled himself with the knowledge that after a hard night's ride and a few quick shots exchanged with half a dozen scared cowboys, they'd be back in town, a lot richer and even more in control of the town and the area around it. By daylight, such as it was in the gray mist of a rainy morning, they were in position to spring their ambush. Hour after miserable hour, the band of hard cases waited. No sign was seen of the herd, and the second night was even more disappointing than the first.

At daylight, Ace sent several men in a wide sweep to see if they could find the trail of the herd. Jeremy and the others tried to stay as dry as possible while the second day dragged on, the rain falling on them incessantly. At dusk, one of the scouts brought in the news that the herd was, in fact, headed northeast, toward Shreveport, in Louisiana, instead of Fort Worth.

"I don't figger it," Ace complained to a thoroughly soaked and short-tempered Jeremy. "There ain't no reason fer taking the cattle to Shreveport. Ain't no buyers there, and no stockyards neither."

Jeremy chopped the air with his hand. "I don't care where they're headed. We're gonna hit the herd and scatter it good, so as soon as it's light, git these bastards mounted and catch that herd." Jeremy turned his back on his underling.

By riding hard, they had closed to within two or three hours' ride of the drive by dark the next day. Ace insisted they stop for the night. "The men are tired and need to rest. Luckily, the rain has quit, so we'll git a decent night's sleep and hit 'em hard first thing tomorrow."

They picked a secluded clearing, well off the trail left by the cattle herd, in case anyone rode back to look for strays. Soon, a warming fire was burning, and after the last of the food they'd brought was finished, a couple of bottles of whiskey started their way among the weary men.

Leroy Scroggins galloped into the night camp around ten. Travis and Alex were sitting by the fire, about ready to crawl into their bedrolls for some needed sleep.

"Doc Sasser," he panted. "Jake says to tell you that thirteen men is back there about two hours' ride. He says fer you to come quick with some men, and we'll catch 'em by surprise."

CHAPTER 17

Travis motioned for Alex, laying against his saddle, across the small fire. "Time for a conference, Alex. Gather up the men, they all need to hear this." He waited until all had assembled around the campfire. The flickering flame cast its warm glow on the curious and concerned faces. The murmur of low voices quickly fell silent as he repeated what Leroy had just told him. The dark sky still held the heavy clouds from the storms they'd endured, even though it was not raining at the moment.

Travis outlined what he was thinking. "I'm sure the men behind us are hired guns working for the land-grabbers. The point is, you men hired on to drive cattle, not fight professional hard cases. I'm going back with Vernon to hit these fellows before they hit us tomorrow. Will any of you volunteer to go with me?"

To his gratitude, every man stepped closer to him. "You bet. Of course . . . Count me in." The babble of the group drowned out any coherent sentences. Even the crippled Pete and Ollie stood forward, and Ollie's aversion to any type of physical danger was well known.

"Whoa," Travis shouted. "All right, I surely appreciate your support. Let's see . . . how about you, Joe. And Larry, you and Skeeter, and Jasper. Alex, you'll stay and guard the herd with the rest."

"Hold on," Alex replied. "This is my fight, too, and I'm going with you." He held up his hand to stop Travis's retort. "Don't even bother trying to talk me out of it, 'cause I'm going, and that's that." He looked at Pete and Ollie. "If somethin' happens to me and the Sassers, you two git these beeves back to the Diamond S, understand?"

Ollie nodded vigorously, probably grateful to be one of those left behind. Logan tried to talk his way into the group, but was shut off by his father. "You can't ride and shoot with a busted wing, son, and you know it. You watch the remuda fer Jasper and help the boys with the herd if somethin' goes wrong."

Jesus Gomez stood forward with the two Mendez brothers. All three shuffled shyly, nervously clutching their big sombreros. "Señor Travis, we are once again vaqueros for the Diamond S. We wish to help in this fight." He smiled and continued while holding out his hand. "Please, señor, allow us this honor."

Travis grabbed the outstretched hand of his father's longtime Mexican employee. "All right, Jesus. I'll take you and Xavier. Pedro will stay to help return the herd to the Diamond S, if we fail. Is that agreed?" The three vaqueros carried a shortened ten-gauge, double-barreled shotgun instead of the customary rifle favored by the Anglo cowboys. The spray of buckshot they put out would be a deadly intimidator in any firefight. They'd provide a substantial increase to the group's firepower.

Jesus happily bobbed his head at the decision and started to give instructions to Pedro in Spanish. Jasper moved over to the hobbled horses and started to saddle his favorite roan. "Damned if it don't feel like the old days with the Butternut Raiders. I just hope we come out better this time than we did at Chattanooga."

Travis walked over to Paco's wagon and retrieved the stolen Union army doctor's medical bag. "Here's hoping I don't need much of this," he muttered to Vernon. He couldn't help but feel pride and appreciation for the men who were riding with him. They'd cast their lot with him without hesitation. It gave him a warm feeling of confidence.

In a few minutes, Leroy was leading the nine heavily armed men back the way he'd come. The dark night was alive with the sound of crickets, frogs, and night creatures. The rain-softened earth muffled their ponies' hooves, making it unlikely another person would have heard their passage if they had been thirty feet away from the trail.

As they entered their second hour of hard riding, Jake suddenly appeared out of the black night. "Looks like you brought enough to do the job," he whispered. "Quiet. They're just on the other side of this rise, camped by a little grove of trees. They're not a bit concerned about being discovered. Don't have but one guard out, and he's just watchin' the horses."

Travis issued an order. "Vernon, keep the men and horses here, while Alex and I sneak ahead on foot with Jake." He glanced at the old scout. "Let's take time to do this thing right. Lead the way, Jake."

Jake led the other two men around the small hill. Across the shallow bank of a small creek, a large campfire burned brightly. Several voices were trying to outtalk one another. The quarter moon was peeking through the broken clouds providing just enough light to see the horses tied to a lariat strung between two trees behind the campsite. A single guard was leaning up against one of the trees, seemingly half asleep. Travis saw movement around the blazing fire and heard a whining voice complaining about his soaked bedroll.

"Seen enough?" Travis whispered to Alex and Jake. At their nods they crept back to where the rest of the men waited. The noise of the men around the fire and the creek frogs singing their mating songs drowned out any sound of their exit.

As soon as they reached the others, Travis backtracked with his men about a quarter of mile to a small cluster of trees. Silently, the men tied off their mounts and gathered around

Travis and Jake.

Travis knelt down and in the dim glow of lit matches, traced an outline of the camp in the mud. Pointing with a short twig, he described the plan he'd conceived only moments earlier. "They're unprepared for a surprise attack. If we take our time, we can sneak up on them and hit 'em just as they get up at sunrise." He traced the routes to the outlaws' camp in the muddy ground with the tip of a twig.

"Alex, you take Larry and Skeeter, and come in from the south. You'll have the farthest to go, so get started right away. Jake, you take Joe and Leroy, and come in by the horse corral. You'll have to take out the sentry just before dawn. I'll take Jasper and sneak in from the west. Vernon, you, Jesus, and Xavier get atop the little hill across the creek from them."

Travis pointed at the outline drawn in the dirt. "When we open fire, some may break for its banks to find cover, and if they do, you'll have them in a cross fire. The sun will be at your backs, and it should stop 'em cold from either escapin' or forting up and trading shots with us. Unless you're discovered, stay quiet and wait for me to start the soirée. I'll try and get them to surrender first, if I can."

Jake spoke up, "Don't take any chances with these skunks, Doc. They're bad characters and can't be trusted." The men grabbed their rifles and joined their assigned groups.

Alex and his two men slipped away to work their way up on the bushwhackers from the south, and shortly thereafter, Travis and Jasper started around to the north, followed by Jake and his men. As they crossed the creek, a hundred feet north of the campfire, Travis could hear sounds of men drinking and talking. If their luck prevailed, he felt confident they could sneak up close to the quarry undetected.

He moved cautiously, taking his time, and as quiet as possible, led Jasper in a wide swing to the west, and then back to the campsite. He could hear Jasper behind him, passing through the brush and wet trees. The sound of Jasper's raspy breathing made more noise than his footsteps on the soaked ground. They eventually were at the edge of the tree line and the bright glow of the fire was visible. The outlaw's horses were only sixty feet away, and one softly nickered at their presence, but the guard leaning against a tree trunk was too sleepy to notice.

Travis settled behind the stump of a lightning-blasted tree stump, waiting for dawn to break. Jasper moved over about ten feet to his right and crouched behind the same fallen tree trunk. Putting his single-shot Spencer carbine over the trunk, the lanky cowboy leaned back and folded his arms in silent resignation, gazing up at the few stars twinkling in the cloudy sky.

The few hours left in the night passed slowly. It was long after midnight before the camp grew quiet and the drunken men settled in for the night. The horse guard changed about four, while the rest of the men slept unaware that grim, determined men had surrounded them. Travis looked for a sign of Jake or Alex, but saw nothing. He hoped that they'd made it to their positions, and waited for sunrise.

He found himself comparing Clarissa and Marie. The differences in the two women were now very obvious. The courage and intelligence of the beautiful Confederate spy contrasted sharply with the calculating selfishness of the adulteress Clarissa. How on earth had he been so blind? He decided to search for Marie once the cattle were disposed of. He'd make more of an effort to present himself as an honorable suitor this time. He hoped she had not been hurt or killed in the last days of the war. The way she looked the night they parted settled into his thoughts. Her striking beauty flashed in his brain, again and again, like summer lightning.

Surprising him with its sudden appearance, the first pink tinge of dawn softened the eastern sky. He cursed his lapse in vigilance. The trees he had seen as a dark mass soon became defined in the pale light of early dawn. Damned if he hadn't mused the night away.

He heard a muffled gasp and shuffle of feet to his left. The horse guard was nowhere in sight, just his hat, lying beside the tree. Jake had slipped up and knocked the guard unconscious. Jasper must have heard something, because he turned and knelt behind the tree, watching the camp. Travis glanced at him and caught a nod in return. It was almost sunrise. Travis looked back at the smoking campfire. He could make out several huddled forms rolled up in ponchos around it.

A man threw his blanket off and sat up, his back leaning against his saddle. He yawned and stretched his arms over his head. After scratching his tousled hair, he pulled on his boots and stood up. "All right, you yahoos, get up. We've got us a cattle drive to stampede. Come on, get up, damn you all, anyway. Serves you right for drinking that rotgut all night."

Travis recognized the speaker. It was the grim-faced gunman who'd watched him that day in the land office. He looked just as disheveled and disagreeable in the early morning light as he had then. The others stirred around in their bedrolls and several rose to their feet, just as the sun peeked over the little hill across the creek. It was time.

Swallowing back his nervousness, Travis shouted at the surrounded men. "You fellows in the camp. Stand still. Don't make a move. You're covered. Throw down your guns and get your hands up."

Faster than he'd believed it possible, the dark-bearded man drew and fired his pistol toward where Travis was hiding. The bullet thudded into the broken stump, showering Travis with wood chips. Instinctively, Travis pulled the trigger on the Henry repeater and jacked in another shell. He sensed more than saw the dark-bearded man throw his arms wide and fall back against the saddle he'd used for his night pillow. The air was full of the familiar *crack, pow* of gunfire. White billowing gun smoke drifted heavily on the damp, morning air, obstructing Travis's view of the camp. He rapidly fired the twelve rounds left in his rifle, as fast as he could jack them into the chamber, and then drew the Colt .44 from his holster. He could hear the mighty roar of the vaqueros' shotguns booming loud in the morning air.

As suddenly as it started, it was quiet and he heard a voice calling, "Don't shoot. We quit. Don't shoot, damn it."

He also heard the keening cry of a man in deep agony. Carefully, he stood and called again. "Throw down your guns and stand, your hands in the air."

As the gray haze of gun smoke cleared, he saw two men, standing by the blackened remains of the campfire, their hands empty and held high overhead. Down by the creek, two more were kneeling, looking up at the knoll, their hands up as well. Beside them lay two still bodies, their blood coloring the stream red.

Jake stepped out of the brush to his left, and then Alex and Skeeter from the right. Travis saw Vernon, his smoking pistol in hand, moving down the hill toward the creek. Motioning with his gun, Vernon spoke to the two kneeling men.

"Do as the man says, and get back over there, and keep them hands high. Give us no trouble and you might live to see sundown." Vernon motioned with his pistol, the grim look in his eyes underscoring his command.

Travis looked around at his friends. "Anybody hurt?"

Alex nodded. "Larry has a bullet in his left shoulder." He called out to Skeeter. "Skeeter, go help him."

"Leroy was nicked on his hand," Jake replied. Jasper hurried to check out his cousin.

Travis and Jake inspected the fallen bushwhackers. Five were dead, including the one who'd fired at Travis. He'd been hit in the mouth, and blood had spilled over his fancy pinto vest. Travis felt a momentary wave of nausea. It was the first man he'd ever killed. The screaming man was Jeremy Asherton, still wrapped in his blankets, with a smashed elbow. The arm was nearly blown off and Travis knew the pain was probably excruciating.

He sent Jesus and Xavier to bring up the horses, including his medical bag. In the interim, he tied a tourniquet around Jeremy's arm and the arm of another wounded man. Three of the wounded men's wounds were not too serious, including two with numerous buckshot pellets in their backside and arms. One, with a nasty-looking belly wound, wouldn't see another sunrise.

Travis saw a half-full bottle of whiskey sticking out of one of the saddlebags still by the fire. "Pour this on that scratch," he instructed Leroy. "By next week, you'll have to look hard to find the scar." Travis ripped the cloth away and inspected Larry's arm wound. It was clean and should heal up nicely. "You'll not be roping steers for a while, but it won't bother you long," he reassured the shaken cowboy. Larry's face grimaced and then he managed a small grin. "Thanks, Doc."

Jesus rode in with the medical bag, and Travis tended to the wounds he'd just helped create. He had the five dead men wrapped in their ponchos and placed on the backs of their horses. "Don't you want to bury them varmints?" Vernon asked.

"Nope," Travis answered. "I want to send 'em back to Nacogdoches with the rest. Those land-grabbers need to see what's in store for anyone who goes up against the Diamond S." He saw the look of terror that passed over Jeremy's face when the bloody forms of the dead outlaws, including the dead Ace and his blood-soaked vest, were laid beside him.

"Jeremy." Travis knelt by his wounded adversary. "I'm afraid your arm has to come off. Do you want me to do it?"

Crying in pain and mortification, the stunned man gasped out, "Don't you touch me, you damned butcher. I'll have the law on you when I get back. Oh, God, my arm is killing me."

Travis stood up. *So be it, if that's what you want,* he thought as he looked down on the moaning man. "Jake, have the men build travois for the wounded men, and get them on their way back to Naggi-doch. They'll not cause us any more problems, with their boss all shot up."

Jake walked over to Jeremy, still lying on the ground, moaning piteously. He knelt down beside him. Pulling out the ten-inch-long Bowie knife that he had on his belt, he put the point under Asherton's eye and lightly cut a shallow groove. The wounded man uttered a new shriek of fear and pain. A thin trickle of red dripped down the terrified man's cheek, mixing with his tears into a pink stream.

"Buster, I'm gonna settle in the valley with the widder Gunther. I don't think there's room enough fur both of us. You be gone by the time I git back. Move to one or another of them Yankee cities. You don't want to come to Texas ever agin. Hear me, sonny?" He flicked the sharp point against the underside of Asherton's nose, cutting a painful nick in the sensitive flesh. "The next time I see ya, I'll make it so bad fer ya that today will seem nicer than a picnic by the river. Git my meanin'?"

Screaming in pain and fear, Asherton cried out, "I hear, I hear, I will. Don't cut me anymore. I promise," he blubbered. Jake nodded in satisfaction and got up, sliding the fearsome knife into its scabbard. He glared at the cowed prisoners and commanded, "I reckon you boys best git to buildin' those travois, like the Doc said, and be quick about it."

It didn't take the gunmen long to finish the task, and the beaten and disarmed men were sent on their way, dragging the dying gun hand and the moaning Jeremy in the Indian-style travois. It would be the last any of them would see of the bunch again. The beaten gunmen were soon run out of town by the local citizens and scattered into oblivion, not missed and rarely remembered by anyone. By the time Travis returned to Nacogdoches, Jeremy and Clarissa had moved away to Chicago. He heard years later that the crippled-armed Asherton became a wealthy man in the stockyard business. Slaughtering pigs seemed to be exactly what he was cut out for.

Chapter 18

The sun had yet to reach its zenith when the victorious group of excited cowboys galloped up to their campsite. The men who hadn't accompanied the raiding party clustered around the fire to hear their stories of the fight. As one after another spun their tale, it seemed that in each telling the feats of bravery and acts of raw courage grew ever more astounding.

"Come on," Alex finally demanded. "We've got half a day of sunlight left. Let's get these cows a'moving."

"Vernon," Travis spoke to his older brother. "Take the point and find us a place near Shreveport to hold the herd. I want to give the men a little time to get cleaned up and dry before we move on toward the Mississippi River."

The herd was soon underway and before nightfall the next day was bedded down in a rolling meadow south of Shreveport, on the northwestern side of the State of Louisiana. The vaqueros and Alex agreed to stay with the herd while the rest of the men rode off to enjoy the liquid and physical delights of the local saloons of the sleepy town.

Travis, Vernon, and Jake rode in together. The town had a decent hotel, where they booked rooms and had a refreshing bath before meeting in the dining room for dinner.

"I'm off first thing tomorrow," Vernon announced. "I'll head for Baton Rouge first and look for barges and steamboats. If I can find enough there, I'll be at the Vicksburg crossing about the time you get there. If I have to go clear to New Orleans, I'll be about three days later."

Travis chewed a bite of his steak and nodded. "It doesn't matter. We'll find a grassy area close to the river and wait you out. Get enough to float the entire herd. I'll give you five hundred dollars in greenbacks to leave as deposit to the barge owners and steamboat captains."

"Hell," Vernon replied, "that'll be more than enough to rent all we'll need."

"Vernon oughta have someone ride with him, Doc," Jake cut in. "That's too much money to be carryin' alone in times like these."

"Good idea," Travis replied. "Who do you want to go with you, Vern?"

"I'll take Jesus. He uses that shotgun of his like a fiddle player wields his bow. Now, if you'll pardon me, I'm gonna catch some shut-eye in the soft bed up in my room. I reckon I'm getting too old for the hard ground anymore."

Travis and Jake sauntered over to the local saloon and checked on the men. Several were well on their way to a head-splitting drunk, but nobody seemed to be causing any trouble. Jasper and Leroy were sitting at a table with several strangers and waved the two men over.

"Doc, Jake, this here is Harvey Pressel and that's Bob and Raymond Kirk. They're out of work saddle bums. They was wondering if you wanted any more help."

Travis thought for a minute. "You know, I believe I do. Did Jasper tell you boys anything about our plans?"

The older man, Harvey, nodded his head. He was prematurely gray, and showed the ravages of long months fighting in the Southern army. "Yep, he did, for shore. We'll be right proud to sign on with you. Ain't that so, boys?" The other two bobbed their heads in agreement. They were as undernourished and rawboned as their older friend, but every man's eyes showed steady and honest to Travis's gaze.

Travis made a quick decision. "Harvey, could you get me ten or so other trusty men to join up for the rest of the drive?"

"Shore can," Harvey answered. "There's a passel of waddies hangin' around, a'lookin' for any job paying hard money in times like these."

"Fine," Travis replied. "Have them here at sunrise tomorrow, ready for the trail. "I'll give every man who finishes the drive a bonus as well. That's all right with you, isn't it, Jake?"

"We really don't need any more, you know," was the laconic reply, between sips of his whiskey. "We got plenty o'men right now."

"Maybe so," Travis replied. "But, I got the money to pay 'em, and these fellows need the work. Besides, with the extra men, nobody'll dare mess with us."

"You're the boss, Doc," Jake replied. "Might as well spread the wealth, as long as it lasts. Besides, some o'these boys were in the fray at Shiloh Church with me. So I reckon we do owe 'em a little somethin'."

Harvey jumped to his feet with gratitude evident in his face. I'll have a dozen men here first light," he promised as he rose from the table. "Come on, boys, we got some visitin' to do."

After they left, Travis looked at Jake. "I think we'll have enough men to scare off any problem now, don't you?"

Jake continued to sip his whiskey. "Yep, airy enough to handle any trouble that comes our way, I reckon."

Travis smiled at his unflappable friend. "Jake, I want you and Leroy to scout ahead the rest of the trip. Find us a good spot to camp each night, and keep your eyes peeled for highwaymen and scavengers. We're getting close to the end of our drive, and we don't need any more surprises."

"Me and Leroy will do jus' that, Doc, don't you fret. I suspect we'll find little to bother us, except worried farmers afraid our cattle'll knock down their fences." Jake finished his drink and rose, wiping his mouth with the back of his hand. "I think I'll ride on back to the herd to make sure that everything's quiet. See you in the morning."

Travis went up to his room and slept soundly, dreaming of a black-haired beauty who drifted in and out of his subconscious dreams. The morning sun was still a sliver on the horizon when he walked down the stairs and out of the hotel. Harvey was there with the promised men, packed and ready for the trail.

Only four had horses, so Travis was grateful he had purchased the Skogginses' string. Travis led the new men out to the herd and introduced them to Alex, who gave them their orders and then started moving the herd east on the packed dirt road that ran across the top of the state to the Mississippi River. The three thousand cattle were stretched out for over a mile on the road, and the extra men Travis had engaged were soon busy keeping the animals moving and contained. The rate of travel increased from what they had averaged as they moved across the countryside. But with the extra men, the herd was kept to the roadway and not allowed to straggle.

Vernon and Jesus left the drive when they reached the cutoff to Baton Rouge. Vern looked back at Travis and Alex before he trotted out of sight, a proud and determined vaquero riding guard at his side.

Alex hooked a leg over his pommel and rolled a quick smoke, as he commented, "I guess Vernon has shaken off the miseries over losing his arm. He sure seems to be in better spirits now."

"All he needed was to realize that he can still succeed, even if he's lost an arm," Travis answered. "Well, it's up to you, Alex. Get us to the river, so we can sell these smelly cows to hungry Yankee soldiers."

They drove the herd hard that warm June day, making nearly twice the miles they were accustomed to. The cattle grazed on the grass growing beside the rutted road and seemed content to stay within its boundaries. Occasionally, they came to a section of land that had been fenced with split rails. Alex was especially alert to insure the cattle didn't push in the fencing. They didn't want angry farmers pursuing them down the road demanding payment for ruined fences and torn-up fields.

Paco traded the hindquarter from a lame steer for some fresh vegetables with one of the farm wives and fixed a delicious stew for the evening meal. Alex routinely doubled the night guard, to ensure against stampede or excessive drifting of the herd.

The first three days went smoothly, with only a few impatient travelers complaining about being forced to the side of the road for thirty minutes while the milling stream of cattle moved past, taking up the entire roadway. One morning, Travis saw Alex talking with several men beside the road. He trotted Colonel over to have a look. The men were ragged scarecrows, their clothing in tatters. They had the look of men who'd been a long time on the road.

"Howdy, men," he greeted the bunch. "Where you all headed?"

"On our way back to Texas and home. We was mustered out last month." The leader, as disheveled as his comrades, spoke tiredly. He looked as if he was about done in, unable to go another step. The men were trail-dusty and hungry-looking.

"Who were you fellows with?" Travis inquired.

"Cobb's Legion," the oldest man replied. "We was with him at Appomattox, when Gen'l Lee surrendered. Been on the road since, headin' back home to west Texas."

"Damn," Alex muttered in sympathy. "You boys have sure come a long hard way."

Travis's feeling of pride in the tattered men's resiliency almost choked him up. Battered but not beaten, they took the bad times in stride. "You men take it easy, and after we pass this herd by, we'll cut out a steer for you. It should give you some decent food for a spell." He dug into his vest pocket. "Here's fifty dollars paper money. Buy a drink on me when you reach Shreveport. We're on the way to Vicksburg with this herd, or we'd stop and visit. Any of you need any medical attention?"

"Thanks, mister." The spokesman grabbed the money from Travis's outstretched hand. "We're fine. Don't think we have any problems now. With what you've given us, we should make it to Fort Worth easy. After that, it's all downhill. Thanks again and God bless ye boys fer the help." He joined his comrades beside the road, under a shade tree, and watched the herd of cows stream by. "There goes one square gent," he remarked to his men, as Travis cantered off. "The first drink we get will be to wish him good luck."

As the evening of the next day approached, they stopped the herd just east of Monroe. Travis ate quickly and then rode into town to visit with Mr. Durmon, at his livery stable. The former agent for Marie LeMont was pleased and surprised to see Travis again so soon. He listened with interest as Travis described his return home and the cattle drive to save his family's ranch.

"Have you seen Marie since I was here?" he questioned Durmon after finishing his story.

"Why, yes, she came through about three weeks ago, headed back to her plantation," Durmon answered. He looked at Travis with a question in his eyes. "You thinking about visiting her?"

"I'd sure like to, but I guess it'll have to wait until I get the herd sold, I reckon. Was she all right?"

Durmon shrugged. "Sure was, only she didn't stay long. Went on down to Bawcomville to her place. I don't know why, as I was told it had burned last year. Her family all died during the war and the place went to seed. She wouldn't hear of staying here with me, though, danged stubborn gal that she is."

"If you see her before I get back, Mr. Durmon, tell her I'm

coming. Don't let her leave Monroe without you knowing where she's going. I'm gonna find her and marry her, if she'll have me."

"That's good to hear," Durmon replied. "She needs to settle down and get back to being a regular woman again. I didn't like her doing all that spy stuff. That sort of business ought to be left to men folks, anyway. No telling her that, though."

They both smiled at the thought of Marie's response if she had heard such a judgment. Travis was still beaming as he rode back to the herd later that evening. He insisted Alex go into town to have a bath and a good meal, while he stayed with the herd. He even rode the late shift on night herd with Harvey Pressel as his partner.

The warm, dark evening was still and pleasant, with a hint of breeze. He and Harvey talked quietly as they rode round the herd. Most of the cattle were contentedly chewing their cuds or lying quietly. "You have any idea what you're gonna do once the drive's over?" Travis asked.

The lanky Harvey threw his cigarette in a lazy arc toward a patch of bare ground and lit another. Already, he was filling out from eating Paco's good, Texas-style cooking. "I reckon me and the Kirks'll find us a steady job somewhere. We've been together since the start of the war. Rode with Cunningham's Horse Artillery for nearly four years. We're about the only ones left out of two hundred what started from Fort Worth in the summer of sixty-one."

"I have a place for you on the Diamond S if you want it," Travis answered. "That is, if we get these damned cows to the river and get 'em sold to the Yanks."

"Thanks Doc. I appreciate the offer. I'll have to speak to the boys, but I'm certain we'll be saying yes." Harvey started to sing an off-key melody he'd heard around the campfire and grinned happily at his riding companion. Life was beginning to look a lot brighter for him and his two comrades.

Travis continued to think about Marie. He was doubly eager for the drive to finish. He would find Marie, court her, and bring her back to the Diamond S Ranch as his bride or fiancée, if she'd have him. As soon as he was sure the ranch was back on its feet, he would turn it over to Alex and June's husband, Ray, and go to Austin with Marie. There, he would open up an office and return to the practice of medicine. He missed it now that he'd had a chance to relax and distance himself from the horrors of the war.

"Now, big shot, all you have to do is convince Marie," he muttered to himself.

"What's that, Doc?" Harvey asked.

"Nothing, Harvey, I was just mumbling about the way these danged cattle stink when you're up close to them," he replied.

Harvey laughed, "You haven't even begun to smell yet. Wait until we get three or four hundred on a barge together for two or three days. Now that's gonna be a smell." Harvey's voice drifted off as he sought to imagine the stench.

The next night, they were drenched in a loud and long thunderstorm. Fortunately, Jake had found a small meadow, surrounded by loblolly pine trees. The cattle didn't have any place to run, and Alex kept most of the men on horseback all night, circling the restless cattle. In the morning, not more than a few head had escaped from the herd, and as soon as everyone had some hot coffee with biscuits and bacon, Alex had them all on the move.

Travis watched his brother-in-law with satisfaction. Alex would be just the man to run the ranch. He could combine both his ranch and the family's into one. He was a natural-born cowman, and loved it. The ranch would be a better place with Alex in charge, and both Vernon and himself pursuing what they really wanted.

The eighth day after leaving Monroe, Travis saw Leroy come galloping around a bend in the road to his front. The taciturn cowboy rode up to Alex and spoke a few words. Alex motioned for Travis to ride over to his side of the point.

Alex motioned to the east. "Leroy says the river is just ahead. Jake has found a place for us about a half mile back from the water, in a big field. I'm gonna ride on ahead and look it over. You keep the herd moving." Spurring his paint, he galloped off.

They settled the cattle in the big meadow, waist-high in green grass and with a stream running down one side. It was nearly sundown but Travis rode over the small hill and stopped Colonel where he could see the lazy brown ribbon of water, the mighty Mississippi River. He grunted in satisfaction, they had arrived and with most of the herd. Jake rode up behind him and stopped his gray beside Colonel. For a moment, they gazed in silence at the slow-moving water of the mighty river.

"Looks good, don't it, Doc?" Jake spit in pleasure.

"I never really was certain we'd make it, Jake. And with most of the herd to boot. I'll bet we haven't lost fifty of them. It's almost too good to be true. Now, if Vernon can only find us some barges and paddle wheelers."

Jake chuckled, "I reckon he can do it if anybody can." He chucked at his horse and started down the hill. "Come on Doc, we gotta figger how we're gonna load three thousand hard-headed beefs on to them barges when they get here."

Travis sat for an instant without moving. He'd never considered how they'd get three thousand ornery longhorns on the barges. He spurred Colonel and caught up with Jake. "Damn it all," he grumbled. "I never gave it a thought. How are we gonna get 'em loaded?"

"Well," Jake replied as he spat a stream of tobacco at the dusty trail, "I been thinkin' on it fer you. Once't I was in Chicago, afore the war, and saw the railroad unloadin' beefs fer the stockyards. Ya never seen so many cows. Well, they used a ramp to get them cattle out of the cars, slick as you please. I figger we can load 'em the same way. All we need is a dock to tie the barges up to."

They rode down to the edge of the wide brown river. The landing dock for a ferry jutted out into the swirling water before them. "That'll do fine," Jake exclaimed. "We'll build some fencing to keep the dumb critters from fallin' in, and run 'em right on the barges, one, two, three."

The next two days, they stayed with the cattle, waiting for Vernon. The animals filled up on fresh grass and all the water they could drink. Alex figured they had three days before they had to find a place to unload the stock. "They'll be plenty thirsty, but they can last that long without trouble."

Travis was sipping his wake-up coffee the next morning when Jake galloped into camp. "Here comes the barges," he shouted. "Yippee fer Vernon. Come on, you mangy saddle bums, take a look."

Nearly every man in the camp jumped on a horse and rode pell-mell for the river, Travis included. There, chugging up against the current, two paddle wheelers pushed ten empty barges toward them. Dark smoke boiled out of the smokestacks, and as Travis watched, a white plume of steam signified the momentary sound of the steam whistle greeting the waiting men.

Jake was fairly jumping up and down as the first boat nosed up to the dock. "Howdy, Vern," he shouted up to the beaming one-armed Vernon, standing on the bridge deck. "Looks like you found us plenty of barges. Hooray fer you."

As Vern walked down the spiral staircase of the decrepit old paddle wheeler, he laughed. "Hell, I could have got us thirty if we'd a needed 'em. This will be the first real money these river men have earned since the war ended." He grabbed Travis's outstretched hand. "Howdy, little brother. See you made it."

"Thanks to Alex and the men. Yep, we're here, with nearly three thousand cows." He glanced at the weather-beaten look of the two riverboats. "Sure these things'll get us to the Yankee forts?"

Vernon laughed, "Don't worry, these barges are just a bit scruffy 'cause of no paint or money to keep 'em fixed up proper. They'll get us there and back, or they don't get the rest of the lease money. Come on, I'll introduce you to the captain and owner." He led the way back on the docked boat and up the staircase. "By the way, I went over to the Yankee quartermaster in Baton Rouge while waiting for Captain Bekins to get his crew together. He took one look at the letter from General Kelso and bought a thousand head. Twenty-five a head, delivered to Baton Rouge. How 'bout that?"

"Great job, Vern. Hell, if we don't sell another steer, the drive's a success. Let's get these barges loaded and out of here. I'll explain to both you and the captain how we're gonna do it."

By the end of the day, the ten cotton barges were loaded with nearly three hundred head each, and while it was obvious the cattle weren't too happy with their new quarters, they were too packed in to do much about it.

Travis summoned the men to the shade of a tall cypress tree and divided them up. "Vernon will take half of you with him downriver, and I'll take half up. After we sell the herd and get them unloaded, we'll meet back over yonder at Vicksburg before returning to Texas. Jake will go with me, and Alex, you go with Vern." He looked around the group of men. "Any questions?"

Vern spoke up, "Let's meet over at the Magnolia Hotel, top of the hill on River Street. That way we'll be comfortable while we're waiting."

"All right," Travis agreed. "Only, any man who gets put in jail for drunk or disorderly behavior while in town will have to get out on his own. Vern, stop over in Vicksburg and see if the army quartermaster there wants any beef. Meanwhile, I'm off to Memphis. I'll meet you back here in about a week."

The two ships parted, and the men waved to each other as Travis's boat chugged around the bend, pushing the five barges with their unhappy bovine passengers upriver against the sluggish current of the mighty waterway. Travis and his men walked around their new floating home a bit before settling down. For most, it was their first time on a paddle wheeler. They talked in excited voices of their impressions of the ride. The only unhappy occupants were the crowded cattle, but standing jammed together in the wooden confines of the cotton barges, what could they do but voice their discontent in mournful bellows?

CHAPTER 19

"I think we should go to Memphis first," Travis explained to Captain Bekins. "When I was last there, it was the headquarters for numerous nearby posts, all of which have to be supplied." He idly watched the prow of the side-wheeler cut a white, rolling swathe through the brown river water.

"Fine by me, Mr. Sasser. I'll push these here cows to Saint Louie if you want. The only thing is, it'll take three days to make it. Yur cows'll be mighty dry by then, I imagine."

"They'll make it, and I'm betting I can sell the whole load there, or close to it."

As soon as Captain Bekins had the boat and barges tied up to the wharf in Memphis, Travis and Jake hurried to the regional commander's office. After cooling their heels in the outer office for over an hour, they were ushered inside the inner sanctum of the commander, Memphis Military District. The general read the letter from General Kelso in Austin and looked up at Travis and Jake, a calculating expression on his whiskered face. "I wonder what you two ex-Rebs did to get this letter from Kelso. However, if he's okay with it, so am I. I'll fix you up with my quartermaster and he can decide if and how many of yur cows to buy. I suspect he'll be happy to take all you got, as we're always short of fresh meat these days."

The general's prophecy was spot-on, and the cowboys were busy within the hour unloading cattle into the waiting arms of the beef-hungry occupation soldiers. By the end of daylight,

Travis and his comrades were headed downriver toward Vicksburg, a government voucher for nearly forty thousand dollars burning a hole in his pocket.

Exactly one week from the day he left Vicksburg to head upriver, Travis rode Colonel up the hill from the riverbank to the heart of Vicksburg. The riverboat had landed at the ferry dock on the Louisiana side only a couple of hours earlier. After bidding Captain Bekins farewell, he had saddled Colonel and paid a young black man to ferry him across the river, anxious to see if Vernon had returned. The black horse had endured the river crossing with ill-concealed impatience and was happy to be back on solid ground. Colonel was frisky, eager to go, now that he was out of the meadow where he'd waited for his master to return.

Leroy and Jasper had stayed behind to watch the horses while the other men escorted the cattle on their one-way trip on the river. The horse had been well cared for, but had not been ridden in all the time Travis was away. Travis patted the smooth, silky muscles of his horse's neck. "Take it easy, old fellow. Tomorrow we'll be on the road again, and you can work the kinks out of your system."

The graceful city on the high bluff overlooking the Mississippi River still bore the scars from the long siege by General Grant's army in '63. Several buildings showed the effects of the months of shelling by the Yankee gunboats. The Magnolia Hotel had a new roof, and a six-pound solid cannonball was still embedded in one of the twelve-inch-thick wooden columns that supported the upper balcony.

As he walked up the wooden steps to the front door, he paused to allow a white-winged butterfly to flitter down the sidewalk as if it owned the space. Its path took it right past the embedded cannonball. Travis observed that it was smooth and rust free, as if people had been rubbing it when they passed.

Perhaps, just for luck, he thought. He did, too, just in case. If Vernon had been as successful as he, their luck was better than he'd ever dared imagine just three weeks earlier.

The first person Travis saw as he pushed through the wooden doors was his older brother, sitting on a black, horsehair, circular couch, which enclosed a miniature Magnolia tree. Vern was dressed in a new brown frock coat with a smoking cigar in his hand. The empty sleeve on his new velvet-trimmed coat was neatly pinned up and shiny new boots adorned his feet. Vernon was animatedly engaged in conversation with an older gentleman and didn't see Travis until he was nearly beside him. His face lit up when Travis stepped into his view.

"Travis, glad to see you back. Where've you been?" He ground the half-smoked cigar in a nearby ashtray. "I've been back for two days, jus' waitin' on you. Oh, excuse me, Mr. Ende, may I introduce my brother, Travis? Travis, this is Herbert Ende, who has a plantation east of here with a season's growth of cotton on it. We were discussing me brokering it for him in New Orleans and using your barges to transport it downriver. You did bring them back empty, didn't you?"

"Yes I did, but you'd best get one of the boys over to the Louisiana side of the river. Captain Bekins was talking about steaming back down to Baton Rouge as soon as he restocked his woodpile."

"Pete's in the bar. Excuse me Mr. Ende, I'll bring him right over there." Vern hurried off. Travis and Ende exchanged small talk until Vern returned, announcing he had found Pete and sent him off.

Mr. Ende rose to shake Vern's and Travis's hand and then excused himself. "I'll check back with you over supper, Mr. Sasser. I know you want to spend some time with your brother. A pleasure, Mr. Sasser, and good afternoon to you, Vernon, until seven o'clock in the restaurant."

Travis and Vern watched the old plantation owner slowly walk out of the lobby and turn toward the bank across the street. Travis turned to Vernon and grabbed his arm. "Tell me, how did you do?"

"Why, we did just fine." Vern tried to act casual, but the pride visible in his eyes gave him away. "I sold the thousand in Baton Rouge, just like I expected, twenty-seven a head, in a government voucher. I took the other five hundred to New Orleans, where I got twenty-five a head and got paid in gold. How 'bout that!" He paused to light up another cigar and continued.

"We got back here two days ago, I gave the men their wages, and I've been waiting for you ever since. Oh, I told the boys they'd have to wait until they accompanied you back to the ranch to get their bonus. Most are out buying things they've been without since the war started. I bought this new suit and met Mr. Ende over a small card game. I'll make a bundle if you'll let me have enough to make a down payment on his cotton crop. Only five hundred dollars, plus a couple of hundred more to carry me until I sell the cotton in New Orleans."

Travis smiled at his older brother. He seemed to be on top of the world. He hadn't even asked how well Travis had fared. As if Vernon was reading his brother's mind, he suddenly spoke.

"How'd you make out with your half of the herd? You're back sooner than I'd expected, so you musta done fine. Come on, you can tell me all about it while I buy you a glass of cool beer in the bar." Grabbing Travis's arm, he propelled him through the swinging bat-wing doors to the small saloon off the lobby.

"I did fine," Travis answered as soon as Vern gave him a chance to speak. "We sold the whole herd in Memphis, and then hurried back to meet you. Got twenty-five too." I'm carrying thirty-eight thousand five hundred in government chits. What'd you do with all the gold?"

"Relax brother. It's in the bank, locked in their safe, except for the five thousand I kept out to handle expenses. I've already spent about five hundred of it, payin' off the men, buying me some new duds, and the rest is in my room, under the mattress." Vern grinned. "Damn, brother, do you realize we're rich? I hate to give you a swelled head, but your idea to sell to the Yankees was sure a good one."

Travis smiled. "We were lucky, no doubt about it. Now we'll have enough to buy cattle from other ranchers and drive them here again. It'll save those of our neighbors we have left from losing their homes as well. Ma and Pa will be able to stop their worrying now. The ranch is safe." He cast a concerned gaze at Vern's happy face. "You comfortable leavin' so much gold under your mattress?"

"I have the two Mendez brothers sitting on the bed, each with a shotgun in his arms. They sleep in the next room at night, so don't be alarmed."

Vernon looked around. "Where are your men? You didn't have any fall off the boats, did you?"

Travis laughed out loud. "Jake's bringing 'em across now and then he's buying 'em a long drink on me at the first bar they find." Travis laughed, "What a mess it was getting those danged critters out of the barges. Old Ollie and Pete were ready to quit, they were so bamfuzzled. We could always get most to come up the ramp, but there were a few stubborn ones that weren't gonna do it, no matter what. The boys had to go down into the barge and lasso 'em, and we'd have to drag 'em out."

He paused, chuckling again at the memory. "The floor was slippery with cow piles and piss, and smelled like a manure wagon in a heat wave. If you could have seen those boys slippin' and slidin', trying to hang onto a foul-tempered longhorn until they could get him close enough to the side for the rest of us to get a rope around his horns. We could hardly help 'em for laughin' so hard. Ollie swears I gave him the chore because I was jealous of his roping ability." Travis sipped some of his beer and continued, "Anyway, Jake thought they'd best have a few drinks to reward their hard work before they check into the hotel."

He finished his beer and wiped his mouth with the back of his hand. "Come on, let's get me cleaned up and over to the dry-goods store. I want to buy a few things myself before we start home tomorrow. And, yes, big brother, you can have your money. You earned it."

They met with Herb Ende for supper, and finalized Vern's deal for the cotton. Jake and the others with him showed up, none the worst for their sojourn into the lower regions of Vicksburg. Travis gave the excited men their earnings for the drive. He offered jobs to any who wanted to return with Alex to the Diamond S, and six of the men agreed. It meant the ranch would have a seasoned crew to start a second drive of cattle later in the summer.

At dawn, the next morning, he led his yawning band of cowboys down the hill to the ferry landing, and across the river by ferryboat to Louisiana. Vern came down from his room to make his farewells, as he was staying behind to supervise the loading of his cotton. Then he'd be off to New Orleans, and the life he wanted. Travis was satisfied his brother had passed over the hurdle of losing his arm. He turned and waved at the one-armed figure, just before he disappeared in the morning mist.

"Be seeing you," he shouted. "You come home soon. I want you to meet Marie. So long." Vern waved back and turned to reenter the hotel. Travis had noticed that Vernon rubbed the embedded cannonball every time he entered the door. Just for luck.

The day was hot and humid, with a real threat of thundershowers in the dark clouds to the south. Travis and Alex led the way, with the gold in their saddlebags. The rest of the crew was strung out behind them. Everyone rode easy and the men passed the time recalling stories of the trip up or down the river. Poor old Ollie and Pete took a large measure of ribbing from the men about their troubles pulling out reluctant cattle from the barges.

"Well, I declare," the old cowboy grumbled. "I reckon you'd have the same problem we did. How'd you get them dagburned critters outta the barges?"

"Hell," Jasper Skoggins answered, "Vernon told the Yankee officers to git some men and they just lined up shoulder to shoulder and run 'em out slick as you please. We just stood on the bank and watched."

Ollie cast an exasperated glance at Travis. "Well, I reckon my boss wasn't clever enough to think o'that. Fer sure, I'm gonna go with you next time. I still ain't got my boots clean."

Even though Travis was a little nervous carrying so much money, the sight of twenty heavily-armed cowboys would deter anyone who might consider trying to rob them. He felt watching eyes on his group, more than once, but they saw nobody. They kept a guard awake at night and arrived in Monroe without incident. They checked into the hotel and got a bath and a hot meal. Travis bade farewell to the men who were leaving their group when they reached Texas, as he would be leaving the others in the morning.

Alex and Jake argued with Travis over the hot supper at the hotel's restaurant. "Doc, you best come back to Texas first and then go after Miss Marie. We've got to git them army vouchers converted to cash money right away. You set it up with Major Richardson, don't ferget."

"Easy, Jake," Travis soothed his old friend. "You were there too, and Major Richardson knows you. I think you should take Alex and the men and ride straight through to Austin, without stopping at the ranch. Exchange the vouchers, put the money in the bank at Naggi-dosh and then return to the ranch. I'll find Marie, however long it takes. Alex, you make sure Jake gets to Austin without trouble." Travis paused and then continued, "I have a feeling I ought to find Marie, while I'm close, rather than wait until I go back to the ranch. It's a feeling I can't shake."

"Well, dad-gummit, Doc," Jake persisted. "You can't be traipsing around the countryside alone or with a gal along. Some skunks'll get on you fer sure. They'll see you as easy pickin's."

"Jake's right, Travis," Alex chimed in. "At least take a couple of the boys with you. I'd feel a whole lot better knowing you had some help if you needed it."

"All right, I'll take the Mendez brothers with me. They're good traveling companions and those shotguns of theirs will deter any hanky-panky. Maybe make 'em feel a bit more useful as well. Satisfied?"

"Not really," Jake grumbled, but he didn't know how to stop the determined man across from him. Jake was a little surprised to realize just how much he was yearning to see his widow lady again, so he appreciated the feelings his young friend had. "You just tread softly, Doc, you hear, now?" The two friends remained silent the rest of the meal, each engrossed in his own thoughts of the future.

As the party of happy Texans reached Monroe, Travis and the two Mendez brothers watched the rest of their group ride on toward Texas, before starting down the rut-filled road to Bawcomville. Because it was only about fifteen miles south of Monroe, they could make the ride an easy one, in no real hurry except for his desire to see Marie again. He looked over the packhorse they'd loaded with provisions, including his medical bag. All was secure, and he had two hundred dollars in gold eagles hidden in his saddlebags.

"Come on, compadres," Travis said as he swung up on

Colonel's back. "Let's mosey on over to Marie's place before the sun gets too high. Git going Colonel, time's a'slippin' away, to quote my friend Jake."

He led the two vaqueros out of Monroe and toward the little village where Marie's plantation was located. It was all he could do to keep from singing, even though he knew the two men with him would gallop after the others if he started. It wouldn't be long now. His thoughts had been on the dark-eyed beauty most of the time, now that he'd rid himself of the burden of the cattle. The ranch was safe, Vernon was back in the saddle, now it was time to think of himself.

Tall, stately cypress trees with long tendrils of Spanish moss hanging from their branches flanked the road. Travis reminded himself to buy some saddle blankets from Mr. Durmon on his way through Monroe as he headed home. Blankets woven from the moss were said to be the best and coolest saddle blankets available in the West. The big black he was riding deserved no less. He absently patted the neck of his horse as he trotted toward the woman he hoped to marry. He could hear the two vaqueros softly chatting away in Spanish as they followed their patron.

As they were speculating as to the new lady's probable charms and attributes while riding along, Travis turned and smiled at them while asking in Spanish, "Is everything all right with you, my compadres?" He didn't want them to say anything that might embarrass them if they had forgotten how well he understood their lingo.

"Sí, Señor Travis. Muy bien," Xavier replied. Their remarks took on a more decidedly neutral character for the rest of the trip.

The bucolic farming community of Bawcomville was typical of the small towns in the area. Several small stores, a single main street, some homes on the dirt side streets, and an overall look of poverty, caused by the war. The town saloon was apparently empty, and the only person Travis saw on the sidewalk, braving the hot noon sun, was a one-legged veteran of the war, hobbling toward the general store on his handmade crutches. The faded blue stripes of an infantry corporal were still on the ragged, butternut gray jacket he wore.

"Pardon me, Corporal, but could you direct me to the LeMont plantation?" Travis climbed off his horse, so the man wouldn't have to look up into the sun at him.

"Possible I might. Who wants to know?" the man replied as he shifted his weight off the crutches to his single leg.

"My name is Doctor Travis Sasser, late of Hood's army. I'm a friend of Miss LeMont. These are two of my vaqueros. We've just finished driving a herd of cattle to Vicksburg. I wanted to stop off and see her before returning to Texas."

The crippled veteran scrutinized Travis for an instant, and then made up his mind. "All right, I reckon. Miss LeMont's place is about three miles south, out that road yonder. It's the first turnoff after you cross the stream." He pointed with one of his crutches and then skillfully caught the silver dollar Travis flipped his way. Nodding his thanks, the crippled veteran hobbled on toward the store.

The trip was uneventful, with only the sound of the horses hoofs' plodding on the hard-packed dirt road to break the silence. Travis watched anxiously for the stream the man mentioned and felt growing uneasiness as they cantered across its bubbling water. The turnoff was up the road a few hundred feet. A weather-beaten sign declared *LeMont Plantation.* Nailed on it was a sheriff's notice, weather-beaten and worn. It had been there for some time. "This land, with its legal description as listed, will be sold for taxes, Jan 31, 1864."

Travis's heart jumped to his throat. The same land thieving was going on here as in his part of the country. Travis cursed softly and spoke aloud. "The damned taxmen taking hardworking folks' land 'cause they don't have any money to pay their tax bill." He hoped Marie was still here. He hurried Colonel down the tree-lined lane toward the white brick house in the distance. Upon closer inspection, it showed the effects of a fire. The roof was gone from most of the house. Only the west wing seemed to be undamaged. As he rode into the front yard, the place appeared deserted. Only the presence of a big, white leghorn rooster and his numerous hens scratching in a small garden at the west side of the building showed some sign of life. The place was quiet, almost foreboding, it seemed to the anxious young Texan.

"Hello, the house," he shouted as he stopped by the front steps. He shifted in the saddle; almost ready to step down, when he heard a low squeak from the front-door hinges.

The front door opened only slightly, and the gaping bores of a double-barreled shotgun poked its way out, pointed right at him. "Git, you white trash," a determined voice called from the darkness behind the gun. "You take dem chili peppers ridin' wif you and gits now or I's gwinea blast you clear back to de front gate. You hear what I says, white man?"

Travis swallowed his surprise and held up his hands. "Hold on. I'm a friend of Miss LeMont, come to see her. Is she here?"

"I don't know you, and Miss LeMont don't want no visitors. Now git, and I means quick."

"Please, tell Miss LeMont that Doctor Travis Sasser is here to see her. If she doesn't want to see me, I'll go, but please tell her I've come to . . ."

He couldn't say any more before the door swung open, and a huge black woman, with a faded red bandanna around her head and wearing a shapeless gingham dress, peered out. Holding the old shotgun with obvious familiarity, she stepped out on the fire-scarred porch. With relief in her voice, she spoke, "Did you say you is a doctor?"

Travis nodded his head, his hands still held high. The two vaqueros sat in stunned silence. Was this how the patron's woman's servants greeted their new boss?

"Oh, Mister Doctor, climb on down and gits in de house. Miss Marie is bad sick, and I'm afeerd she's gwinna die. Praise de Lord, a doctor done come jus' lak I asked Him."

Waving the big double-barreled gun for emphasis, she repeated her order. "Climb on down offa that horse and come with me. Hurry up, my little lamb is sick to death."

Chapter 20

Travis leaped off his mount and hurrried to the packhorse, grabbing his medical bag. "Pedro, you and Xavier take care of the horses, and then come inside and wait for me. We may have to transport Miss LeMont to Monroe."

"Sí, Señor Travis," Pedro replied. He took Colonel's reins from Travis and led the horses around the house toward the weathered barn.

Travis hurried up the steps and motioned to the black servant. "Where is Miss LeMont? Take me to her."

The old black woman was close to tears. "Oh, Masser Travis, don't tell Miss Marie I called you white trash. She's awful sick, and don't need to be worryin' about my bad manners. Come on, I has her back here in de bedroom."

The massive black woman hurried down the burn-damaged foyer and entrance hall toward the east wing. As they approached the portion of the house that had escaped the fire, Travis saw furniture and boxes, probably saved from the flames, stacked and covered with white sheets. The place was a sad reminder of what it once had been.

"Where are Miss LeMont's field hands? By the way, what is your name?"

"I'm Mammy Lulubell, Doctor Travis. I's been Miss Marie's mammy since she was borned. Her pappy done died two year ago in Vicksburg of de flux and her brother Pierre drowned when his boat was sunk by dem damned Yankees last year. Miss

Marie is all alone 'cept fer me and Roland, the head butler. All the other field hands done run off when de Yankee soldiers come through in sixty-four. The sheriff says this place don't belong to Miss Marie no more. He says we has to leave when de new owners come from back East."

Mammy Lulubell led Travis up some stairs to the second floor. "Miss Marie been staying in the visitors' wing. It be the only place not damaged in de fire last winter. Me and Roland saved all the furniture and stuff we could, but we couldn't do nothing about de house. Iffen it hadn't started to rain, de whole place would have burned right down. Praise de Lord for His favors."

She stopped in front of a bedroom door. "Here we is. Oh, Doctor Travis, please save my baby lamb, I beg ya."

Travis brushed past the overwrought Mammy and hurried to the bed where a still figure lay. His heart caught in his throat as he looked down on the wan face, framed by the silky black hair. Sweat glistened on her upper lip. Travis gently placed his hand on her forehead and confirmed her high fever. The touch of his hand was enough to wake the lightly sleeping woman. Her glazed eyes widened at the sight of the face peering down at her in concern.

"Who? Oh, Travis, it's you. I can't believe it." She licked dry lips and swallowed with effort. "I hoped you'd come for the longest time." Her eyes squeezed shut as a spasm of pain racked her frail body. "Oh, oh, God that hurts. Travis, please help me. I can't stand much more of this pain." Once again, her face contorted in agony, and she shut her eyes. "Help me, Travis, help me." She drifted off in a fevered sleep.

Travis pulled down the coverlet and unfastened the sweat-soaked bodice of her dressing gown. As he carefully peeled the soaked garments from her body, his eyes ran over her, looking for the source of her pain. The stark outline of her ribs, and the flaccid sag of the once-firm breasts indicated a rapid loss of weight. The stomach was taut and hot, and Marie moaned in pain when he gently pressed the lower-right quadrant below her navel. Travis carefully pulled the shift away from her feet and grimly looked at the naked body of the woman he loved. He realized he was looking at death, as sure as if she had taken a bullet wound in her stomach.

While at medical school in Boston, he'd seen the young men and women come into the hospital, with similar pain and symptoms. After a while, the patient would experience severe diarrhea and vomiting, rapid loss of weight, and soon thereafter, death. Those he'd been able to autopsy had a lower abdominal cavity filled with infection, known as peritonitis. He'd seen the ruptured vermiform, or worm-like appendix. The bodies of healthy soldiers with stomach wounds that he'd cut into had a different-looking appendix. Theirs were healthy pink, and not distended, nor filled with pus.

Unfortunately, Travis knew from bitter experience that any invasion of the abdomen by surgery would usually prove fatal. He was certain the dirty conditions of the battlefield hospital exacerbated the problem, but the record was clear. He wondered if he dared operate on Marie. If he allowed infection into the abdomen, he would be killing the woman he loved. If he didn't, she would probably die of a ruptured appendix. For certain, he dare not try and take her to Monroe. The bouncing journey would likely prove deadly.

"How's my baby, Doctor Travis?" Mammy inquired. She stood close beside the stranger who silently studied the naked body before him. "You's been lookin' at her long enough to save her twice, I reckon," she declared, a hint of self-righteousness in her voice.

"She's bad sick, Mammy. I think a little thing in her stomach, called the appendix, has become infected. It'll burst soon and the poison will spread to the rest of her system. Nobody survives that when it happens, nobody, damn it to hell."

"Well, what cans we do, Doctor?" Mammy gently pulled the coverlet over her baby. She felt uneasy letting this man look so long at her sweet child, naked and all. It wasn't right, even if he was a doctor.

"Mammy, you need to get some cool water and wash her thoroughly. Keep a wet rag on her forehead. I'd like to get her temperature down if possible. Then get some coal oil. You have any?"

Mammy nodded her confirmation. "We has a little bit in the storeroom. I was savin' it fer special occasions."

"Good, heat it as hot as you can stand and soak a rag in it. Then put the rag right here." Travis pulled back the coverlet and pointed at the red area on Marie's abdomen. "Keep changing it as it cools. Sometimes that made a difference at the hospital. While you're doing that, I want to talk with Roland." He walked out of the room, his nose suddenly aware of the stale smell of illness. His chance at happiness was perilously close to death. He had to decide, should he let her try and recover on her own, although that didn't seem likely, or to cut into her abdomen and risk killing her through induced infection. Neither decision appealed to him.

Travis walked out of the house onto the back porch, his brow furrowed in thought. A stooped, black man with a snow-white crown of hair above the ears, surrounding a shining bald top, was hoeing weeds in the little garden. Travis walked over to him.

"Pardon me; you're Roland, I guess."

"Yes, sir," the man replied with solemn dignity. "You are fortunate, sir. The last man to get off his horse with Mammy's shotgun on him is buried right next to the elm tree yonder." He motioned with his chin, still chopping at a stubborn weed.

"I'm a friend of Miss Marie. My name is Travis Sasser. I'm a doctor, so Mammy was lenient with me."

"That is wonderful, sir. My mistress is gravely ill, as I'm sure Mammy has told you. How may I be of service, sir?"

"Roland, I wonder if you have any liquor around the house?"

Travis saw the flash of disappointment that showed in the butler's eyes. He explained, "I need it to clean a table where I can operate on Marie. I want to use it to make sure my hands and instruments are as clean as possible. I promise, I won't take a drink until I'm done."

"Yes, sir," Roland answered. "I've got several bottles of brandy and some jugs of corn liquor hidden in the smokehouse. Shall I get some?"

"Yes, all you have, and start some water boiling. Also, find any clean sheets you have and bring them to the kitchen. If I decide to operate, it will be there. It's cleaner than any other room and the light is good. Go, get started." He watched Roland hurry away, while he stood immobile, considering his options. He had to do something. He couldn't stand by and watch Marie die.

Travis called out for the two vaqueros. "Pedro, you and Xavier come here, please."

The two men exited the barn and rapidly walked to him. "It's too late to take the lady to Monroe. We'll have to operate on her here. Come with me, compadres. We have to scour the kitchen until it's clean as a hound's tooth."

Under Travis's critical guidance, the room was soon as clean as the three men could make it. He wiped the inlaid wooden dining table that had come from the burnt-out dining room with a rag soaked in Roland's white lightning. Several pots were filled with boiling water, which Travis used to wash his instruments before placing them on a folded towel next to the head of the table.

"Roland, can I depend on you to administer the sleeping potion to Miss Marie? I'll show you how to do it, but you can't quit once we start."

"Doctor Travis, you can depend on me," the solemn butler answered.

"Pedro you and Xavier will have to hold the lanterns high while I'm operating. If you feel sick, then look away, but keep the light up so I can see, understand?"

Both vaqueros nodded their assurance. He knew that same bravado would disappear as soon as the blood started to flow from the first incision. He just hoped they wouldn't faint, as some medical attendants did the first time they assisted with an operation.

For a few seconds, he stood by the table, collecting his thoughts. The chances that he would kill the woman he had come to love were immense. Only the knowledge that Marie was certain to die if he didn't try kept him from throwing up his hands at the thought of operating on her. He settled his resolve and turned toward the stairs. "Everyone come with me," he commanded.

At the entrance to Marie's bedroom, he paused and asked the other men to await his call. Tapping softly on the door, he entered and silently moved to the bedside. Mammy was sitting beside Marie's quiet form, sponging a damp rag across her forehead. "Shhh," she whispered. "She's asleep now. De cool water and hot oil done helped her to rest."

Travis smiled appreciatively at the protective Mammy and gently shook Marie's arm. "Marie, Marie," he insisted softly, disregarding Mammy's fierce glare. "Wake up, Marie."

The dark brown eyes flew open, and Marie gasped out, "What, what do you want?"

"Marie, you've got to listen to me. I want you to know what I'm preparing to do. Do you understand me?"

"Yes, Travis," she replied, while shuddering at a sudden spasm of pain. "I hear you. Please, Travis, help me. I hurt inside, something awful."

"I know you do, Marie. It's what is called your appendix. I'm sure it's infected. I've seen it before." Travis paused and then plunged ahead. "Marie, if I don't remove it, it will burst, and you'll probably die of abdominal infection." Mammy gasped at the statement, but Marie just looked up at Travis, with pain-filled eyes.

"I can't take you to Monroe. It's too late for that. If I cut into you here, and remove it, you may die from the effects of the operation. You're aware most wounds to the stomach are fatal. I'll try, my dear, unless you don't want me to. What do you want, Marie? Shall I try?"

Shuddering with pain, Marie held out her hand to Travis. "I'm certain if anyone can do it, you can. Anything is better than this pain, so go ahead, do what has to be done." She closed her eyes as if to go back to sleep. "I love you, Travis, darling, I have since our time helping the wounded at Fort Pillow. You saved those wounded men. I'm confident you'll save me." She squeezed his hand fiercely and lay silent on the bed, her eyes clamped tightly shut.

"What's you mean?" Mammy whispered protectively. "You ain't gwinna cut into my little lamb. Over my dead body you ain't."

Travis sat for an instant, his heart thrilled at Marie's declaration of love. "Mammy, I am, and you're going to help me do it. Now hush up and do what I say." He turned to the door, where his men were peeking in. "You men, come here and each grab a corner of the sheet Miss Marie's lying on. Carefully now, let's carry her down to the table in the kitchen. Mammy, you stay at her head, and hold it up."

Aside from a shallow intake of breath when she was first

moved, Marie made the trip without a murmur. Gently, the men laid her on the wooden table. Travis thought of the many times he'd operated on wounded men on dining tables during the war. Using some of the alcohol, he washed the rigid and hot stomach area of his patient, and then draped clean towels around the region of her body where he planned to operate.

For a moment, he stared at her alabaster white skin, then moved to the head of the table where Roland waited with the chloroform bottle and the gauze mask Travis had given him. "All right, Roland." Travis placed the mask on Marie's face. "Give her a drop every twenty seconds until I tell you to stop. Just count to thirty between drops. Here, let me show you how. Then you take over."

"Please, Doctor Travis," Roland's voice cracked in shame. "I am afraid I can't count. I'm sorry, sir."

"Damn," Travis grumbled. "Pedro, you count for Roland. Count to thirty, and then start over. Keep counting until I tell you to stop."

"Por favor, Señor Travis. I cannot count, either. Xavier can, can't you, Xavier?"

"Sí, but only in Spanish. Will that be permissio?" he asked with a worried frown.

"Yes, yes," Travis answered in exasperation through clenched teeth. "When you reach thirty, point to Roland. Roland, when he points, you add a drop of chloroform to the mask. Watch me and do it exactly the same as I do."

Travis placed the gauze mask over Marie's face and eased a drop of the liquid onto the mask. He counted to thirty in Spanish and added another drop. Soon, Marie's shallow breaths deepened as she passed into the chemically induced sleep. Thank God he had the chloroform. He'd done enough surgery with the patient awake and screaming in his ears.

For several minutes Travis continued to drop the liquid, and once convinced she was sedated, gave the bottle to Roland and looked at Xavier. "Start counting, Xavier. Remember, signal every time you reach thirty." Returning to his place next to the exposed abdomen of Marie, he locked eyes with the worried Mammy, standing at the foot of the table. "Mammy, you stand beside me and hold the dishpan with the instruments in it. If I ask for more bandages, put it down right here, where I can reach it."

Mammy took the pan filled with corn whiskey and the instruments from Travis's medical bag. "Whoa, what's you got in this here pan, Doctor Travis. Smells suspicious like that whiskey I knows that rascal Roland's been sipping when he thought I wasn't around. You ain't plannin' on sipping whiskey whiles you cut on my baby?"

"That's what it is, all right. It will help to keep the instruments clean, and that's important." Travis dipped his hands in the pan one last time before starting.

"Wall, it shore ought to do that," Mammy agreed. "It'll clean paint right off the walls."

Smiling grimly, Travis reached for the shiny scalpel lying in the bottom of the pan filled with the potent-smelling liquor. Between the fumes of the chloroform and the whiskey, he would be hard pressed to keep his senses sharp. And he knew how important it was that he be a better doctor than he'd ever been in his life. He prayed that all those mangled men he had operated on in the army would now allow him to save the single person on earth that he cared about most of all.

Taking a deep breath, he drew the sharp blade across Marie's white skin, leaving a thin red line in its path. Dimly, he heard the sharp intake of Mammy's breath at the sight of Marie's blood. Even dimmer was the muttered counting of Xavier, and Roland's mumbled praying.

With fingers flying, he clamped and tied off the bleeders, using the finest silk thread in his supply. Cutting and tying his way through the abdominal muscles, he soon came to the shiny, semitransparent peritoneum. Much like sausage skin, it contained the organs of the lower abdomen. Travis knew that once he cut through it, any infection that entered would probably prove fatal.

Breathing through clenched teeth, he sliced an opening into the abdominal cavity. For an instant, he looked into this wondrous creation of God. The organs that gave life to the woman were exposed to his view. Not daring to pause an instant, he enlarged the opening and looked at the glistening pile of intestines lying coiled within the stomach cavity. The large intestine lay below the many feet of the smaller intestine. Where they joined, he saw what he expected, the little worm-like appendix, not limp and small, as it should be if it were healthy, but swollen and filled with yellowish pus. As he grasped it with his hand, he could feel the heat radiating from it. It would burst soon, spraying the abdominal cavity with the foul matter contained within, causing peritonitis and agonizing death.

He tied off the appendix at its base, and a quarter inch down, tied it off again. Then, he carefully cut between the two ties, and lifted the hot appendage out of the hole in Marie's stomach. He could hear Pedro trying to keep his stomach down and the almost hysterical counting of Xavier. Mammy was mumbling a litany of promises if the Lord would save her baby lamb.

Travis glanced up at Roland. The solemn black was biting his lip, but every time Xavier said "Trienda," he placed another drop directly on the mask.

Travis dropped the inflamed appendix in one of the bloody rags he'd used to wipe Marie's cut. "Bury that after we're done, Roland," he told the butler.

Wiping away the sweat that had accumulated at the juncture of his upper lip and his mustache on his left forearm, he wiped the raw stump of the appendix with a whiskey-soaked rag. It oozed a small droplet of blood, and then nothing. After a few seconds, he took the needle and fine silk thread lying in the whiskey-filled pan. Then he sewed together the tough peritoneum, pushing the needle through the rawhide-hard skin-like covering much as a shoemaker sewed a shoe together. He stitched his way out of the wound, sewing up the layers of muscle a little at a time. Finally, he sewed shut the amazingly tough subcutaneous and outer skin, using many small stitches as a master tailor would on a fine suit of clothes.

Finished, he breathed deeply as he rinsed his hands in the whiskey and nodded to Roland. "You can stop the chloroform now. It's all done. All we can do from here on is pray that I haven't hurt her more than I've helped her." He looked at the stressed faces of the people around the sheet-draped form. "Thank you for your assistance. I couldn't have done it without you. Each man grab a corner of the sheet, and let's carry her up to her bed. Mammy, you stay with her. Call me if the wound starts to bleed. I need to go outside and get a breath of fresh air." The smell of the room, its penetrating odors of whiskey, chloroform, and the brassy smell of blood nearly sickened him. Had he saved the woman he loved or killed her? Only time would give him an answer.

Chapter 21

The setting sun was transforming the western sky into a brilliant orange hue, boldly tinged with purple and grays where it met the horizon, before Travis felt like reentering Marie's half-burned house. The fresh air had cleared his head of the operation's noxious odors, and the vivid sunset helped to settle his nerves. He climbed the stairs to Marie's room and entered, delighted to discover that the young woman was sleeping, the reassuring bulk of her devoted nanny hovering nearby.

"The child's still sleeping, Doctor Travis. I's been watching the cut, and it ain't bled but jes' a drop, since we put her to bed."

"That's a good sign," Travis replied. He took Marie's pulse and checked her breathing. She seemed to be simply asleep, with no overt problems. "When you tire, call me and I'll take over. If she tries to move, in her sleep or when she wakes, don't let her. The incision must not be opened before it starts to heal. Call me if you need me; otherwise, I'll come back around twelve o'clock and sit with her a while."

He tiptoed out of the room, satisfied that Marie was in good hands and resting comfortably. Roland had cleaned the table and prepared a meal of chicken and red beans, which Travis ate outside, anxious to stay away from the room with its unpleasant memories. Eventually, the mosquitoes drove him back inside. He restlessly lay down on the davenport in the parlor and tossed and turned until he relieved Mammy around midnight.

After checking her temperature and the incision, Travis settled into an overstuffed chair next to Marie's bed while she slept the night away. He passed the hours dwelling on their time together and her growing importance in his feelings. The night passed uneventfully and about daybreak, Mammy shuffled into the bedroom to resume her vigil at Marie's side. "You gets some rest, Doctor Travis. I'll call you iffen Miss Marie wakes up. Roland, he made some chicken soup for the child. It be all right fer her to eats it?"

"I think so, Mammy. Don't give her anything solid just yet, only soup, wine, and water. If everything goes well, in a couple of days we'll try something more substantial." Travis yawned and walked to the door. "I'm gonna get some sleep, but call me if you have any problems."

He was exhausted and slept until late afternoon. After washing the sleep out of his eyes, he returned to Marie's bedroom. She was awake, talking with Mammy. "Good afternoon," he intoned in his best bedside manner. "How are you feeling?" He took her wrist to feel her pulse. With his other hand, he felt her forehead. The fever was almost gone. Her face lit up at his entrance.

Marie smiled at him, eyes bright and pain-free. "I'm feeling much better, thank you. There's a little pain in my side where you cut me, but it's bearable." She waited until he put down her wrist and looked into her eyes. "Mammy says you cut the whatever you called it out of me. Am I going to get well?"

"Appendix, and yes, I think so," Travis answered. "We have to be very careful to prevent infection. We were in a very dangerous place. For the time being you must lie still, until the incision heals. Don't take any chances of tearing open the stitches. We're not out of the woods yet." He gave her a warm smile, affection written all over his face.

Marie grew very quiet, looking up at him. "I missed you, Travis. I hoped that you'd come see me, but I really didn't expect it. What happened to, you know, the woman you were so, so faithful to?" She looked at him with a look of both wisdom and humor. "There was one, wasn't there?"

Travis nodded. "She turned out to be a bad penny. Married someone else while I was in the Yankee prison. Just as well, since she didn't measure out too solid against you."

"You mean you . . ."

"I mean I'm here to present myself to you, Miss LeMont, as your suitor. As soon as you're well, that is. The first thing is for you to start feeling good again." Travis grinned at her, and she laughed softly in return.

"Thanks to you and your skill, I'm confident it shan't be long before I feel fine." Marie flashed him a smile of blinding loveliness. "Thank you, Doctor." Her smile faded, and a determined frown crossed her face. "You haven't forgotten that I'm very angry at you for taking that Yankee money, have you? I may not choose to be courted by a common bank robber."

Travis sighed, "So far my dear, that money has saved three ranches in Texas from foreclosure, and started Homer and Irma on their lives together. I will however, if you insist, turn myself over to your authority for life. I accept you as my permanent jailer, answerable for any and all crimes against the South. Until you can take up your new duties, you must try and rest. I want you well as quickly as possible."

"Then get me something substantial to eat. I'm hungry enough to chew the bedpost off, and all Mammy will give me is chicken soup and a sip of brandy."

Travis stood. "You listen to her. She's the best nurse I ever saw. Please, rest and save your strength. I'll be back later." He smiled at this woman he had saved and loved.

Mammy swiftly moved to the bedside. "You heerd what he

said, child. You lays back and rest now, and I don't want no sass."

Travis went down the stairs and out into the yard. Roland was at the garden, and the two vaqueros were brushing the horses at the stable. He walked over to Roland. "Why don't you ride into town with my men and buy whatever supplies you need? I'll give you a list of things I need to help Miss Marie recover. Pedro, you and Xavier come here, I've got a chore for you. Hitch up the wagon and take Roland to town."

By the time they returned, it was full dark, and another night passed without incident. After hearing Marie's pleas for solid food throughout the day, Travis relented and gave her some of Roland's baked chicken for her supper.

By the time a week had passed, it seemed apparent that Marie was not going to suffer an infection from the operation. Travis spent a lot of time with her, telling of his plans, what he'd accomplished for his family, and how much he hoped she'd be a part of his life in the future.

Marie recovered more of her strength every day, enjoying the attention she received from the handsome young doctor and skillfully reeling in the willing fish her charms had lured. Finally, one evening, they kissed long and deeply, before Mammy shoved him out of the bedroom. "So's my lamb could gets some rest." For both, the embrace set the world spinning with a desperate longing for one another, stronger than either believed possible.

The next morning, Travis rode Colonel into town and talked with the county sheriff. "It's a done deed, honey," he reported when he got back. "Some Yankee speculator has bought your place and the three others next to you. When he shows up, you'll have to leave. The sheriff is sorry, but says there's nothing he can do about it."

"Then, let's leave now," Marie flared. "Why wait for the inevitable? Let's pack my things and be gone from here." She looked at Travis with bitter eyes. "You'll have to take me as is, without much dowry, I'm afraid."

"I'll take you with gratitude, Marie. You don't need a dowry. Besides"—he smiled mischievously—"you still have a share of the loot coming to you. That's dowry enough."

In exasperation, she punched his arm. When he started to fight back, Mammy shouted out, "Don't you mess with that sick child. Leave her alone, you hear me."

Laughing at the protective Mammy, they kissed and parted for the evening. Travis slept the sleep of the just, content in his world and longing for the future.

The next day, he left at dawn with Pedro and Xavier for Monroe. The first stop was to see Mr. Durmon, at his livery stable. They returned with an almost-new carriage, painted white with blue fringe on the trim, pulled by a pair of handsome grays. If one had to guess, it would appear to be a Union army officer's carriage that had a fresh coat of paint over the standard Yankee blue. That wouldn't be possible, however, since no Yankee carriages had ever been reported missing.

Pedro and Xavier each drove sturdy wagons, with fresh teams to pull them. They arrived to find Marie sitting outside, enjoying the late afternoon sun. "Hello," she called as they drove up. "What do you have there?"

"Moving as many household goods as you have requires more than an extra saddlebag," Travis answered.

"Oh, Travis, you dear. You mean you'll let me take my furniture with me when we leave?"

"Of course," he replied as he swung down from the carriage. "That is, if you'll marry me as soon as we get back to the Diamond S. Is it a deal?"

With a squeal of joy, Marie spread her arms for his embrace. "Of course, you silly goose. What do you think I've been hoping for these last two weeks?"

As their lips drew apart, she murmured, "I can take Mammy and Roland with us, can't I?"

"Certainly. I've grown accustomed to them as well. Only thing, Mammy doesn't accompany us on our wedding trip, agreed?"

"Agreed, my darling," Marie giggled. "That will be for just you and me. Will I be completely healed by then? I would like that, and even better, so will you." Her attempt at a lecherous lear brought laughter to both parties.

Travis swung the laughing young woman up in his arms. "Time to go in. Supper's ready, if I understand Roland's look. Come on, Miss LeMont. It's time you dined at the table with us."

"Sweet Jesus," she shouted happily. "Real food, at last. I was afraid you were determined to starve me into submission. To the table, MacDuff. I'm so hungry, I could eat Jake's cooking."

Marie's recovery accelerated in the days that followed. Soon, she was walking around the house and yard without difficulty. Mammy rubbed cottonseed oil on her scar every morning and night. Travis had removed the exposed sutures and attended to the healed scar closely, and it appeared strong.

At dinner that night, he announced, "I believe you're ready to travel, Marie. What say we start loading the wagons tomorrow, and leave day after that?"

Marie's eyes lighted in anticipation. "How long then until we reach your ranch?"

"About six days, if we take it easy," Travis answered. He looked at his dining companion. "You'll be my wife this time next week if all goes well. I love you, Marie."

"And I love you, Travis. I'm as happy as a person can be. Yet, a month ago, if I'd had to leave this place, I'd have been devastated." She looked at him across the table. "I have you to thank for the change in my life. For my life itself."

"I'll take my payment in love, one day at a time," he replied. "For the rest of forever."

A week later, he told Roland to stop the carriage at the top of the hill overlooking the Angelino River. With the afternoon sun high overhead, the ranch house was a bright and beckoning beacon in the distance.

"There it is my dear." Travis pointed. "There's the place where we start on our personal road to happiness." He glanced back at the two following wagons, loaded to the canvas with all of Marie's belongings. They sat silently, savoring the moment.

Marie held his arm tightly and looked up at the man she loved. "Darling, I'm so happy." Marie sighed, "You know, don't you, that you'll have to be the most successful doctor in Austin to afford a place big enough to hold all our furniture. Not that I have any doubts that you will be."

Travis laughed and inhaled the sweet scent of the silky, raven-colored hair resting against his shoulder. "Frankly, my dear," he whispered, softly kissing the dainty lobe of her ear, "I can't wait. Let's get started?"

ABOUT THE AUTHOR

Thom Nicholson was born in Springfield, Missouri, and grew up in Northern Arkansas and Southwest Missouri. He graduated from Missouri School of Mines with a bachelor's degree in nuclear engineering. During the summers he worked out west for the US Forest Service in forest fire suppression.

After college he briefly worked in a uranium mine in New Mexico before joining the US Army, where his first assignment was to play post football at Fort Knox, Kentucky. He then graduated from the Officer Candidate School at Fort Benning, Georgia, of which he is now in its Hall of Fame. After graduation, he attended parachutist training. Following an initial assignment to the mountain brigade at Fort Carson, Colorado, he joined Special Forces and trained at Fort Bragg, North Carolina.

His initial overseas assignment with Special Forces was with the 5th Group in South Vietnam, where he was the XO of Camp A-224, Phu Tuc in the highland mountains of II Corps. His camp was actively engaged in interdiction operations against the Viet Cong. Upon his return he was assigned to Fort Leonard Wood, Missouri training recruits for several months before he returned to Special Forces, first to Panama and then back to RVN, where he was assigned to CCN, MACV-SOG, engaged in behind-the-lines interdiction operations against the North Vietnamese Army. He was the S-3 Plans Officer, then the S-1 personnel officer, followed by Company B (Hatchet Force)

Commander until his return to Fort Bragg, North Carolina, where he was the chief of Phase IV training to enlisted Special Forces soldiers.

After his discharge from active duty, he joined the 12th Special Forces (Reserve) and served in the active Reserves until his retirement in 1996 as a full Colonel with thirty-three years of service. He worked as a Professional Engineer in his civilian status, obtaining his MBA from Pepperdine University through the GI Bill. He is a Registered Professional Engineer, a graduate of the Industrial College of the Armed Forces, and an Enrolled Agent of the IRS. He has worked for thirty years as a football official, both in high school and college. He is married to Sandra, a public school speech pathologist, and lives with her in Highland Ranch, Colorado, where they are retired. He writes Western novels while working on his golf game in the summer and skiing in the winter. They have five grown children, scattered from Washington, D.C. to Portland, Oregon.